THE LAST
NIGHTINGALE

THE LAST NIGHTINGALE

A NOVEL OF SUSPENSE

ANTHONY FLACCO

BALLANTINE BOOKS

NEW YORK

A Ballantine Books Trade Paperback Original

Copyright © 2007 by Anthony Flacco
Dossier copyright © 2007 by Random House, Inc.

Published in the United States by Ballantine Books, an imprint of
The Random House Publishing Group, a division of Random House, Inc.,
New York.

BALLANTINE and colophon and MORTALIS and colophon are registered
trademarks of Random House, Inc.

The design of the title page features an incorporation of the photograph
"St. Dominic's Church, Bush and Steiner Sts. Brick and masonry structure
upon sand and alluvium of no great depth," which was featured in the
Carnegie Report on the great San Francisco earthquake of 1906. It can be
found in the J. B. Macelwane archives at Saint Louis University, and at
http://mnw.eas.slu.edu. Reprinted by permission of the Department of
Earth and Atmospheric Sciences, Saint Louis University.

ISBN-978-0-8129-7757-8

Library of Congress Cataloging-in-Publication Data

Flacco, Anthony.
The last nightingale : a novel of suspense / Anthony Flacco.
p. cm.
ISBN-13: 978-0-8129-7757-8 (pbk.)
ISBN-10: 0-8129-7757-2 (pbk.)
1. Police—California—San Francisco—Fiction.   2. Orphans—Fiction.
3. Serial murderers—Fiction.   4. San Francisco Earthquake, Calif., 1906—
Fiction.   I. Title.
PS3606.L33L37 2007
813'.6—dc22   2006101090

Printed in the United States of America

www.ballantinebooks.com

2 4 6 8 9 7 5 3 1

Book design by Simon M. Sullivan

TO SHARLY
for the magic of believing

ACKNOWLEDGMENTS

I am most grateful for *The Last Nightingale* to be among the works that Mortalis, as a new imprint, has selected for its publication list. The work done there in preparing this book for publication has proved their intention to make Mortalis a house of distinction. Editor Paul Taunton brought his eye for logic and detail to the honing of the manuscript, and the finished book is a better one for his involvement.

Agent Sharlene Martin took my early manuscript to this emerging group, so I thank her for the opportunity to work with such a smart, energetic, and creative publishing team. She and they make for delightful colleagues, because of their shared enthusiasm for building something to be proud of in the publishing world, and their intelligence and dedication in doing so.

Fair mention must be made of my local favorites among the next generation, approaching fast in the rearview mirror and therefore offering me constant inspiration to get it done sooner rather than later: Scott and Jill in Seattle, Nicole in Los Angeles, brave Jordan far at sea, with Matthew and Daniel in San Diego, not far from Drasco and Nikola. These are the good ones. You know the kind I mean, just a few of the many reasons why all the future doomsayers may yet turn out to be wrong.

Even if The Last Nightingale could be revived,
How would it tolerate the cure?
Knowing that Life merely awaits
To devour it again.

—PRESUMED SUICIDE NOTE IN THE POCKET OF
TOMMIE KIMBROUGH'S LAST VICTIM,
WASHED ASHORE NEAR THE GOLDEN GATE.

THE LAST NIGHTINGALE

CHAPTER ONE

WEDNESDAY, APRIL 18, 1906
5:12 A.M.
THE FIRST SHOCK WAVE

RANDALL BLACKBURN'S MUSCLED FRAME did not strain at the long uphill hike, even though the route led from his policeman's beat in the waterfront district all the way back to the City Hall Station. At thirty-two years of age, he was able to power his long legs up the steep terrain with such speed that he could leave his beat at five in the morning, traverse more than a dozen blocks uphill, plus a few short connecting streets, and still be at his desk with enough time to jot down a brief nightly report and quit the shift by six.

The strenuous hiking routine usually helped to calm him down after a long night. This morning, it barely had any effect. He was coming off of an unusually rough beat patrolling the "Barbary Coast" district, whose grand name was a façade for a strip of bottom-feeder saloons and dead-end flophouses down near the waterfront. The whole night had been filled with more violent rampage and general disturbance than he had ever seen on a single shift. He spent most of his shift dodging punches from drunken gamblers and avoiding knife blades flashed by syphilitic whores. Their mania was contagious among them all night long and more so with every passing hour.

He had never gotten used to the place, even though the dangerous foot patrol assignment was routinely meted out to him by his station chief. Blackburn realized that the continual Barbary Coast beat was intended as some sort of an ongoing affront to him, and that it was being done for the benefit of the rank-and-file officers. He just didn't have any good ideas as to what to do about it. His reputation as a widower who was far too obsessive in his police work naturally pleased the upper brass, but it also placed a lot of pressure on fellow officers: men with families, lives away from the job.

Then some bright soul up in the command office figured out that with Blackburn's overactive code of ethics, he would work just as hard in the dangerous district as he did anywhere else. And so week after week, the dreaded assignments sent a morale-soothing message to the rank and file:

> Don't worry about Sergeant Blackburn,
> no matter how much of a fanatic he might be.
> Look at where he is.
> Nothing matters unless the right people
> like you.

While he strode along the sidewalk, Blackburn tried to tell himself that the real reason he constantly drew the graveyard shift and the Barbary Coast assignments was because of his superior physical capability. But a voice in his head accused him of being the author of his own predicament. The back of his neck tightened at the unwelcome truth of it.

On any night, it was a relief to leave the district behind at the end of a shift. That was especially true this morning; it had been a real "ladies' night" along the Barbary Coast, and between the women and the men, the street corner hags were by far the most dangerous. Those bottom-rung females lived in a drunken haze, battered by lives of nonstop torment. He approached every one of them knowing that they would eagerly offer sex to a policeman to buy his tolerance, or just as eagerly snatch away his sidearm and shoot him in the face. Most were prepared to either live or die in the attempt, and it was all the same to them.

Lately, while he kept a sharp eye out for their flurries of random rage, he also knew that the Department strongly suspected that at least one of these doomed women had somehow become highly skilled at throwing heavy-bladed knives. Blackburn himself had seen the grim products of the mysterious killer's work. Each of her victims had almost certainly fallen to the same knife, which left identically deep and wide cuts. The crime was always committed as a fast kill, always under cover of darkness. The consistent knife-point entry at the back of the neck indicated surprise or ambush. The victim's spinal cord was usually split by the thick blade.

Over a dozen such victims had turned up in less than nine months, with never a clue beyond a couple of reported glimpses of a "small-framed woman" seen hurrying away. No one even knew if this woman had any actual involvement in the crimes. That's how thin the evidence remained, after all this time and all those victims.

Blackburn had personally found three of the bodies, on three separate occasions. Every one was castrated with precision and skill, postmortem. Not a single victim was robbed. It seemed as though the taking of the victim's life and the removing of his use-less manhood were enough to complete the desired experience—one longshoreman's body was even found with a sizeable wad of cash right inside the vest pocket.

When the press got wind of the story, with macabre humor they dubbed the killer "The Surgeon." The SFPD publicly speculated that The Surgeon was almost certainly a physically fit young woman, probably one who had fallen into ruinous ways. Perhaps she grew up on a farm, where she had learned her skill with the knife. Possibly butchering hogs.

Since then, on most nights along the Barbary Coast, Blackburn had nothing more for company than the inevitable castration jokes that seemed to come from all directions. The night-beat clientele generally agreed that as long as they weren't the ones being killed, the best thing to do was to laugh it all off. And since Blackburn was under Chief Dinan's orders to keep an ear to the street, he had no choice but to spend his nights asking the same questions about the killings, over and over, and listening to the same handful of jokes in response.

No one actually voiced open approval, but he couldn't help noticing that the sidewalk ladies were uniformly ignorant of any useful facts, free of any helpful theories. None was inclined to so much as guess who the ghoulish killer might be. And while they never went so far as to openly cheer The Surgeon's grisly work, that extra bit about slicing off the cocks of the dead men usually made them giggle whenever the topic came up.

As for the killer—Blackburn still hoped that there was only one. But throughout the past night's shift, with that crazed charge hovering in the air, he had half expected to trip over a collection of bled-out corpses at any moment. He kept fearing that a few of the other violence-prone whores might have started to find The Surgeon's behavior personally appealing.

So tonight he was doubly glad when his shift ended without major trouble. He took extra long strides back to the station, making good time even though the predawn light was absorbed by the fog. With the gas streetlamps still burning at every corner, he could see just well enough to keep up his pace between the isolated pools of weak yellow light while he moved through the chilled mist. The sound of his heavy boot heels ricocheted off the cobblestones and echoed around the silent brick storefronts.

The smell of early morning ham and egg breakfasts floated from a number of homes, tempting him to get back home to a meal of his own. He paused to check his silver pocket watch when he passed through a circle of pale gaslight near the corner post office at Mission and Seventh. He was only a few blocks away from the City Hall station, and it was only twelve minutes past five: record time. He liked that. It was as if more of the night's prickly energy had risen up from the ground and soaked through the soles of his boots with every step, filling him up as fast as he burned it away.

He pocketed the watch and started to take a step outside of the lamplight, but just as he lifted his foot, the entire street jerked sideways and pulled itself out from under him. His footing vanished with such power that, for an instant, he thought that he had stepped on some drunk's sleeping blanket and gotten it snatched out from under his feet.

Half a second later, the street's cobblestone surface jumped up and hit him with the rude force of a blind-side fist in a bar fight. His body slammed to earth and he took the pavement as a full frontal blow, barely reaching out in time to protect his face from the cold bricks. Spots filled his vision and his head rang with waves of pain that throbbed in time to his heartbeat. He heard his own voice cry out, "It's an earthquake!" even as he fought to avoid blacking out.

Instinct brought him to his hands and knees, moving his limbs with natural magic while the ground shuddered under him. But he remained in place. After a boyhood in Northern California, Blackburn had enough experience with earthquakes to know that it wasn't time to get up yet. He reassured himself that at least he was awake and knew what was happening—he hadn't been ejected out of a warm bed and onto a cold floor, as most of the city's residents no doubt were. And most of whom were probably now lost to confusion and panic.

Until the rattling died down, there wasn't any safer place to go. If he moved out of the range of falling bricks or stones from one building, he would only move into range of another. He thought about taking shelter in a doorway, but rejected that. In the heavy stone buildings that lined both sides of this street, a doorway might only prove to be a good place to get buried alive when the keystones gave way. He knew that if any structural damage had taken place during the bigger shock, then a building might only need another little rattle before coming apart.

He told himself that with any luck, this first shock wave would be the worst of it. But just as he began to rise from his hands and knees, the street began a hard swirl that threw him onto his side. This movement was much stronger, coming not thirty seconds on the heels of the first shock wave. It rolled with such power that the best he could do was to scramble back down onto all fours and remain there on the ground.

Beyond that, the shuddering earth was already telling him everything he needed to know. That first wave, he now realized with a cold rush, had not been the real earthquake.

It was only a foreshock. Blackburn did not know if he yelled the words or not.

And then it was more than just the idea of a major earthquake that leaped into his mind. It was all the dire implications that went along with it for a brittle city of bricks and mortar.

They quickly became real. The violent rolling motion of the earth was joined by a vertical rise and fall. The ground dropped out from under him, then slammed back up again. Blackburn found himself clutching the back of a lurching beast. It was all so unreal that the first icy shot of mortal fear had not even hit him yet. All he knew, at that moment, was that he had never been through an earthquake like this one.

Then abruptly, the ground's vertical movements slowed.

All movement stopped.

Quiet descended . . .

And within seconds, everything was shrouded in a deathly silence. The air felt like a thick wet blanket that did not transmit sound. There was nothing reassuring in the absence of noise.

The silence lasted for eight or nine slow heartbeats.

And then a deep rumbling began. A pulse throbbed, far beneath the earth's surface. It was indescribably deep, so low on the tonal scale that he felt it in his bones and deep in his chest. For an instant, his memory flashed a boyhood image of putting his ear to a railroad track, listening for the vibrations of a faraway locomotive. Except now there was no track and no train. This rumbling sound was wrong, completely out of place.

It was then that the first burst of real *fear* stabbed through him, stronger and colder than anything he had ever felt. It cut through his training, his life experience, and at that moment, if the rolling earth had allowed him to climb to his feet, the fear would have owned him and sent him screaming into the night. His instincts already sensed what the rest of him was about to learn.

When he glanced down Mission Street, he stared into an impossible sight—a massive surge of energy was running toward him, underneath the surface of the earth. It hurtled through the ground like a wave of curling surf.

Solid earth was rolling like the sea itself.

His brain seemed to freeze while the invisible monster shot toward him and trailed upheaval in its wake. Brick storefronts buckled and exploded. Granite paving stones blew upward like kernels of popping corn. By the time the energy wave hit him, Blackburn was a paralyzed statue of astonishment. The wave tossed him into the air. When he landed and the street curb crashed into his ribs, the blow knocked all of the wind out of him. Then he could do nothing more than lie helpless: ten seconds, twenty seconds, fighting the sensation that he was drowning on dry land.

He rolled onto his hands and knees and managed to take a clear breath, but by then the invisible wave was long gone. The din of destruction overpowered his hearing. Behind him, the roof of the post office was gradually collapsing, and those sounds were only part of a much larger chorus. In all directions, buildings of every size were still shedding their stone exteriors like giant reptiles casting off skin. The ones that collapsed upon themselves expelled thick clouds of dust out the windows and doorways, coughing their guts into the streets before they died.

He turned his head in a circle and caught shadowy glimpses of Armageddon. Never since losing his wife and child had Blackburn felt the overpowering need to cry. Now the choking sobs took him as if they had only been gone for a day. He cried out in wordless despair. It was several seconds before he regained control and strangled the feelings back down. The noises around him diminished at the same time that he managed to squelch his own outcries. In a self-conscious flash, he felt thankful to know that even if anybody was awake and looking out of their window and right at him, they were certainly far too distracted to have noticed his slip of emotion.

Meanwhile, another eerie silence was returning to the ruined landscape. It felt especially unnatural, because people should have been calling out, screaming in pain or crying for help. But instead there was a complete absence of voices.

He realized that survivors had to be out there: random miracles, mixed in with the rubble. They were scattered underneath the ruined buildings all around, just as surely as the silent dead were buried alongside them.

But still nobody screamed. No voices at all. Only the random sounds of falling debris punctuated a silence that was as deep and cold as the black waters of the bay. Blackburn had no idea how long it took him to stagger a block or so, but it was only then, after that much time, that the sounds from victims finally begin to drift up from the giant piles of rubble. The first cry that he heard was a long, ghastly wail. It started low, then quickly rose in pitch, like the sound of a distant hunting dog.

That initial outcry triggered a ghoulish chain reaction—other victims quickly sounded out from hidden and entombed places. Their voices carried a tone that Blackburn had never heard in his twelve years of hardscrabble police work. He knew the desperate sounds might as well be the wail of graveyard ghosts.

When a terrible scream sprang up through a rubble pile directly in front of him, he couldn't help himself. He abandoned the trip back to the station and began clawing his way toward the trapped victim.

Just as he closed in on the anguished sounds, he glanced up from his work and saw the first living person since the earth had attacked—a healthy-looking young man was scrambling across the rubble. He looked like he was running from a rabid dog.

"Hey! Over here!" Blackburn bellowed to the man. "Police! Help me dig!"

When the man ignored him, Blackburn bellowed in his strongest voice, "I said *police,* damn it! Stop right there!"

The fellow scuffed to a halt. For an instant, the young man swung around and stared straight at Blackburn, eyes like saucers. He paused there, just long enough to adopt an attitude and make a decision. Then he spun on the balls of his feet and disappeared.

Blackburn swore in frustration. He resumed digging and didn't bother to call for help again. Within a few moments, he managed to pull a large man free. The victim was bleeding from several wounds and seemed too injured to get very far. The man immediately began to wail in a thick Greek accent, "My wife! Where she is? My wife!"

Blackburn could only holler for him to stay put until someone could carry him out of the area. Then he stumbled away in search of the next buried victim. In the space of a few moments, screams were beginning to rise from everywhere, and there was still no able-bodied help to be seen.

It only took another couple of steps for him to reach the next source of cries—children, clearly, two of them—their shrill voices penetrated his bones. He abandoned himself to such a fury of digging that he did not feel the skin shredding from his fingers and his palms. Any object that his hands could latch onto was hurled to the side, in movements that he repeated over and over while the dust-filled air seared his lungs.

But soon, in spite of all the distraction, he noticed a new smell in the fouled air.

Smoke. Oily and thick, the source was somewhere nearby. He resumed digging, but within moments, the screams of the other trapped victims began rising higher. By now these people smelled the smoke too, and they grasped what it meant for them if they failed to get out of the path of the fire. Every breath that he took held less usable air. He began to go light-headed. His body started to fail him, in spite of his determination. His hands became clumsy paws. His thoughts ran thick. He tried to force his memory to tell him what he was supposed to be doing. He got no answer.

It was the feel of a tiny hand that brought him back. He had opened up a pocket of space that held two small girls, perhaps six and seven years old. They pounced on him, crying out in a language he couldn't identify while they grabbed at his uniform sleeves to pull themselves free.

He saw that both girls were bleeding, but before he could think of how to help them, they scrambled over him and scurried away, hand in hand, shrieking in panic. There was nothing else he could do for them. More trapped victims were calling out everywhere around him and his strength was quickly draining away. His only choice was to get to clearer air, and to gather reinforcements at the station: men, tools, water. Water most of all.

When he finally made it far enough up Market Street to a spot where random air currents had carved a trough of better air, his thoughts began to clear. He felt some of his strength return. But when he stared through the faint light at the place where he knew City Hall was supposed to be, the sight stopped him in his tracks.

Only a few days before, a fellow officer named Leonard Ingham told of a nightmare that had kept him up for hours; the entire city was wiped out in one massive conflagration. Blackburn remembered laughing at Ingham and chiding him for spending too much time around the Gypsy fortune-tellers down on the waterfront.

But here he was, staring at the spot where the high-domed City Hall was supposed to be, and most of it was reduced to rubble. The great dome's steel frame remained standing, but it had shucked most of its limestone covering, just as Ingham described. Worse, with all of the early morning cooking fires that had been burning at the time that the quake struck, the massive blaze that Officer Ingham's dream had predicted was certain to be close behind.

Blackburn hurried over to the ruined building. A dozen or so able-bodied officers were clearing space for a makeshift command center out on the broad front steps. In their midst was Police Chief Dinan, pacing back and forth, bellowing orders at anybody within earshot. The chief had already spotted him.

"Sergeant Blackburn! Thank God you're alive!"

"Yes sir, I was almost back here when it—"

"We need a man with your strength!"

"I'll do whatever I—"

"Most of the City Jail inmates are still under the building! We've opened a passage down to their cells. Check 'em out one by one. If they're dead, leave them. Any that are injured too bad to work, leave them, too. Round up everybody else at gunpoint and march 'em all down to Portsmouth Square!"

"Portsmouth Square? Sir, that's a long way from—"

"Shoot any man who breaks ranks!"

"Sir, there are already fires. Maybe we could draft the prisoners to work the hoses?"

"What are they going to *do* with the hoses, Sergeant? Use 'em to beat the flames out?"

"What?"

"A runner from the waterfront just came up—every water main in the city is busted. There's not gonna *be* any water for these fires. But you can bet there'll be bodies to deal with. There are exactly two graveyards on this peninsula, and both of them are full. So you march those men down to Portsmouth Square and start digging trench graves!"

The chief grabbed Blackburn by the lapels and drew him close enough to blast him with a hoarse whisper. "We've got *plague* down in Chinatown, you understand me? And now the rats will be coming up out of every busted sewer line! Think about that, will you? You want to know how important this is—even though we've only got one motorized patrol car, it's not gonna do anything but ferry bodies down to you. That means our rescue work is all gonna be on horseback or most likely on foot, hear me? Just so you can get the bodies we send you into the ground, fast as you can."

The chief dropped his voice again. "And make sure to cover them too deep for the rats. We can rebury everybody later. Somewhere off the peninsula. Oakland, maybe."

Blackburn felt a flicker of worry that Dinan had gone over the deep end. "Chief, if you mean the Black Death, I've never heard about any plague in San Fran—"

"You weren't *supposed* to hear!" the chief bellowed. He forced his voice back down to a croaking whisper, "*Nobody* was, except a few of us! We've been hoping that those few cases that have come up were brought directly in, but that the plague itself isn't really here. Nobody knows for sure. And now you can keep quiet about it too, or I swear I'll bury you right along with the—"

"Yes, sir! I'll go right now!"

"You sure as hell will if you want to stay upright, Sergeant! And mark me, now—these inmates, tell them you've got orders: If any man even *looks* like he might try to run, you're gonna *shoot him down!*"

Blackburn hurried to comply. But there was hardly time to get down into the cell area and holler for the attention of the captive men before the next big aftershock struck, thirteen minutes after the initial wave.

Just when he announced to the inmates that he had a proposition that could get them out of their cells, the earthquake rolled through with a force that dropped all of them to the floor. The basement area was claustrophobic, making this second quake feel much more powerful than the first. Blackburn was sure that if it didn't subside within twenty or thirty seconds, the rest of City Hall would collapse into the basement and make a grave for all of them.

Luck gave them a nod; this shock wave faded quicker than the first, and when he was able to pick himself back up and peer through the dust, he realized that his sales pitch to the men could not have had a better opening. He saw the same death panic in their eyes that he had felt inside of himself. There was no need to use force. He asked for volunteers and got a general show of hands.

They all smelled the thickening smoke.

He and his two officers were so heavily outnumbered that they had to move with great care in hooking up their chain gang. It used up valuable time to get the men organized by height, for equal stride length, and then shackled into teams on long leg bindings improvised with sections of wagon harness. The sun was well over the horizon by the time the big sergeant and his young patrol officers marched away with their twenty-five conscripts.

By now massive smoke columns were rising up in every direction, joining together high over the city in a ruinous pall that blocked out most of the daylight. The three officers marched their charges into what was becoming artificial twilight, armed only with a rifle and a double set of sidearms for each man. Blackburn had instructed them to make it a point to look like they were itching to use their guns, and for a while at least, the simple theatrics worked. The trembling "volunteers" felt less fear of marching deeper into the burning city than of the bullet in the back they were convinced any man would receive if he attempted to escape.

At 8:14 A.M., another powerful aftershock set everything to rattling, and this time it was too much for dozens of the city's brick and stone buildings; they finally shattered and crumbled into the streets. Block after city block began to take on the appearance of a rubble-strewn artillery field.

A score of major fires now burned unchecked in every direction. Full daylight barely penetrated the shroud of smoke swelling over the ruined city. Blackburn lost large chunks of time in guiding his men around the worst of the damage and the emerging fires. The streets were so choked with obstacles that a hike which should have taken less than half an hour consumed nearly three. They only sustained that modest speed because they were marching under a firm order not to stop for any rescue work, no matter how vital it might appear to be. His confidential order from Chief Dinan was simple:

Nothing gets priority over saving the city from a rampaging outbreak of the Black Death.

The desperate focus of that order became plain when the same sea breezes that were feeding the fires began to lift the smoke clouds. Blackburn hated what his eyes told him. As far as he could see in all directions, the city's large buildings were in various states of collapse. The few that were still standing amid the billowing smoke swayed with every new aftershock.

Some of the city's able-bodied survivors had recovered enough of their humanity to begin working to rescue trapped survivors, but there were others who made no attempt to disguise their looting. From time to time, Blackburn fired over their heads to scatter them, but it was clear that they would only move on and strike again.

There were three different occasions when he actively interfered with events by ordering one of his armed men to chase and shoot at gangs of looters. But each time, he remained within his orders by keeping the group of inmates moving while his assigned officer made sure that the perpetrators either took a bullet or were frightened away.

It never slowed the group down. When he marched his men past one half-buried victim who stood trapped below his waist among twisted iron beams, the young man begged to be shot before the advancing flames could reach him. The approaching fire proved that his fears were true. Blackburn didn't even have to issue the order—his corporal quickly stepped forward and shot the man through the back of the head. The convicts watched, astounded, and felt themselves reminded that the penalties today were swift and harsh. They fell into step with added determination.

In the absence of recognizable landmarks, Blackburn's group lost direction several times. They were picking their way across the crumbled remains of the Emporium Building before he realized that they were at the corner of Market and Powell streets. He ordered the men to take the slight left turn onto Powell, and corrected their course whenever he spotted something familiar. Still, by the time they reached the intersection at Jackson Street, a stone's throw from Portsmouth Square, it was already a quarter past ten—and they were off course again.

He glanced around at the beautiful neighborhood's simple houses. The modest family homes were still standing, built with flexible wood beams instead of rigid bricks and mortar. He found himself hoping that the prevailing winds would change, just so these simple homes might be spared the swarming fires.

But just after his men rounded the corner and began to head down Jackson Street, he heard a woman's screams. The sounds stopped him cold. Piercing, deathly screams were coming from inside one of these peaceful-looking houses. The screams were as primal and intense as anything he'd heard yet that day, an equal mix of terror and pain. The unreal aspect of it was that they were coming from somewhere inside an untouched house. No motion could be seen in the home, and the neighbors either did not hear or were choosing not to react. The entire neighborhood was otherwise silent.

But Blackburn had already marched his men past so many other miseries, there was no time to investigate this one. Portsmouth Square was getting close, and the sour-faced inmates were starting to look as if they realized how heavily they outnumbered their captors.

He took a last glance back at the peaceful-looking house. Exhaustion pulled at him, and the main work detail hadn't even started yet. There was nothing else to do but make a mental note to come back to that place later on, and try to check into the source of those terrible, out-of-place screams.

If he ever got the chance.

CHAPTER TWO

10:15 A.M.

FIVE HOURS AFTER
THE GREAT EARTHQUAKE

AT THE SAME TIME that Blackburn marched his men away from the house on Jackson Street, twelve-year-old Shane Nightingale was inside, curling his thin frame tighter inside the small kitchen pantry. He tried not to listen to what was going on just a few feet outside, but the words stabbed into him like nails.

"It's the end!" the stranger's voice hissed. "A day of atonement for you. You're starting to appreciate that now, aren't you? My job is to empty you out! But don't worry. We'll take all the time we need."

The sounds coming out of Shane's adoptive mother had mostly dissolved into infantile shrieks and babbling, while the madman responded to Mrs. Nightingale with icy precision, mimicking the sounds of her deathly terror. He did it with such energy and skill that he seemed to be playing to an audience.

To Shane, it felt as if the killer somehow realized that there was a terrified and helpless twelve-year-old boy hiding only a few feet away, and was taking additional pleasure in his torments by drilling the event deep into Shane's mind, toying with him until the moment came to throw open the pantry doors and drag him out to suffer with the others.

Then abruptly, Mrs. Nightingale went quiet. The room took on a silence as thick and sour as old buttermilk. It was several long moments before the stranger began to speak again. This time he kept his voice to a reverential whisper.

"Ah! Now you're perfect! Safe from any more sin! The sins of that arrogant man you people call husband and father."

All of the horrors laid upon Mrs. Nightingale were still not enough to satisfy the maniac, even though he had surely killed her. Shane felt a vague sense of relief that she had finally come to the end of her suffering, and that the lovely lady who adopted him out of St. Adrian's would endure no more of it. Shane knew that she had been the one who influenced the family's decision to rescue him from that place. Her husband and daughters would have passed him by and left him there. Even though she didn't allow any real closeness, he had always loved her for saving him.

His relief sank under an overwhelming flood of guilt. Shane knew perfectly well that even a scrawny kid of twelve was expected to find the strength to fight off such a monster. Instead, from the moment that the brutal attack began, his terror had owned him. His legs went numb and useless. His throat seized shut. He couldn't even control his bladder.

How long had it been? He could barely see inside of that darkened place, but the pocket watch that he won by pitching pennies now hung from a little hook on the back panel. He had placed it there when he moved in because he could read it by a thin beam of light that penetrated the slight warping of the door frame. Now when he craned his neck to see it, the watch showed that it was almost ten-thirty.

Early that morning, when Father Nightingale saw that nobody in the family was injured, he ordered everyone to get out of the house and into the safety of the front yard, just in case another aftershock rolled through. Then he shouted that his dry goods store was at the mercy of looters, and he hurried away in the family's four-seater buggy, carrying his shotgun and a sack full of 10-gauge shells. The last that they heard from him was when he called over his shoulder for everyone to stay outside until he returned.

The family obeyed him for a while, but eventually both girls convinced their mother to go back in and set about putting away the toppled things in the parlor and kitchen. It was as if they all agreed that the earthquake was the worst thing that could happen that day; the rest was simply a matter of cleaning up. Once they finished, Shane had persuaded them all to return to their rooms and rest, then he had gone straight into the kitchen and crawled back into his makeshift retreat in the pantry, where he fell into an exhausted sleep.

He awoke to the sounds of the girls screaming and Mrs. Nightingale hollering in protest, and of people being brutally dragged downstairs. The intruder sounded like he was searching through the house, bellowing, "Where's your husband? Where is he?" Mrs. Nightingale cried over and over that her husband was out guarding his store, but the intruder was determined to search the whole house himself. Shane could only lie paralyzed. He knew that his grim hiding place was sparing his life.

Early on, Mrs. Nightingale had screamed Shane's name twice. She kept herself mercifully quiet about him, after that. The killer made no reaction to the name, as if he either had not heard her or was already convinced that nobody else was around.

Shane wondered if perhaps she hoped that he had somehow escaped and run for help. Maybe she thought that by keeping quiet, she was giving herself and her girls a chance at rescue.

The girls never had the chance to put up any defense. When they were dragged into the kitchen in the first place, each one had only managed a couple of wordless screams before they were silenced. But he recognized those brief sounds. He knew them from his days at St. Adrian's. There, unsuspecting children who got themselves targeted for punishment frequently had the experience of a Helper coming up from behind and grabbing them—snatching them up off of the ground by an arm or leg, pulling them like a sack of grain. Sometimes the Helpers would yank so hard that the child made the same kind of involuntary yelp of shock and fear that Shane heard from both of these two girls.

Back then, there was never anybody around to help either.

Amy and Carolyn had grown up in a loving household and had no powers for battling such cruelty. Shane wondered if mere shock had sealed their lips; his own terror, after all, was keeping his voice silent and holding him as still as cold plaster.

The intensity jumped higher when the perpetrator began a nonstop diatribe about his motives, to explain and justify his actions. Since there was no way for Shane to ignore the dreadful harangue, he was a captive audience at a demon's lecture.

The hanging watch told him that it had been nearly three hours since the invader took Mrs. Nightingale and her girls captive. Obviously, the killer felt no concern about making a quick escape. In the general chaos that was surely going on all over the city, he was gambling that help was unlikely. It went on and on, long after the woman of the house stopped making any sound. When Shane finally realized what the madman was actually talking about, he had to bite his teeth into his tongue to silence himself. The man was actually asking his two surviving victims to agree with him, to tell him that what he was doing was all right. He wanted to hear them concur that his reasons were sound.

Amy and Carolyn began kicking out at the floor, against the cabinets, against their restraints.

At that point everything became more than Shane could take in. His need to escape the lunacy overtook him and his brain began to shut itself down. His eyelids turned to lead. He plunged into a sickened and delirious blackness. The ability to rouse himself was nowhere inside of him.

Later, when Shane felt himself coming back, his eyes were already open. He blinked hard and blinked again, stunned that the world had not somehow gone away.

Now it was quiet. An amber split of lantern light bled through the crack above the pantry door, and the thin beam showed his pocket watch: nearly straight-up midnight. A whole day, gone. He wanted to think that Father Nightingale had somehow returned and vanquished the demon, and that it would now be safe to crawl out from hiding. Before the thought could fully form, he realized that of course the man of the house never came back. The sounds of struggle would have roused him. Shane wondered whether he could have made himself burst out of the pantry and somehow join in the fight.

But it had never happened, and now the awful sounds were beginning all over again. The demon was killing Amy. Shane's blood pounded so hard beneath his skin that it felt as if it could burst through his flesh. The demon rendered her unconscious again and again. Each time, he revived her at the last instant, godlike, and granted her another few minutes of life before starting the process all over. It was happening to sixteen years' worth of beauty and charm bundled into a feminine form so lovely that Shane had spent his entire first year in that house trying to avoid falling in love with her. He had always squelched his feelings, never doubting that if he gave himself away the entire family would judge him perverse. Amy would have been repulsed. They might have even sent him back.

Any worthy young man would leap from the pantry, determined to fight like a warrior, all in the nick of time to save beautiful Amy. But Shane's legs wouldn't take him anywhere. He couldn't even feel them.

Briefly, he wondered if he could at least do something as simple as to cry out. Could he buy Amy a few more moments of life that way, while the startled killer left her side to search for the source of Shane's voice? He began with a quick swallow, in hopes of opening up his parched and swollen throat a little bit wider. Then braced himself to scream with all of his power.

"Stooooooooooppp!"

Only a hiss of dry air came out. It was not enough to penetrate the simple wooden doors. The sounds outside the pantry never even slowed down, and soon were more brutal than anything that anyone should hear. Shane lay on his back and positioned his numb forearms to cover his burning ears. Amy's degradation was private. He would not listen to any more of it. The powerful swirl of torment spun inside of him until it carried the rest of him away once again and pulled him deep into a trance.

More time passed.

When Shane finally came to, he snapped back to consciousness at the sound of the terrible voice—

"Time to wake up!"

The monster had found him. Shane's heart slammed hard in his chest as he fought to focus his eyes inside the dim pantry—and then he realized that it was still dark in there. The doors were still closed.

And so the monster was not talking to him. The only one left was Carolyn, the youngest. An instant later, Shane heard her muffled cries. *Where in God's name was Mr. Nightingale?* What could possibly keep him away for so long? Shane noticed that a strong smell of smoke was drifting into the house. There was fire out there, not far away.

Crashing sounds began in the kitchen. They were harder than anything he'd heard throughout the long ordeal, so despite his terror, Shane dared to peer through the crack just above the door. Through that razor line of sight, he saw Carolyn being whirled about the room in a profane dance with the devil.

Now she was crashing into furniture. Slamming into walls.

Shane caught glimpses of the killer, but never saw enough to gather anything more than that the man was dressed in nondescript workman's clothing and that he seemed to have a small and wiry build. But there was no hint of weakness about him. He moved like an attacking dog. Shane pulled away from the dangerous crack and shrank back against the wall. A wave of delirium washed through him and held him in its power while the attack went on and on.

Daylight crawled by. Twilight fell. Only then, after all that time, did silence fall back over the Nightingale house. Most of the night passed before Shane's awareness drifted back into the moment. He found himself in the growing light of sunrise.

A day and a half had passed, and during all of that time the Nightingale house had been used as the stage for a play more furious and foul than anything an earthquake could do.

"Hello? Hello, inside! Anybody here?"

A man's voice. At the front of the house.

Scraping noises now, just outside the pantry. The demon is visible through the crack over the pantry door, staggering across the room in fear. The demon scrambles to the window and peers outside.

"Shit!" the demon hisses. Even from inside of the pantry, the demon can be heard while he stumbles to the rear of the house . . . throws open the back door . . . makes his escape out through the yard . . .

And as quickly as that, it was over. The killer was gone.

There was more loud banging at the front door. Then sounds of the door being forced open.

"Hello inside? Police! We're evacuating the area!"

Heavy boots, coming closer, entered the kitchen. A booming male voice called out.

"Sergeant Blackburn! Three bodies here, no sign of life!"

More boots thumped into the kitchen. Now Shane could see the man through the door crack—he was big, strong-faced, with dark hair like Shane's. He and his men were all filthy, covered with streaks of dirt and blackened by smoke. They looked half dead with fatigue. But something else was wrong. The sergeant did not cry out at the sight of the dead women. Shane could see all three cops there in the kitchen, and none of them seemed surprised by what was on the floor in front of them.

Shane still could not make himself cry out. The heavy boots moved on and quickly made their way throughout the house while the sergeant and his two officers searched the other rooms for any signs of life.

How could these men have no idea what they had just seen? But the sergeant ordered the men out of the house, shouting that the fires were coming, that this house was done for. There were still three more homes on the block to be searched.

The boots stomped away. No one bothered to close the front door.

Silence returned. The smell of smoke was becoming strong, now. Overpowering. The fire was nearly upon the place. It was the awful feeling of choking on smoke that finally roused Shane. His arms were nearly useless and his legs felt full of lead, but somehow the pantry doors opened for him. He rolled out and onto the floor. The change was instant and powerful—as soon as he left his little shelter, the heat coming from the advancing fire was blistering hot.

Without meaning to, Shane glanced over at the three bodies. He quickly turned away, but that one glimpse was enough to show him why the police failed to realize what they were seeing. Mrs. Nightingale was almost completely covered by the dish cupboard. It might have been knocked onto her during the killer's frenzy with her daughter, or perhaps deliberately placed over her later. Only her lower legs protruded; she looked like a casualty of the earthquake.

Amy lay under the overturned kitchen table, mostly concealed by it. The parts of her that could be seen gave no sign of the horrors she had endured. And although little Carolyn was more bruised and bloody than the others, within all the wreckage and chaos she would also be mistaken for an earthquake victim, battered by the violent shaking. These dead could speak nothing of the evil they had seen, certainly not to men hastily conducting a hunt for survivors. And now, with the fires nearly upon the house, Shane realized that he was going to be the only witness. There would soon be nothing left to see.

He closed his eyes against the horror show and crawled out of the kitchen, muscles numb, pulling himself along on all fours until he reached the front of the house. At the entrance, he grasped the doorsill and hauled himself to his feet. Then he turned to face the daylight world for the first time since the great earthquake had struck the city.

The whole planet seemed to be on fire. Even the sky.

He blinked into a reddening artificial dusk to see a shattered and smoking landscape that stretched in all directions. Brick buildings were nothing but shells. Most of the wooden buildings were ablaze. The streets were full of rubble. And everywhere, refugees stumbled along. Some carried mounds of belongings, others pulled carts by hand. A small few had managed to find draft horses somewhere, and put them to work pulling wagons loaded down with hasty piles. Everyone was retreating before a wall of flame and smoke. He stumbled out into the road and stood among them.

The sun was mostly blocked out by the massive columns of smoke and their message of ruin. He gazed into one giant swirling cloud and for an instant his burning eyes told him that he caught a glimpse of a face, twisted and horrible.

Shane felt something hard and small clutched in his fist and opened his hand to see his watch. He had grabbed it off the hook and carried it with him, with no idea he was doing so.

A hand grabbed his shoulder and spun him, nearly stopping his heart. Before him stood a woman who resembled Mrs. Nightingale so much that a cold rush shot through him. The woman spoke to him in a coarse whisper.

"Are you going through Chinatown?"

"Why?" Shane asked.

But to his surprise, the word "why" didn't fully emerge. It stuck halfway across his lips and hung there like a toothpick that he couldn't spit out. "Whuuh . . . Whuuh . . ." The sensation was so foreign that at first, he forgot to be embarrassed.

The woman ignored him and continued, "Somebody said that there's only one working telegraph left in the whole city! At Post and Montgomery. Chinatown. Do you hear me?"

"Yes," Shane answered.

But "yes" didn't come out, either. All that came out was, "Yehhh . . . Yehhh . . ." And this time he felt the distinct sensation of words sticking in his throat.

She went on. "I walked all the way out to Ocean Beach because there was a rumor that the Atlantic cable is still working, but it only goes overseas. My family's in Oklahoma! What are we supposed to do if our families are here in *this* country?"

Shane barely heard her. Why wasn't his mouth working? "Chinatown is just a few blocks that way," he meant to say, instead of "Ch-Chi-Chinatow, tow, town is juhh, juhhh." And by now he was disturbed enough that the woman noticed it on his face.

"Are you all right?" she softly inquired. "Because I could sure be glad for somebody to walk me through Chinatown. You know, in case the Coolies want to get back at us. Now that everything . . ." her voice trailed off. She looked more closely at him, regarding him as less than likely to represent a solution.

"Nnnn-nnnn-no. I—I'm not guh-guh-going tt-tt—"

She spun on her heel and walked off before he could finish the sentence.

His stutter took away any small desire he might have still had for communicating with anyone else. Now he wanted nothing so much as to dissolve into the landscape. When he looked around one more time to get his bearings, he noticed that most people seemed to be migrating generally southeast, toward the open expanse of Golden Gate Park. It was the opposite direction than the woman was traveling in, which seemed reason enough to go that way; some small part of him hoped that if he kept quiet for a while, his speech problem would magically disappear. He fell in step with a loose crowd of wanderers that moved in defeat toward the bay.

To his relief, no one took notice of him. People bumped into him without seeing him, without even slowing down. Everyone stared out of haunted faces through hollow eyes. Their expressions seemed to confirm what that faceless, solitary demon of the kitchen said over and over while he destroyed the Nightingale family.

This was surely the end.

Shane let himself be swept along with the others, moving away down the street. Even within the chaos all around, he was eager to be gone, just in case Father Nightingale returned to see what Shane had allowed to happen. When he turned for one last look at the house, falling sparks had already set the roof on fire. The place would burn down fast. He was glad for that much. Even if Father Nightingale was still alive, he would never have to see the awful remains of his family.

With that, he realized that of course Mr. Nightingale was dead. No matter what kind of difficulties he might have had with his store, what man would leave his family alone for a day and a half while the shattered city burned to the ground?

It was good that the anonymous crowd could swallow him. He didn't want anyone, not a living soul, to recognize him for what he knew himself to be: He was a contemptible creature. He was a failure as a young man, even as a human being. His rightful place was in the grave.

Just don't look them in the eye. He learned it so fast that the lesson seemed to arrive complete, a gift of instinct. *Move along quietly, keep it smooth, no jumpy motion. Nobody ever thinks a twelve-year-old is doing anything important. Be invisible.*

And in that fashion, Shane Nightingale moved undetected among the living, seized by the overpowering impression of being a dead thing trapped inside of someone else's moving body. It was a mystery to him that no one seemed to notice.

CHAPTER THREE

THE SECOND DAY AFTER
THE GREAT EARTHQUAKE

RANDALL BLACKBURN HAD LOST all track of time. He guessed that it was pre-sunset on Thursday afternoon. But after nearly a day and a half of fighting the Chinatown fires whenever he wasn't filling temporary graves, he was dangling from the point of collapse. All he knew for certain was that his mission was blessedly close to ending.

There was no longer enough emergency work to justify the extra risk of inmate labor, so he had finally been able to send his exhausted inmate workers off to Army holding pens across the bay in Oakland. He knew that in truth, the battle against the fires was brutally lost, for the most part. In spite of everyone's best efforts, the fire was burning its way all around Portsmouth Square and throughout Chinatown. Nearly everything was laid to waste for many blocks in every direction, or soon would be.

At first, most of the residents had stayed around to fight the fires. Even after all was lost, quite a few remained and took to makeshift shelters erected in the open areas of the Square. It was only when a squad of soldiers showed up to reinforce the police gravediggers that the refugees were finally swept off to less crucial areas.

Blackburn deliberately worked beside two whining underlings, Officers Gibbon and Mummery, trying to control their potential damage to morale. *They're doing everything wrong, for new recruits with careers to consider,* he thought with disdain. Gibbon and Mummery were nearly ten years junior to Blackburn and should have both had more energy for the task. But they allowed their work to make them sullen, and that was something rare in the lower ranks. Most young cops appreciated that police work was a respectable and secure livelihood, and so they kept their attitudes in line. Such things were especially important for a young family man, as nearly all new cops happened to be. But these two dolts were behaving like men who had gotten their jobs easy, perhaps from relatives or through bribes.

They clearly failed to see any reason to adopt Blackburn's dedication. And there was no practical way to punish them under the circumstances, something that these two had already figured out. It left a bitter taste in Blackburn's mouth that all he could do was to give firm orders, then make sure that they saw him going about each of the jobs himself in the way that it was supposed to be done.

He employed the most careful efforts in handling the remains of victims, but still held to his central order and refused to permit anyone on his squad to quit before all of the bodies that had been pulled from the rubble were safely interred—and protected from the rats—or until all of the park's available ground was filled. There was still open grave space left when the delivery system broke down. It happened somewhere back along the way, no one knew where. With a fraction of the city's officials still living, and with the city's physical resources hardly functional, the remaining workers' growing fatigue was now causing the work process to decompose faster than the corpses they hoped to save. He lost count after burying fifty.

All of them were planted deep.

Fatigue settled in like fog. It was natural for anyone who had ridden out the Great Earthquake, as it was already being called, to function on fear and adrenaline for the first few hours. Many were too traumatized to sleep at all. But halfway through the second day,

even the healthiest and strongest felt their physical resources de-
pleted. Even simple tasks became confusing.

Blackburn could see that anarchy was snapping at their heels,
and he could only hope that the rest of the city's dead were being
reduced to ash in the unchecked fires. Protected, at least, from the
final indignity of feeding the rats that roamed everywhere, free as
cats and dogs. The fires, in the end, were proving to be good for
that much. No one could know how many San Franciscans and
hapless travelers died in the Great Earthquake and fires, with all
trace of their existence wiped away. Human remains joined thousands of abandoned pets and even large draft animals in mass cre-
mation. Thankfully, uncountable swarms of rat populations were
converted to ash and bone as well.

But rats were always the first to run and the last to get caught. If
he and his men failed to go deep enough, the rats would be at the
fresh graves the next day. And yet he was nearly delirious with exhaustion. If only his bosses would let him get some sleep. He had
managed to snag a few catnaps here and there, but with waves of
uncontrolled flames rampaging through the city and raining hot
embers, there was never time for anything more.

Only when the last of the bodies were taken care of did he manage to spend a couple of hours sound asleep, facedown under the
nearest tree, before some lieutenant shook him awake and ordered
him to form up a detail. He was to lead a top-speed, house-to-
house search for survivors in those neighborhoods that stood in the
path of the advancing flames. He and his crew would have to keep
themselves moving just ahead of the firewall, in a final pass through
the standing homes before the firestorms consumed them.

His stomach was already twisted with hunger; his bones ached.
He wondered how the two soft recruits were going to take to an-
other difficult assignment. But he was pleasantly surprised to see
Gibbons and Mummery actually perk up a bit under the challenge.
The necessity of it was plain, even to them.

Unfortunately, there weren't many victories there. Most of what he saw within the masses of tilting wreckage was an endless repetition of mangled bodies, long dead. A small few were still alive, but trapped beyond saving in the few moments before the flames found them. Most of the living victims wanted to be left alone to tug at their restraints. But three of them, strangers trapped together, all begged to be shot, just as the young man had done on the first morning. He took a deep breath and obliged every one of the three in the same way that his father taught him to dispatch game—shoot quick, take them by surprise if you can, and show mercy by getting it right the first time.

Before another hour passed, Blackburn realized that he was at that strange house where he and his men had heard the woman's terrible screams during their long march to the square. He sent his men in, but decided to join them and check for clues about the source of the screams.

It turned out that there was nothing there, only more of the endless dead, beaten by the quake. He got his men out of there with scant minutes to spare. There wasn't even time to examine the bodies. His team had done all that they could, and it was no longer possible to keep ahead of the fires. He sent them back to Portsmouth Square to get some rest.

He doubted that there was anyplace else for him to go back to; his apartment building stood within the previous day's burn area. At the moment, he felt more upset about not knowing where to go to get some uninterrupted rest than over the loss of his home. As far as his apartment was concerned, there wasn't much to lose. The place itself had merely been somewhere to store clothing and to sleep between stretches of overtime. The only possessions that held any grip on his affection pertained to his work, and those were still safe inside his sergeant-sized police locker in the more fortunate part of the station.

Despite his efforts, he realized that the earthquake had taken a much smaller toll on him than the majority of the people he was paid to protect. Something about that felt right to him, since he lived in such simplicity and diverted nearly all of his energy to his career. But there were days, now that he was over thirty, when he found that the world had little patience for a single man, a widower (how he hated the word) who had been alone for nearly ten years without ever coming close to remarrying. Society in general tended to dismiss him as a confirmed bachelor and a social standoff. In his bleakest moments of reflection, Blackburn found that the idea of close friendship between men, or of romances with women, somehow seemed more like the performance of an exotic play than something he might actually find in daily life. But now with the fires continuing to eat up the city, he couldn't let go of the desire to rush home and try to retrieve something, anything, and join the treasure hunters sifting the rubble for their own belongings.

The lieutenant was not a fool and could judge how close to cracking from exhaustion all of his men were, so he ordered Blackburn and a few of the others to crawl into the nearby police command tent. They were advised to get a few hours of rest but then stay put until needed. The lieutenant reminded him that there was no point in trying to go home, anyway. Everything was gone.

Blackburn was too drained to argue, especially now with the chance to sleep. He found himself lying on a blanket pad in the police tent without remembering how he got there. The instant he closed his eyes, he fell into a deep slumber filled with sensations of physical torment and images of disaster. As awful as these things were, they barely raised his pulse. There was nothing in the realm of nightmares that hadn't already been exceeded in the waking world.

Shane Nightingale stayed with the same crowd of refugees that he had joined in front of his house, even after they turned northward and trailed along in front of the dynamited mansions on Van Ness Avenue. Within an hour, maybe two, his band of wanderers made it all the way up to the boat docks at the top end of the city. Their journey over the rubbled streets and through the smoky air was made in silence, mostly broken by nothing but the scuffing of the relentless footsteps. If anyone spoke at all, it was almost always in a whisper.

Shane understood that. A sense of shame tends to keep anybody quiet. After the last three days of his ordeal, his own sense of shame was so strong that it attuned him to the same sort of things in others. He could see the signs of it all over them. To him, the crowd of wanderers resembled children who have just been severely scolded. Back at St. Adrian's, the other boys in his dormitory used to look like that after they had all been subjected to severe whippings, convinced by the friars that they had deserved it.

After all, everyone in San Francisco was aware that their town had a reputation for providing easy access to sins of every stripe. Throughout the seaport city, even people who never partook of the temptations offered by the sin trades nevertheless benefited from the money that sin brought to the local economy. The city's prosperity was related in countless ways to the infamous solicitations and brothels of the Barbary Coast's dark corners and to the hidden dens of Chinatown.

These wanderers around Shane had all been among the lucky citizens living off of the surplus prosperity boosted by such things, up until that very morning when all of them bore witness to the destruction of their world. Even as the impromptu band searched for ways to get out of the city and escape the relentless firestorms, it seemed apparent to Shane that all of them were wondering just how much personal stock they held in the city's collective guilt.

And how can this city's guilt be doubted? Look at what had befallen them—it stretched out in all directions. For all he knew, for all that any of them could know, the entire planet was being shaken to pieces and burned to ashes, and there was nothing to do but watch. What difference would it make, if they ran in one direction or another?

He overheard a couple of new arrivals to the shuffling crowd. They were telling others that there was something of a refugee camp up and running, nearby in Golden Gate Park. The messengers claimed that a few church groups had formed soup lines there.

Hardly anybody turned to head for the park, though.

Shane understood. Nobody wanted to set up residence in a refugee camp; it would be a place full of victims. The emanations in such a place are strong, like the fouled air inside a damp hospital. No one had any desire to stay in smoke-stained tents among others who could only remind them of their broken condition. What they all wanted, as if thinking it with a single brain, was to escape the crumbling city.

The crowd passed squads of military men posted in front of certain mansions to fend off looters. The mansions seemed cruel and arrogant, amid the destruction. It was hard not to hate whoever lived in such places; some of these guards were looting the homes themselves. Shane just looked away and said nothing, so ashamed over his failure to stop the Nightingale murders that he couldn't feel superior to anybody. Twice, he and a few of the other young men found themselves pulled from the crowd by Army unit commanders and conscripted to help move rubble off of stranded victims. It was not necessary to talk in order to do the work, and he liked the feeling of being good for something. Still, every time they released him, he ran ahead to catch up with his shambling group of familiar strangers.

The crowd reached the marina at around three in the morning. There was no one to help them. Any sort of seaworthy vessel had already sailed out. Rumors spread about a couple of ferries that would come and take anyone across the bay who could afford to pay profiteers' rates. A few of the refugees decided to wait for that uncertain rescue, but the rest of them began to drift. Within a couple of miles, they came to the Pacific shoreline at the western edge of the Presidio Military Reservation. The soldiers on duty there didn't look happy to see the crowd. They ordered them all away, saying that every vessel had already been conscripted to help float soldiers in from nearby Fort Baker on Horseshoe Bay.

The crowd had no choice but to cooperate—the soldiers raised their rifles and announced that Mayor Schmitz and Commanding General Funston had declared the city under full martial law. Any citizen who disobeyed a soldier's orders was to be shot. No prisoners would be taken because there was no place to put them.

Nobody made any strong objections. Everyone moved on. They kept up their slow pace until sometime around four A.M., when they came to the flats of Ocean Beach. Predictably, everything resembling a boat had already disappeared from there, too. People began circulating the same rumor that Shane had heard before: something about an intact telegraph cable in the area. Some of them wanted to send messages out, but Shane couldn't picture sending a message to anybody. He wondered what could possibly be said about any of this, even if there was someone to hear it.

A small group peeled off to search for the rumored telegraph station while Shane and the others walked away. This place had been their last hope of finding a boat, a ferry, even a raft to get them away from fires that appeared poised to burn all the way out to both horizons. Now there was nothing else to do but begin a walk of many miles, all of the way off the San Francisco peninsula. Most of the group were poised to go.

Just when Shane had decided to make the long hike with them, half a dozen mounted soldiers rode up at full speed. They reined in long enough to call out for able-bodied help. One of them spotted Shane, who found himself yanked up onto the horse and plopped down behind the saddle before he could object. The soldiers all wheeled their mounts and headed directly back toward the center of the city.

He was drafted onto a cleanup crew in the Mission District, the oldest part of the city. His particular group was sent off to the famous old Mission Dolores to do brick and stonework. At that moment, the prospect of labor seemed like good news to him—he had no idea of where to go anyway. As long as he worked hard, nobody seemed to care that he didn't want to talk, so it seemed that the Mission Dolores work crew could be a good place to lose himself for a while. He knew a little about the Mission, having learned from the friars back at the orphanage. It was the oldest Christian church in the city, dating back to the 1700s. He had even seen pictures of the Mission in a history book at the Nightingale house. As soon as his crew arrived, he recognized the famous lines of the Mission walls. It felt good to be in a place that seemed familiar, even if the feeling only came from someone else's photographs.

One of the soldiers told Shane that there was a list of sites inside the city that were to be restored right away. The list was written by a so-called "Committee of Fifty," made up of the town's most prominent citizens. This Mission Dolores was right near the top of that list.

The news got better. The "Committee" apparently realized that good labor depended upon a good food supply, and so a bread and soup line was in full swing outside the Mission doorway. The aromas reminded Shane that he hadn't eaten since the night before the earthquake. Suddenly it was all he could do to stay on his feet long enough to get through the line. He ate until he became sick out on the street, then he went back through and ate a second time.

By the time the sun was all the way up, Shane was full and the food was staying down. The hours began melting by while he worked in a hand-to-hand brick line, helping to carry away fallen bits of the newer church that had been built next to the old Mission. He tried to give the appearance of confidence by doing an impression of a man who knows how to work. Even when he smashed his fingers, he didn't allow himself any more reaction than to gasp at the pain. The second time it happened, when he couldn't keep the tears from rolling, he managed to wipe them off with his shoulders while he kept on working. He was almost certain that no one spotted him.

The task got him all the way to lunchtime before the work ran out. He took another helping of bread and soup, and had just enough time to choke it down before being drafted into another small crew. They were to reset the gravestones around the Mission's old cemetery, a small plot of land that was packed full with San Francisco's earliest settlers. It was relatively easy work, so the crew alternated their graveyard labor with spells of firefighter duty within the surrounding neighborhood. When the flames came and burned through, Shane saw that there wasn't much to be accomplished against the fires. Somebody said there was a rumor about hoses that were going to pump ocean water all the way up from the pier, but there weren't any to be seen.

It seemed to Shane that they were all only there to witness the destruction. There was no way to do battle with it, other than helping to pull trapped people out of the fire's way, or by helping to move important belongings. The thick adobe walls of the Mission and its clay-shingled roof were easy enough to save from the fires, however, and while the city founders' gravesites had taken some damage, the cemetery struck Shane as basically unscathed and beautifully peaceful. He immediately understood why the "Committee of Fifty" included this place on their list.

The physical work was perfect for him, easing his tightened muscles and numbing his scrambled emotions. Meanwhile, the food line stayed active and a few more trips carried him through the rest of the day. By evening, the little cemetery almost looked as if nothing had happened there.

Shane's team of exhausted conscripts finished for the day just as thick rain finally began to blow in off the sea. The workers sent up a spontaneous cheer. Shane even felt the gnawing ache lift off his chest for a few seconds, borne up by the sound.

Most of the drafted workers were allowed to leave at that point, but Shane dawdled around. He hated the thought of leaving the food line before they took it down. One of the grateful Mission friars noticed that Shane was making it a point not to leave, and asked if Shane wanted to lay down on a sleeping blanket there under the Mission's strong roof. The simple generosity of the question caught Shane so off guard that his throat seized up. He couldn't bring himself to risk an answer without breaking down, and he was grateful when the friar accepted that Shane could only nod. The man handed him a sleeping roll and pointed to an isolated corner.

Shane eagerly rolled out the mat and lay down. The padding was just thick enough to soften the floor; he could still feel the cold stone beneath. That did not matter. It was a kingly luxury to remain sheltered in that dry and quiet place, while outside the Mission a forgiving rain gradually began to quench the city's smoldering ruins.

Blackburn smelled the thick char in the air before he heard the words.

"You awake? Come on, now, Sergeant—you awake?"

He opened his eyes and looked up into the face of another young SFPD lieutenant. The lieutenant's face glowed orange and yellow in the light of his field lantern. He repeatedly jabbed Blackburn's bare foot with his boot heel.

"I'm *up!*" Blackburn groused.

"You *sure,* now?"

"Wide awake."

"You don't *look* wide awake, Sergeant. You know what day it is? It's Saturday evening, almost seven o'clock. You been out cold, all day long!"

"God's sake, Lieutenant! I went straight from digging graves the first day to fighting the fires when they came through here."

"Are you being insubordinate, Sergeant?" the lieutenant asked with a sneer.

"No. Sir. I am trying to say a man has to have some rest."

The lieutenant clucked his tongue in the way he reserved for men of lesser rank. "Now, them volunteer ladies over there got a coffee wagon set up. Go get yourself some and stay awake. I'm gonna have orders for you."

The lieutenant turned away to check a sheaf of notes in a leather-bound notebook, and walked off muttering, "And then by God, I'm gonna get some sleep myself. Somebody else can try to shovel their way through this shit pile."

Alone now, Blackburn strained to see out into the night. Countless points of orange glow marked the horizon in all directions. There were deep fires that hadn't succumbed to the rain yet, even though the surface fires were mostly extinguished. After hours of light drizzle, thick trails of steam rose from the downed buildings all around the edge of Portsmouth Square. The stench of burning things drifted everywhere.

The scene was how his boyhood pastors had described Hell to him. He rose to his feet, painfully stiff, and headed for the coffee wagon.

Before he took three steps, the young lieutenant called out, "All right then, Sergeant! The next thing on this list is the Mission Dolores. Their messenger said it's *muy importante*. Take your coffee and hike over to Sixteenth Street. Check up on the Mission's cleanup progress. The town bigwigs want to make sure our civic heritage is protected."

The lieutenant stepped close to Blackburn for emphasis, and went on, "Offer them police assistance to guard the place, but listen to me: *Convince them that they don't need it*. Truth is, we couldn't get around to helping them for days, and we don't need word about police weakness getting around."

"I'll try, sir."

"Don't *try*, Sergeant, accomplish your task. Encourage them. Flatter them if you have to. Slather them with bullshit if that works. Just convince them that they can handle it on their own. People congregate at a famous old church like that. They trade gossip, you get it? If the city realizes how badly overwhelmed we are—"

"Well God damn it, Lieutenant, is there some mysterious reason we can't draft civilians and maybe make some real progress?"

The lieutenant raised the lantern to include Blackburn in the glow. He glared at him. "Your problem is your mouth, Sergeant. Now, I know what a fine job you did here, but your mouth could be the one thing that winds up holding you back. Get your coffee and get going. When you accomplish your task at the Mission, take a few hours off. Rest up. Check the ruins at your apartment, though you'll likely be wasting your time."

"Thank you for the advice, sir!" Blackburn said with too much enthusiasm. He saluted, waited for the return, never got one. The lieutenant was gone. Blackburn lowered his arm, turned around and headed for the coffee table. That was something, anyway.

Instinct told Shane to lie still on the Mission floor and do his best to fake being sound asleep. He heard boot steps, along with the scraping of a pair of sandals. Through squinted eyes, he watched the same kindly friar who had given Shane his blanket roll. Now the priest shuffled along beside a police sergeant—the same man who had just been in Shane's dream, the one who was actually in the Nightingale house.

He was too stunned to react while the footsteps came close . . . The footsteps paused . . . Shane could hear the big man's breathing.

"So that's it, then?" the sergeant's voice boomed. He stepped into view, just a few feet away.

The Mission assistant quickly drew close to the sergeant and raised a finger to his lips, then pointed down to Shane's makeshift bed. Shane dropped his eyelids closed the rest of the way and heard the sergeant mutter "Oh," then lower his voice before continuing. "So you haven't really had any other problems here, right?"

"Sergeant Blackburn, I get the distinct impression that you don't want to hear what I've been telling you."

"Oh, now, don't say that. You just don't realize how much good work your volunteers already accomplished here. Maybe they helped keep thieves away, just being here! Amazing teamwork! No outbreaks of trouble, no fistfights, no need for a police presence at all."

"Sergeant, this Mission is a valuable part of the city's historical—"

"All right! All right. Listen, Padre, my head is splitting open. Tell you what; let me get a couple hours of shut-eye here, and after that we'll talk."

"You should tell your commanders at City Hall that my position will not change. We need a sizeable labor crew here, and that will require police presence. Just because we've had no trouble yet is no reason to—"

"Some rest, Padre," Blackburn interrupted. "It's what I really need. Then we'll talk. Aren't you always more cheerful after you've had some sleep?"

There was a pause. Shane could not tell what it meant, until the padre's quiet voice replied, "I'll get you a bedroll. Take the corner opposite that young man sleeping over there."

Shane bit his lip in frustration. The big sergeant—an unknowing witness to the Nightingale family murder scene—was going to lie down and sleep no more than ten feet from Shane's spot on the floor. The situation mocked him.

He listened to the padre's sandals scuffing out of the room, while his heartbeat hammered so that it felt like it echoed off the stone floor. What if this sergeant could simply take a good look at Shane and somehow see his whole dreadful story written on him? What if, with a single glance, the big man somehow realized that the two of them had been inches from one another, inside of a now-vanished crime scene?

Shane could hear the big man breathing, almost sighing. He sounded tired. The sergeant yawned and stretched, popping his joints, until the padre finally returned with the bedroll. The two men exchanged a few pleasantries, then the friar disappeared and left the sergeant alone there with him. All he could do was to keep faking sleep while he listened to the sergeant spread out his roll, slip off his boots, and lie down. After a minute, the sergeant's breathing became deep and even.

It seemed safe enough to assume that the big man didn't have any sense of who Shane was. He felt better, but he still had to wonder how anyone could fail to see the guilt boiling inside of him. Strangely, nobody had so far. He wanted nothing more than to remain as a bundle of rags sleeping in the corner, lost among thousands of faceless refugees.

He gradually drifted back to sleep, resolved that if this Sergeant Blackburn of the City Hall precinct was still around when he woke up, he would immediately slip away without giving the man a chance to ask him anything.

CHAPTER FOUR

TOMMIE SIPPED A STEAMING MIX of Oolong tea, honeycomb, and three teaspoons of whiskey while he stood nude but for his slippers before the large window of the top floor study. His Victorian house high atop fabulous Russian Hill stood unscathed by the earthquake and the fire. Such front and center evidence of his essential importance next to the city's ruffian public gave him a heady rush of self-affirmation, to the point that while he gazed out over the ruined city, he could not help but find the rest of its scrambling population disgusting.

The path of destruction stretched in all directions, even though the rain had finally put out the last of the big fires. The rain, it turned out, had been a true godsend. In spite of heroic efforts from the surviving firefighters and police, almost nothing that human beings did to fight the leaping firestorms had done any good.

Death was everywhere. For uncountable numbers of terrified residents who thought that the earthquake and fires signified the end of the world, it turned out to be precisely that. Rats now roamed the city with impunity. Tommie was astonished by how many found their way out of burning buildings. *Only five days,* he marveled, *and they've already learned not to fear us.*

So then, how to move in harmony with this turn of events? Tommie knew that the mayor's office was doing its best to crank out in-

formation to the newspapers and wire services regarding the numbers of the injured and dead. But the simple truth was that nobody
could offer anything better than a well-intended wild guess, and es-
timates would be held down to minimal levels. It struck Tommie
that the authorities were actually trying to cover his tracks for him,
in the interest of the city's reputation. Another blessing.

Tommie was aware of all these things because just the day before, he had ventured out in male clothing to catch up on general
gossip. Although he kept to himself while strolling through the
refugee camps, he frequently paused just long enough to eavesdrop
here and there, so that by the time he got back home, he knew the
state of things all around the city.

For him, those facts merely added to the self-evident truth
demonstrated by the advancing wall of flames, days earlier, when
the majestic conflagration split in two. The two sections each proceeded *around the sides* of Tommie's lovely hilltop neighborhood—
completely sparing his house. His Victorian home came through it
without so much as a singed window treatment. The only necessary
recovery from the earthquake consisted of throwing out a few broken lamps and rehanging some art. Now, all it took was a simmered
potpourri of cinnamon and allspice to conceal the charcoal smells
from blackened ruins only a few blocks away.

He stepped out of the slippers. Now stark naked, Tommie set
aside his empty glass and began to roll his new, electrically powered
vacuum cleaner gracefully across the floor. The diesel generator
down in the basement chugged up more than enough power while
Tommie guided the machine back and forth, back and forth, using
the same slow and sweeping motions that the lady in the magazine
advertisement did. He carefully kept his free hand out to the side,
fingertips extended, arm raised halfway between the hip and shoulder. The invention itself had only been on the market for a few
years, and was priced strictly for the well-to-do. Only the best people had them. He practically danced with the machine.

The Great Earthquake had done nothing less than vault Tommie into his dream, giving him the power of an avenging angel who rises up to mete out justice. And right from the first moment, Tommie had known where to start: that arrogant bag of skin, Mr. Nightingale, the dry goods man. For years, he allowed Tommie to pay off his tab whenever he got around to it. So what if he neglected payment for a year or so? Tommie could have written a bank check at any time and would have forgotten the whole thing by now, never feeling a hint of difference in his daily life. But it pained him to pay out money. It seriously pained him, and it made no difference that he had so much. Each time he paid a bill, it felt like swallowing a dose of poison. As far as Tommie could see it, every price tag, every line of store credit, every invoice that came in the mail, they were all nothing more than coded and toxic messages from a world that wanted to take and take and take until everything Tommie had was gone. And where would that leave a creature such as him? He had to wonder.

It was never necessary for Nightingale to take him to court and win a judgment against him. Everyone knew Tommie was good for it. *They ought to know, anyway.* All of them. They had no excuse for not knowing. Nightingale had shown no appreciation, no respect at all for Tommie's point of view. First the greedy man put a lien on Tommie's house. Then, the day before the earthquake, the fool actually showed up at Tommie's door to dun him for payment. The arrogant bastard had done all this over a few thousand dollars! The foul man had actually come to Tommie's home, unannounced and uninvited.

Nearly catching Tommie inappropriately attired.

And so it made no difference that Nightingale had been out tending to his store, right after the quakes died down. He would have accomplished nothing for the rest of the family, even if he had been at home. Tommie would have just killed him, first thing. The result for the others would have been the same.

A house full of females, in a time of general civic emergency, when everybody's full attention is focused on the earthquake and fires. What a perfect place. What an ideal set of victims for Tommie's new beginning at the true Savoring of his work.

It was all the better, since none of the Nightingales had any idea of who he was or why he was there.

The memories swept over him again, in a small wave of ecstasy. Tommie felt good, all the way down into his bones. The thought struck him, *there's a poem in this*. A fine poem: short, romantic, musical. He picked up one of the notepads that he kept available everywhere in the house, each with its own silver writing pen, and put his calligraphy studies to use.

> *Your horror was so pure*
> *Rays of terror flashed from your eyes*
> *Like the breath of a dying angel*

Those three lines were all it needed. Something about it made him crave a sexual release. Within moments, satisfaction filled him like warm and soapy bathwater. With it came an inspiration—from that moment forward, each of Tommie's deserving ones would get an original poem left behind with them, to commemorate their contribution to the Savored experience.

As soon as darkness fell, he got into full makeup and costume and headed for the Barbary Coast. A brief step backward, for old times' sake. A quick knife kill and an easy escape. The drunks were sure to be back down there, feeding their habits again, earthquake or not. Who among them didn't deserve it? *The poem's the thing.* What Tommie needed most of all was a deserving corpse to pin one on.

CHAPTER FIVE

SHANE'S DOGGED WORK HABITS quickly endeared him to the padres. He became all the more valuable after it dawned on the holy men that neither the San Francisco Police Department nor the United States Army could supply the labor to repair and guard the Mission, despite the good intentions of the Committee of Fifty. The priests already realized that Shane was homeless, so now they asked about his family. All he was able to tell them was that they had been lost to the Great Earthquake. Beyond that, his throat locked up on him when he tried to explain.

Once they understood what he was trying say, they offered him a position there at the Mission. There was need of a grave tender and night watchman for the Mission cemetery, since some of the more desperate earthquake victims might decide to raid the city founders' resting places for buried gold and jewelry. The pay was only a few pennies per day, but meals were included at the friars' table, and they let him set up a permanent living space in an empty toolshed. All he had to do was hang the watch on one of the many nails protruding from the rough wooden walls and he was all moved in. It gave him a place to exist, and some sort of a reason. Work, meals, and rest formed the core of his days.

He quickly learned that the padres at the Mission were generally not like the Helpers at the orphanage at all; they left him alone to his chores and his daily life. One or two of them came around, nearly sniffing at him, but he hit them with his practiced blank stare and refused to respond to them in any way. That gave them the opportunity to think that he was crazy and keep their dignity while they walked away.

Shane hardly felt the time slip by. On the outside, he buried himself in his new job and adjusted to life at Mission Dolores. Inside, he survived his private turmoil with a simple grim march through days that were each the same as the next. Before the quake, a demeanor such as his would have called attention to itself, perhaps gotten him in trouble. Now everybody on the streets seemed preoccupied with their own stock of primal fear, even a lingering sense of doom.

The natural rage over the betrayal of the very ground beneath their feet gave everyone plenty to wake up screaming about in the nights that followed. Even the quiet ones, those who silently swallowed their nightmares and never spoke of them, slept without resting. They clenched their jaws hard enough to crack their teeth and tried to minimize their suffering by denying it. Among people in such a state, Shane had no trouble passing unnoticed.

His state of mind was perfect for the job of tending to a graveyard. He craved the isolation. Inside of those first days and weeks, his method of disguise was to do his best to act normally, but without attempting to speak, and to avoid drawing anyone's special attention until he could get clear of them. He took examples from the non-English-speaking Chinese and Mexican laborers, after he realized that they could get through most situations with a combination of shrugs and hand gestures. His reputation as a good worker soon began to protect him. He found that he was able to do a good enough job at his assigned tasks that it made others appreciative of his presence and less inclined to get suspicious about him. By and large, people left him alone.

Once the friars demonstrated how they wanted the repair work to be done—the careful mixing of fine mortar, the precise fitting and gluing of broken tombstones and statuary—he discovered that he could sometimes escape the grip of his despair for a good hour or two while he was absorbed in his work. There was a small sense of peace and satisfaction to be coaxed from the results, even if the relief never lasted for long. He was grateful to do the jobs right there where he was living, and to spend both the nights and the days among his newly repaired handiworks.

His first serious solo job assignment was to repair the split gravestone of one Catherine Hoban, who had died in 1854 at the age of twenty-six. Shane's mind filled with images from the woman's time, because the strict monks at St. Adrian's had made sure that he knew all about the Gold Rush era. The stone's inscription told that Catherine Hoban lived through the great gold strike of 1849, as well as the following massive surge in the city population, plus the huge influx of young Chinese men imported as labor. Catherine Hoban was alive when San Francisco exploded into an international presence as a seaport, but she died just as the city was emerging, when she and San Francisco were both still young.

Shane carefully daubed the fine mortar all along the two edges of her broken headstone, and while he worked, he tried to feel for a presence in her grave. He wondered, was there something that would indicate whether or not Catherine Hoban had died a peaceful death? Or was hers violent and terrible? The markings told him nothing.

He fit the headstone's two pieces together and made sure that there was a complete bond all the way along the break, then held them in place by hand while the mortar dried. He could have accomplished the job more easily by propping the two pieces in place, but he wanted to give the repaired stone the simple gesture of respect of being perfectly hand balanced.

Since the city was enjoying a brief break in the pounding rain that had covered it the past few days, it was comfortable enough while he held the two stone pieces together that he drifted in memories from more peaceful days at St. Adrian's. The monks there had always told Shane that he was left at their door with a piece of paper, no note. The paper only said "Shane, 4, born January 1." No last name. No other information.

He had always found it hard to accept that he was already four years old when he arrived at St. Adrian's. If that were true, it seemed like he ought to be able to remember something of his life before the orphanage. But his memory of anything prior to being there was blank.

Inside of St. Adrian of Canterbury's Home for Delinquents and Orphans, his daily life had always reminded him of the life of an ant in a busy anthill: a relentless pace of endless chores, one after another after another. Though he was rarely able to leave the orphanage, whenever he had free time he explored the world through the books that the friars taught him to read. And although the friars and their Helpers gave plenty of reason for fear, they employed that fear against their young charges by enforcing the proposition that ignorance was deadly for their Delinquents and Orphans.

The unwavering focus came from the friars' conviction that knowledge might actually make a difference in the lives of these children, who were otherwise guaranteed an existence as social throwaways. They could survive a childhood without ever being adopted, but the friars promised them daily that without education they could choose between growing up to be prostitutes, thieves, or thieving prostitutes. And then they could take their natural places among the other denizens of the Barbary Coast district, down by the shrouded waterfront.

So Shane made it a never-ending point to absorb all of the friars' lessons and to score well enough on their tests so that they saved their worst torments for thicker heads. The way he looked at it, the constant access to books had saved his life in that place.

As for the more intimate arts of family existence, it was only over the past year in the Nightingale house that he ever witnessed and participated in the daily life of an actual family. The most awkward part at first, for a boy of eleven, was the unaccustomed closeness of two "sisters" who were so highly attractive to him. He came to hate his penis for being untrustworthy, and made it a habit around the house to always carry something he could swing around in front of himself if the need arose.

Amy's sense of music filled his heart from the day he arrived. Her voice expressed a light and feminine energy that seemed to just soar up from her, free of self-consciousness. By the time he had passed his first two weeks in the Nightingale house, Shane was convinced that he was lucky to be able to live so close to her, even if that was all he could ever do. He could never forget that there was to be nothing more; life slapped him flat to the ground every day. The worst of it was the simple fact that he was still only twelve, and a sixteen-year-old girl was older by a lifetime. Even if he had come up in the proper social class, she never would have welcomed his affection.

It was Carolyn, most of all, who had always seen him as nothing more than what he was: a house servant. But sometimes she let him hold her hand to steady her while she practiced standing on the tips of her toes. She was so light and graceful, as if her bones were hollow like a bird's. Delicate and full of quiet mischief, she dreamed of being a ballerina. Carolyn ignored parental objections to her dancing and spent about half of every day flying through the air. For one crazed instant Shane wondered how the killer knew that Carolyn was the dancer in the family. For a long time, Shane could hear the madman swinging her body, dashing her against the walls.

It was during those final weeks before the earthquake that Shane felt himself sinking into the family unit and beginning to perceive them in new ways. The constant combination of civilized discourse and household intimacy forced him to learn to work within a family relationship. The little routines of it came to feel good, reassuring.

Now his torment included a palpable sense of loss over this new way of being with others—and the guilt of having done nothing but lie in his hidden pantry bed, soaking his pants, unable to move or cry out while the family was systematically slaughtered. No matter how he reasoned his way through it, in the end, Shane knew that his present-day circumstances were the direct result of his inability to fight against the killer. What if he could have won, somehow, through sheer luck? Or what if his display of boldness and bravery could have *forced* God to grant him a miracle? It was clear that the stuttering kicked in because some part of himself wanted to stop in the middle of whatever else he might be saying, and instead scream out to anyone within earshot that he was a coward.

Shane's muscles began to ache from holding the tombstone pieces in place. He realized that a good amount of time had passed while he held the mortared stones, so he gently tested the glue and found that the bond was strong enough for him to let go. He stood up and looked at Catherine Hoban's headstone, a tall, thin flag of granite. The balance between the two rejoined sections was as perfect as he could make it.

With that, it struck him that he might never be able to find any answers to the questions about himself that tormented him. Still, when he stepped back to admire his handiwork on the gravestone, he felt the simple pleasure of taking pride in the work of his hands.

Randall Blackburn stood alone in the darkened shadows of a garbage-fouled back alley near the Barbary Coast district. He stared down at the dead man's body, which was not that of an ordinary waterfront drunk. This one was a handsome fellow in the prime of his life. He was perfectly dressed, a well-heeled gentleman in an expensive wool suit, groomed down to the details. This was a victim who was going to be missed by somebody.

There was a note on the body. Along with the telltale *modus operandi,* it assured Blackburn that for the second time in nine days, The Surgeon had struck.

The wound from the heavy-bladed throwing knife was visible at the base of the man's skull. While the wound itself didn't prove the knife was thrown, the obvious depth and angle of entry practically guaranteed that there was no other way to cause that exact injury. No other wounds were evident. And tonight's victim was the second to have a fancy note left behind with him. That first note had looked like a crude attempt to use humor to further debase the victim. Blackburn clearly recalled its swirling, feminine hand:

> *Worthlessness is purity,*
> *Making me a diamond*
> *Among the rejected.*

Tonight, by leaving this second note, The Surgeon was using her handwriting to make it clear that each of the two notes was left by the same killer.

Although the newspapers had ruined the Department's element of surprise in their hunt, perhaps tipping valuable information about the investigation, Blackburn didn't believe that he was looking at the work of some deranged copycat. The specific method of brutality, the skill at silent killing, the lack of interest in robbery— these things were more than clues, they were trademarks. No, this Surgeon character was evolving herself a new style. Her tastes were changing.

That single fact was so promising that it made Blackburn feel hopeful. Newness equals unfamiliarity, and unfamiliarity could keep The Surgeon off balance just long enough for her to make a mistake.

For the past several days, the authorities had managed to keep news of that first note away from the newspapers, hoping that by retaining the detail they might gain some kind of leverage in interviewing suspects. Up to this point, secrecy hadn't been much of a challenge; the victims were all broken men, barely noticed in life and ignored in death. But on this night, with a victim who looked like a gentleman, it was plain that the official silence would never survive scrutiny by the various interested parties.

But once again, the crime had happened inside of Blackburn's beat, during his midnight shift. An involuntary shiver ran up his back when he briefly wondered if the killer was deliberately doing this to him. He decided that there was no reason to think anything like that. Yet. After all, the persistent rumor was still that the killer was one of the street hags, and long-term planning didn't exist in their world. Besides, the worst he had ever done was to arrest them and pull them in off of the streets for a night, where they could safely sleep it off and then have a hot meal the next day. For some, jail was the best accommodation they visited all week.

But who then? The question taunted him.

The nicely dressed dead fellow at Blackburn's feet was going to be the spoiler of certain ambitions held by Mayor Schmitz and Chief Dinan, by costing them the secrecy of this new trend with notes, and the potential of using secrecy to trick a suspect into confession. That would have allowed the mayor and the chief to come off as heroes for the newspapers. There was a lot of finger-pointing going on around City Hall; a major public relations event such as the capture of a wanton killer could have served both men well.

Blackburn felt a sinking sensation as he acknowledged that another brazen murder on his watch was a guarantee of continual midnight assignments on the Barbary Coast. It tormented him to know that this time he was going to be in such a deep trench with the brass that he might go for many years and never dig his career back out. He was unaware of how hard his jaw was clenched while he stared down at the victim, until he felt the resulting pain.

He bent close enough to read the handwriting on the small paper note. This one was neatly placed in one of the body's fists. The delicate slip of paper was perfectly smooth and unwrinkled, tucked between two of the dead fist's fingers.

The world has loved me, made me welcome, everywhere I stayed
But I left my wife to disgrace myself on women who are paid
And nothing could have stopped me but The Blade.

"At least this one rhymes," Blackburn muttered. So The Surgeon wanted everyone to know that this victim was a man who deserved harsh justice. The body expelled gas, as if to confirm that this one wasn't going to keep itself away from the newspapers. The Surgeon's new trademark doggerel "poems" would be public knowledge before long, making the Department brass unhappy in the extreme. Although the sun wasn't going to come up for another two hours, Blackburn already sensed that the day was going nowhere but downhill.

He whistled down a mounted officer and told him to hurry back to the station house for a body recovery wagon. The officer cantered away, and then there was nothing left to do but stand guard over the scene.

Shane's new job carried a lot of free time, especially during late night hours. So within his first couple of weeks at the Mission Dolores cemetery, he began trying to undo his maddening stammer by reading out loud. He had accidentally discovered that he could still speak clearly if he was reading, while he was silently going over an announcement on the church bulletin board. He began to mumble the words under his breath. It went on for a while before he realized what he was doing—something about having the words to read and follow allowed him to bypass his stutter. Not only did he speak clearly while reading aloud, it was effortless. With that realization, he began to practice his reading in earnest. He generally did it at night, but he would take time out for it anytime that nobody was around. It soothed him to be able to hear the sound of his own voice speaking clearly once again. It gave him a form of hope.

Besides, he was seldom ready to go to sleep before sunrise, ever since the unthinkable thing. It felt safer to sleep in the daytime—harder for anybody to sneak up on him. Daylight also helped him to wake up faster whenever the familiar nightmares returned.

But at night, alone and safe in the cemetery, Shane wrapped

himself in darkness like a warm wool blanket. It never occurred to him to think of the place as frightening. Instead, he paced among worn tombstones and practiced his reading by lantern light. While the words on the pages flowed easily from his mouth, he concentrated on impressing his brain with the sensation of speaking freely, hoping that the practice would eventually keep his speech from seizing up as soon as he went off of the page and tried to talk.

Most of the time, Shane read without any real regard for the content of the article. Once in a while, though, a story captured his imagination. Especially the society pages, adorned as they were with pen-and-ink sketches, and sometimes even daguerreotype photographs of successful men and women. The shots accompanied articles about High Society's weddings, their births, their graduations, and their charity balls—all of it was news to him. The images stuck to his brain like flypaper. It wasn't the idea of money and power that was so captivating; it was the impression of contentedness. How could it be otherwise for such people, living such lives?

He tried to envision what it must be like for them to live each day, feeling assured that they were a desired presence anywhere they went, always knowing just how to behave and what to do. These people had the world's stamp of approval. Unlike Shane, their conduct brought credit to their families. No doubt, any one of them would have known what to do in the Nightingale house. They would have been able to take action where he could do nothing more than lie paralyzed.

The Nightingale family had given Shane their last name and ended his life as a foundling in order to show him a house where there was decency and discipline for everyone, even if he were little more than a glorified servant. It wasn't an unhappy household; happiness simply wasn't part of the daily roster. Mr. and Mrs. Nightingale were both vocal supporters of hot baths, cool tempers, and cold routines. It felt sterile to him, even though he couldn't imagine what he would actually do differently, given the chance.

He only knew that despite his respect and fondness for people he lived to serve, he never felt any desire to emulate their way of life once he was grown. That was even truer now, when being re-minded of the Nightingale house made his mouth taste of ashes.

Shane became consumed by the urge to study the happy people of the world and discover the secret to living their lives. Most of all, he wondered what they might know that could have given him power to take action, back in the Nightingale house, if only he had known it too. Could learning it guarantee that such a thing would never happen again? That question, especially, began to haunt him.

Now while he read the society pages and practiced his speak-ing, he was also searching for a *particular example*—somebody who might teach him, by personal demonstration, the secret of how to live. But since Shane also knew that privileged people have authority—his experience in life so far had shown him that too much authority tends to turn nice people into mean ones and to make nasty people turn just plain evil—his plan was to select his subjects, then hang back and observe them from a distance. Let them teach him without realizing it. That seemed safer than con-fessing his weakness and asking for help, exposing himself to scorn. Perhaps earning himself a ticket back to St. Adrian's, where children were sometimes heard making those same yelps of sur-prise and fear that he now knew far too well.

Surely these society people were the antithesis of nearly every-thing he had absorbed with the hardscrabble survival skills learned in the orphanage, or the grim and gray discipline of the Nightingale house. He would practice. He would do more than practice; he would study them, copy them any way he could. There was no choice. Until he did, he felt certain that he was missing too many pieces inside to be able to hold his own, out there among the fast-talkers. With lives such as these society people seemed to have, surely they knew how to avoid going through their days feeling like garbage. Surely there was something he could learn from being around them.

"What a thing," Shane said under his breath, "that anyone can actually live like that." His mind sank into the fantasy images while his body exhaled so deeply that the muscles rattled in his shoulders and his legs. "What a thing," he said again, just because it seemed to need saying. He was too preoccupied to notice that he was speaking without any sort of stammer at all.

CHAPTER SIX

LIEUTENANT GREGORY MOSES WAS SERVING as Acting Station Chief at the City Hall precinct house. It was only a temporary position, and he never let himself forget that. The job had literally fallen into his lap with the Great Earthquake, and it had somehow remained there throughout the four weeks since. Nearly everything about the job still felt new, and virtually none of it was comfortable. Moses' decades of experience as the department's Keeper of Records never gave him any reason to expect to find himself as a station chief. And since Moses had never tasted the curse of political ambition, the personality traits necessary for leadership were baffling to him. After so many quiet years in the Record Keeping Department, padding back and forth among the stacks and files, the instant promotion and its never-ending urgencies felt about as natural as a suit of needles.

There was no avoiding it. Moses was promoted at the direct order of Police Chief Dinan on the very day of the quake, after Station Chief Winkle took a fatal brick to the skull. Somebody pulled one of the precinct's old command-succession charts from the City Hall ruins to see who was next in line for the job, but it turned out that every individual above Moses on the list was either dead or missing. Chief Dinan read all the way down to number seven in the succession line, farther down than anybody ever expected circumstances to actually go: *Head of the Record Keeping Department*.

Moses' rank of lieutenant had always been a simple perquisite grafted onto his job, a reminder that confidentiality was of the essence. For many years, the first order of secrecy down at City Hall had fallen to him. All the friends and relatives of the "Committee of Fifty," plus the city's other backroom organizations, were able to carry out their lives inside a zone of official silence. No matter how nasty certain personal events might have become, all of the appropriate sensitive events were reliably covered over and permanently forgotten. While it was true that Moses' line of work made him the custodian of a world of secrets, rather like a father confessor, they weren't the kinds of things that were helpful in running a police station and the precinct that it serves.

Accordingly, each one of these thirty days since the Great Earthquake had felt like a long trudge through knee-deep water. Every moment was impossibly hard. Not only was Moses inexperienced with command, but while he called the morning roll and handed out the daily assignments, his brain burned with a pervasive sense that he was in *highly* dangerous territory.

Back when the news of his fateful promotion had first reached him, Moses experienced it as some sort of dark anti-miracle, something sent by demons—every pound of fat on his body quivered with the realization that this uncanny opportunity had come to him at precisely the wrong moment in his life. He was a good hundred and fifty pounds overweight, having long since passed "portly" and landed firmly in the territory of the morbidly obese. Back in the Record Keeping Department, nobody ever called him to task about it. There was an unspoken agreement that Moses was to be tolerated, so long as he did solid and reliable work, never betrayed any secrets, and stayed out of sight among the stacks.

Until the Great Earthquake struck, he was safe in his humble ambition of efficiently running the Record Keeping Department and knowing that he would be left in peace to slowly die inside of his expanding carcass. And he found that the relief of giving up on life provided a strange form of comfort to his depressed condition. Moses was loath to be the center of attention anywhere, especially in a command position as he was now, responsible for dozens of officers who could see at a glance that he was unfit for the job.

Now he couldn't get the eyeballs off of him. For the last four weeks, his bizarre turn of fortune had forced him to stay on the job as much as eighteen hours a day, seven days a week. He took no time off, hoping to use his sheer level of work effort to compensate for his obvious lack of worth. And since for all that time he had been surviving on little more than soups and cigars, the weight was falling off of him. If he could keep that up, in a year or so he might look normal again. But he knew that without the nearly supernatural level of motivation he'd been experiencing, he would never be able to repress his raging appetite for that long.

For now, it was easy to endure hunger. His hunger pains helped to confirm that at least he was doing what he could about himself. He dreaded having to spend every waking hour in full view of everyone, knowing that he couldn't possibly have the respect of the other officers. It was lucky that the men listened to him at all. What would he do in the event of a general mutiny, break down in tears?

Most of the time, Moses sealed himself inside of his work routines to insulate himself from the hot sensation of people's stares and the implications in their eyes. He stayed so busy with one task after another, hour to hour, day to day, that the business rituals became unseen armor. For a while, the armor helped him to keep away certain other, more difficult aspects of his job. These job aspects were the ones that made it necessary to have an approved line of succession for Station Chief in the first place—they were the reasons that you couldn't possibly fill the position by placing an ad.

It wasn't the labor of the job that challenged him, it was the question of what to do about his predecessor's complex web of favors and punishments in the running of the station. He already knew quite a bit about his predecessor's private agenda, men who were owed favors, payoffs, or reprimands by the precinct. His knowledge of secret things was a clear and convincing sign that he carried a bigger than average nightstick, but how long could that faint intimidation last? If there was any hope at all of staying on in this position—an impossibility that it embarrassed him to consider—much more was going to be required of him.

Most importantly, Moses knew that it was vital to begin sending out a steady stream of authoritative signs to the rank and file. He needed to act as if he would always be the Station Chief, even if that was absurd. So far, he had only been able to put off fulfilling the old obligations because of all the chaos in the recovering city. But his honeymoon period in the new job had stretched to the maximum, and now human nature was kicking back in. If Moses were going to hang onto this awful blessing for even a little bit longer, then he needed to make himself known as a man of action. He had to send all the right signals to the brass and to the men.

The thing that galled him was that the favors were to be done for people to whom Moses owed no gratitude. The punishments were also for those whom he regarded with no malice. No doubt the people on the receiving end of those things, good or bad, were wringing their hands while they waited for a sign as to what to expect from the new management down at the precinct station. The department brass, no doubt, expected him to willingly participate in their ongoing patterns of petty evils, in the name of the greater good. For the greater good: Follow the Devil's map to Heaven. Trust what it tells you and ignore your own senses.

He glanced down at the notation for his next appointment and saw a perfect example of it all: Sergeant Randall Blackburn. Moses was aware that his predecessor had habitually handed out the contemptible assignments of the Barbary Coast district to Sergeant Blackburn, in spite of the man's excellent police work. Blackburn was a sacrifice for the rank and file. Moses saw it as a pitiful sop to all the officers who resented Blackburn's do-or-die attitude. So instead of slapping the lazy and envious bastards back into discipline, somebody up in the department brass figured that it was easier to make a show out of Blackburn's career. They left him permanently on the least desired and most dangerous walking beat in order to set him up as a thing of ridicule, thereby defusing the growls and whines of a bunch of little boy cops who should have been wearing knee britches if they were that fragile.

Moses also knew about Gibbon and Mummery, the two recruits who bought their way into the station's force because their fathers were on the City Council. They drew the best assignments, turned in the worst performances, and suffered no consequence beyond an occasional verbal reprimand. Even the reprimand was performed entirely for show. They sneered their way through most of their assignments and produced results that a child could beat. And proof that there is a Devil: They had both survived the earthquakes.

There were a dozen examples, no doubt with more to come. The real job of Station Chief wasn't roll call and paperwork, it was Lord High Executioner. It was precisely that sort of power that Gregory Moses had always loathed and avoided, the power that brings out aspects of people's personalities he had never cared for at all. It was painfully ironic to him that such cynical petty evils were part of why he had effectively retreated from the dangerous human race, making it so hard for him to work in that arena now. Such things had combined to make it easy for him to give up on the outside world in the first place, to surrender to the private joys of chewing and swallowing.

On the horns of this dilemma, Moses wondered what the surviving officers *actually expected* of him. Were they looking for a signal that the status quo would go on, or did they want him to break out in some new direction?

Worst of all, if Moses tried to make a peace gesture—say, just wipe the slate clean and let it all go—could it backfire on him and send a message of weakness? If that happened, then once they removed him and sent him back to Record Keeping, everyone would know that Moses had failed his golden opportunity. He would have to continue coming to work every day, to a place where contempt for Gregory Moses was going to be the rule from then on, with the safety of retirement still years away.

He concluded that no matter what lay ahead, his only hope of enduring in this position was to carry out the roster of petty evils that had been willed to him. If he did, perhaps these minor concessions to a hungry demon might be enough to let him hold on to this job, this windfall, this unexpected and undeserved boon, for just a little while longer. Because it felt so champagne smooth in those isolated moments, whenever he was alone in a room without eyeballs on him, to look into a mirror and regard himself as a worthy man. How fine would it be, to actually hold on to all of this?

With that, it was time to deal with this business about Sergeant Blackburn. Once he did, his position would soon be widely known, traveling at the speed of gossip. Moses stepped to the door of his office and leaned out to take a look; Randall Blackburn was waiting on the long bench that lined the hallway.

Back in his office with the door closed, Moses leaned against his desk, making elaborate business out of lighting a cigar while Blackburn stood quietly, waiting. Moses sat and got settled before speaking.

"The problem, Sergeant—as I see it, at least—is that the United States Army has done an exemplary job in helping to restore order here. And I mean they did it to the point that they made us all look bad. Let us salute the Army," he added in a voice dry enough to cure meat.

"I think you'll have to salute them for me, Lieutenant. There were soldiers openly looting some of the same houses they were sent to protect in the first damn place."

"Mm. And how do you know this?"

"I saw them."

"Did you stop them?"

"No."

"Did you try?"

"No. I shot over the heads of some civilian looters. Didn't do much good."

"You didn't try to stop the soldiers?"

"I said no. Sir."

"Sergeant! I am *not* in the Record Keeping Department anymore, in case you forgot."

"What do you mean?"

"Your tone of voice! Regardless of how anyone feels about it, my rank is now Acting Station Chief. You need to reflect that in your attitude!"

Blackburn calmly stared back at Moses for three or four more heartbeats. It was just long enough for Moses to decide that he needed to retake control.

"The fact is, Sergeant Blackburn," Moses began, "the thought among our commanders is that this unrestrained behavior by U.S. soldiers—on our turf—is a blow to the reputation of the San Francisco Police Department. Publicly, we are forced to thank the Army for the help. Privately, we'd love to shoot them all in the head. And just between us, the brass have decided that we're going to settle for getting even by outshining the Army."

" . . . Outshining?"

"I told you about your tone of voice, Sergeant."

"Sir. How does it help us, to 'outshine' the Army?"

"It doesn't! It helps the department brass. The politicians. Maybe they're the ones we ought to shoot in the head, eh?" He looked up at Blackburn as if it were time for two fellow conspirators to shake hands and go for a beer.

Blackburn kept his face blank. "You could do that, but there is that other thing about hanging for it."

Moses let out a tired sigh. "My God, Blackburn. You're as tiresome as your reputation, I'll say that." He sat up in his chair. "Now, they appreciate that you were instrumental in keeping down the threat of disease right after all hell broke loose and everything. But they also figure that in times like these, a month is too long for Sergeant Hero to go without doing something else impressive. Especially in the wake of your allowing the soldiers to run riot, and all."

"I was under strict orders from Chief Dinan <u>not</u> to stop for any—"

"What you need to do is solve a big case for the Department. Something flashy. Say, an important murder."

"Sir, I know The Surgeon stepped up from killing drunk sailors with this last so-called gentleman, but every street source I have is looking for—"

"No, you're not going to stick that tired old case into this discussion. We don't know for sure if the new bodies are really The Surgeon's work. Personally, I think that she died in the quakes or the fires. This new one isn't doing the castrations, and I've assured the brass that the last one was faked. No, it's a copycat."

Moses pushed a paper-thin case file across the desk at Blackburn.

"And here's your lucky break, Sergeant—this case is solved already! All you have to do is bring back everything the District Attorney's office needs to guarantee a conviction, in less than twenty-four hours."

Blackburn opened the file. There were only two pages inside. Most of what was there had already been in the afternoon paper. A local society gentleman, former Navy Captain Harlan Sullivan, had been killed by his mistress the night before, when she invaded his home and shot him in the upstairs bath. His nude body was found collapsed across an industrial-sized scale standing near the large claw-foot bathtub. The captain had sustained a single gunshot wound to the back of the head. Witness testimony from wife Elsie Sullivan described how she came home just in time to see the mistress flee out the back. The victim was already dead when the wife got to him.

To the responding officers, she revealed that she and her husband had an "arrangement," and that his mistresses were tolerated by her, so long as he kept them out of her life. She assured the officer that her husband had always followed the arrangement. All she could confirm was that he had somehow lost interest in this latest one and tried to break it off with her. But unlike other mistresses in the past, this one refused to be left behind.

The head butler finally caved in under strong questioning. As the majordomo, he knew everything about the house, and they pressed him hard. He was a strapping man, barely of middle age, but he proved easy to frighten. After a few solid kidney punches, he admitted knowing all about this mistress, and that the husband had recently broken it off with her. When police asked him if it were possible that the wife somehow did it out of jealousy, he laughed out loud; the couple's living arrangement was an open secret. Elsie Sullivan loved the daily banquet of her privileged life. She would never, the majordomo assured them, risk prison for the likes of Mr. Sullivan.

"We arrested the mistress this morning," Moses broke in on Blackburn's reading. "Her name's Marletta Pairo, twenty-nine, very nice looking. They found the murder weapon under her mattress. Not your usual whore, I should think."

"Was he paying her?" Blackburn asked.

"I don't know."

"If she's a prostitute, she has to get paid."

"Sergeant, I don't happen to know *or* care if she—"

"I just mean that a mistress isn't necessarily a whore. She might be blamed for participating in adultery, but sometimes the other woman isn't paid anything at all and really does love—"

"And at twenty-nine," Moses rode over him, "she seems a bit long in the tooth for this sort of work, eh? Anyway, we had to take her in, after killing one of our most prominent citizens and being spotted by his equally prominent wife. So now we have her, we've got the murder weapon, we know she did it. But since we can only hold her for three days, we've got to get her charged, and the brass wants to bring in an unbeatable case."

Moses decided to look directly at Blackburn while he delivered his order, instead of casting his eyes downward the way he usually did. He squinted to get his focus, then used his most direct and authoritative voice.

"You need to return with a solid piece of evidence or some great witness testimony, by tomorrow at noon. This case has all the elements of an open-and-shut deal: important society people, wife pressing for a conviction. Naturally, the suspect claims innocence. You just put the story in a nice box for the prosecution, that's all."

Blackburn stared at the little file, incredulous. There was no official statement from the suspect, no testimony from anyone besides the wife. They had a pistol and one witness. But they "knew" that the mistress did it?

"Lieutenant." Randall Blackburn spoke in low tones. "Do you mind telling me where this order is coming from?"

Ordinarily, Moses would have dropped his gaze under such a direct challenge. Nothing in the life of the Department's official Record Keeper prepared him to go man-to-man with a cop who boxed ten rounds with the local toughs every time he went to work. But this time Moses returned the gaze. He even leaned forward while he replied, "Much higher up than either of *us,* you can bet on that."

It felt good to lie so boldly. The sense of power was wonderful. In that moment Moses became aware of the warmth of his penis lying against his thigh. He continued with added energy.

"You know Blackburn, it seems like you take some kind of pride in being the 'lone wolf.' Except I think you forget that *nobody likes* the lone wolf! Understand?" Moses realized that this last line was dangerously close to how he felt about himself, so he didn't wait for an answer.

"You get away with it because you turn in good results. But since it *has* been a month since your last big moment, you need to bring this one home, and fast."

He ended in feigned innocence. "At least, that's how the word comes down to me. So just go ahead and walk the Barbary Coast beat tonight, but follow any leads you develop, then stay on to work this case until noon. Put in for the overtime."

Moses deliberately capped the order with a shrug, but somehow it didn't feel right. Easy gestures of casual authority were a form of arrogance that Moses had yet to master. With a rush of self-consciousness, he realized that his fake shrug most likely resembled the involuntary spasm of a man who just sat down on a cold toilet.

It didn't matter; the course was set. Moses looked up at Sergeant Blackburn and smiled. The smile came easily to him and went unchallenged, surprisingly enough. Under any other circumstances, Moses would expect a man like Blackburn to wipe the expression right back off of him.

But not today. Probably not tomorrow. And certainly not until that inevitable moment when they removed him from this marvelous position. Until then—

His smile broadened. He couldn't help it. Fat Gregory Moses hadn't felt like smiling in a long time.

CHAPTER SEVEN

THAT AFTERNOON

BLACKBURN SAT AT A thick wooden table in a clammy little interrogation room while the jailer escorted murder suspect Marletta Pairo back to her cell. He had gone straight to the jail to have Miss Pairo brought up to the interview room as soon as he left Lieutenant Moses. He was surprised to discover that the retired captain's girlfriend was remarkably stupid and inarticulate. He wondered how the captain had been able to stand her company whenever they weren't between the sheets.

Miss Pairo tried out a range of attitudes on him and ran herself through a gamut of emotions over the course of the long interview, but her fear and anxiety were as plain as her protests of innocence. Still, she could not explain how the gun got into her locked apartment. It was certainly the murder weapon: handmade, firing a distinct 35-caliber forged lead slug. The barrel still smelled of freshly burned powder and the chamber was minus a round. Miss Pairo's denials added just enough to the case to make his job hard, and to guarantee the need for fieldwork. The rest of her interview was worthless. The poor woman was so terrified that she would eagerly swear to seeing pigs fly if she thought that it would get her off the hook.

It went no better at the home of the late Captain Sullivan. Elsie Sullivan was a self-possessed and well-spoken woman in her forties, a product of a social class that prided itself on tightly controlled emotion. She was heavier than most women, but Blackburn noted that she still presented herself well, with a series of girdles and corsets that held her in an hourglass shape beneath her outer clothing.

She was able to tell her story with relative poise, until she got to the part about finding Captain Sullivan sprawled across the big floor scale. Her voice broke and her face went pale while she described the scene.

None of it did Blackburn a bit of good. Her story fit all the known facts. As a potential suspect, what motive did she have? The family money was hers as well as his. Her closest staff members backed up her story about the terms of her marriage. They all scoffed at the idea of Elsie Sullivan having a fit of jealousy over one of her husband's passing flings. Furthermore, Mrs. Sullivan's attitude with the police was fully cooperative. She was eager to have the guilty party tried and convicted.

And Blackburn didn't believe her at all. Even when he set aside his natural resentment of smug complacency, he still didn't believe her. Her pretty face and polished mannerisms gave her a pleasant veneer, but her eyes left him cold. They reminded him of an animal who knows nothing but hunger and fear.

The brass wanted evidence by noon the next day and he was on his own.

Shane lay on his back, sound asleep, protected in the cool darkness of the little toolshed at the rear of the cemetery. The society pages were draped across him like a blanket. In that day's newspaper, even the usually decorative Society section was given over to crime reporting, elaborating on the scandalous story of Captain Sullivan's murder by his enraged mistress. The drama was deep—she was arrested with the murder weapon in her possession. The article took care to acknowledge the new widow Sullivan's lack of involvement.

And while no reputable newspaper stooped to printing a sketch of Captain Sullivan's body, sprawled wide across the big scale, the scene was described in sufficient detail that the effect was the same.

Shane had grabbed up the newspaper as soon as it hit the corner stand that day, eager to practice reading out loud as soon as he got the chance. But when he came across the Sullivan murder story, it hit him hard, wiping away all the other trivial items. Everything about the case struck him the wrong way, even though he didn't understand why.

For an instant, he wondered if it was because he felt his hope fading for finding a class of people that he could aspire to join. That thought quickly faded. It didn't explain his feelings. This story was simply one family's tragedy, and the Nightingale family had fared no better in their place among the merchant class, especially Mrs. Nightingale.

Something about the news story made Shane remember a time when he spied Mrs. Nightingale while she examined herself in her full-length mirror. A coincidence of geometry and a passing moment had placed him so that he caught her reflection through a carelessly closed door. And in that ambushed moment she presented her full self to him, unknowing, while he silently stared from the darkness and watched her turn this way and that before the mirror. His attention riveted itself to her troubled face and her frustrated breathing while she struggled to get a view of herself that would give her whatever she was seeking.

Mrs. Nightingale was a full-bodied woman, by any standard. Shane knew very well how much she loved to eat, and that she considered any form of physical exercise the antithesis of refined living. But she always dressed so well and walked with such stiff pride that it never occurred to him that she was anything but delighted with herself. And yet at that moment, her principal traits were vulnerability and distress over her appearance. It opened his eyes to the depths of effort that women expended for their appearance, since appearance had a great deal to do with how well they lived. It suddenly seemed clear to Shane that if a woman suffered this hard over the shape of her body, she must be in a constant state of torment in the presence of other women. The younger ones, the prettier ones, the ones with ideal figures—what else could they be to Mrs. Nightingale except constant jabs, reminders of her own failings? Self-criticism was something that Shane knew too well.

She stepped to the mirror and tossed a robe over it, completely blocking all reflection. She turned away in disgust. *The reminder is too much,* he had heard himself say out loud, just as he realized that she heard him, too. She turned in alarm, spun to face him, and locked her eyes with his.

He felt surprised that she didn't appear angry. She simply nodded. *The reminder is too much,* she repeated. Holding his gaze, she gently closed the door on him.

Then it was over. The memory dissolved and sleep carried him away.

Shane woke up to a throbbing headache, with pains so sharp that he had to move slowly while he sat up. He pulled the newspaper blanket off of himself. The paper was open to the Society section, and as he glanced down, his eye caught the realistic pen and ink sketch of Mrs. Elsie Sullivan. She was bigger, much bigger, than Mrs. Nightingale had ever been. *So that's it.* The news article had prompted the strange memory as he fell asleep. He looked at it again. Yes, the accompanying sketch of Mrs. Sullivan showed that she had far more to be concerned about than Mrs. Nightingale ever did, with regard to her appearance. What was Mrs. Sullivan's stance in front of a mirror? Could she stand the view? Or did she cover her mirrors, too?

That's when the key seemed to jump off of the page at him. The large scale in the bathroom, the one where the body was discovered—it was more like something you might find in a meatpacking house. That scale was a heavy-duty item meant to take a lot of use. Mrs. Sullivan would never have brought something like that into the house. What woman would? No, it must have been brought in by Captain Sullivan himself.

And why would he do that? He was a fit man, hardly in need of a heavy-duty scale.

Shane felt the answer before he had time to think it—the scale wasn't there for Captain Sullivan. It was there for her. He was the one who brought it home, but it was there for her.

Shane had plenty of experience at being the object of taunting, and now the same familiar feel was here. What else could the big scale be, he asked himself, besides some sort of goad from Sullivan to his wife? The scale's mere presence in the house presented an ongoing insult. The contraption might as well have been screaming, *This is what it takes to weigh you!* In its power to inflict pain, it could laugh at her in a cruel voice that no one else heard.

Shane wondered how long the big scale had been in the house. Surely every single one of those days held some special new humiliation for Elsie Sullivan. Each one was delivered by the sight of the scale itself, possibly along with the occasional verbal barb from her husband. Like straws on the camel's back, they built up, one after another after another, into a boiling mass of resentment and a murderous rage.

And so she shot him, just right, so that he fell more or less across the thing. And then she left him there on purpose. *This is for your oversized scale, bastard!*

Shane couldn't explain the gun, but he felt certain now that Sullivan's mistress was innocent. It hurt him to think of how terrified she had to be, locked up for this crime. The memory of Mrs. Nightingale's final screams of terror and desperation were stuck in his brain like bullet fragments, and he had to wonder if the Pairo woman's fear was any less. He found himself overwhelmed with the urge to help her. However, the force of it didn't keep him from being baffled as to what he could actually do. After all, was he supposed to go to the police with all this?

To tell them what?

And why should they believe anything that he told them, anyway? Worst of all, what if somebody recognized him for what he was? What if somehow these men who dealt with criminals every day could look at him and see his horrible guilt?

But the picture might as well have been burned into his brain; Marletta Pairo's pain was now linked to the final agonies of Mrs. Nightingale. There was nobody but him to help her now. He had to ask himself if he was ready to abandon another innocent one, ready to lie quiet and piss himself instead of taking the necessary risk. Back in the kitchen pantry, his legs had been paralyzed and his throat sealed shut. But what would his excuse be now, if he kept silent about his suspicion, just to keep himself safe?

What good was anyone's life under that kind of burden? He knew the answer to that.

Shane picked up his newspaper and opened it to a full-page advertisement that left a good portion of the page blank. He tore off the blank part to use for notepaper and went to get a pencil from the Mission schoolroom. There, he addressed the note to the head police officer named in the newspaper article: Sergeant Randall Blackburn.

Shane knew of no other way to try to get the images out of his head, so he began to write down his suspicions.

The freshly minted Widow Elsie Sullivan spent her entire ride to the City Hall station fuming in outrage and plotting her ultimate revenge against that arrogant police officer, Blackman or Blackheart or whatever his name was. The man had not only committed the outrage of summoning her down to the station house, but he had sent hirelings in uniform to arrest her like some petty criminal. Fortunately, none of her friends were in attendance. Still, plenty of servants observed the spectacle of the grieving widow being escorted from her home and driven away.

The few moments that it took to walk with the officers from her doorway to the police cart felt as if they took half an hour. Her blood boiled inside of her all the while. She thought of French royalty being hauled to the guillotine in death wagons.

Fine enough, gentlemen, she seethed. The policeman would play his little game of hauling her in and of flexing his great authority. She would toy with him in his "interview" until he tired of bothering her and "allowed" her to leave. With that, his power over her would be exhausted. And at that point, he would have concluded his little fishing trip with nothing.

Then it would be time for her to demonstrate her power over him. Not the petty, niggling power of a common street bureaucrat with minimal education and excessive brawn, but that of an intelligent, college-educated, ambitious woman with access to half the people in the SFPD who ranked over him. Several were within her active social circle. Thus the more subtle but far more lethal power of her social influence was about to bear down upon this bastard sergeant, and from every direction. A plague of locusts.

Elsie rode along in the police cart enduring simultaneous levels of discomfort. The officers had snatched her away just before she was to begin her bath, and the clothes they made her put on were the soiled ones she had just discarded.

At first she was so taken aback by them that it was almost funny to her. It was unbelievable, the sight of these two officers blithely destroying their futures by treating her this way. They wouldn't even allow her to dress in private, insisting instead that they guard her in plain sight while she went from bathrobe to fully dressed and all phases in between. The officers refused to allow her to don her usual array of support garments: unmentionable straps and elastic wraps, layers of squeeze-tight underthings that supported her hourglass shape. Instead the men had barely given her time to put on her outer clothing.

With her flesh unsupported, Elsie Sullivan's naked body usually felt, to her, like a bundle of moist rubber sacks. But once she was safely ensconced in her lifts and wraps and girdles, she transformed into a formidable warrior woman. Men were respectful and a little shy in her presence, and most women didn't even try to give her any sort of trouble.

Today, however, without the needed strength that should have been supplied by her fabric exoskeleton, she found herself arriving at the station as a glob of moist and overlapping rubbery bags. Her own odor was excruciating to her. The assault on her senses caused her backbone to shiver uncontrollably several times.

By the time they pulled into the station and escorted her inside, she was only able to maintain a ladylike composure by concentrating on her breathing and avoiding all eye contact. They have *no idea* what they are doing, she kept reminding herself. *They have no knowledge of the sort of strings that I can pull. They are servants.*

She didn't take their actions personally, as compared to those of the sergeant himself. Elsie Sullivan held a complete grasp on the appropriate care and feeding of servants, and of the delight that their proper use delivers. She would be satisfied to simply have them fired. But she was convinced that something had to be wrong with this Blackbeard fellow. His clumsiness in dealing with her begged for retaliation, cried out for it so loudly that she felt a wave of pity for the foolish man—not that it lessened her craving for his violent destruction. That was a foregone conclusion.

Elsie Sullivan had never entered City Hall through the police doors before, and she was shocked at how primitive and nasty things were below the station. The inner offices looked like they had been carved out of a cave, dimly lit, clouded by fresh cigar smoke, sour with the residue of old tobacco. The two officers, who did not yet realize that their careers were dead, escorted her into a small and bare office. There was nothing more than one large wooden table in the center of the room, with two hardwood chairs. The professionally doomed men sat her down at the table with a few polite, empty words, then walked out and left her there alone. She heard a key turn the door's lock.

Elsie could only stare around the bare room in silence. A powerful knot of dread appeared inside of her, inviting her to panic. She vowed not to give in to it. Instead, she committed herself to turning its energy toward fueling her anger, and to focusing her mind while she waited for a weakness to appear in the situation. Then Elsie Sullivan, a grieving widow who had entertained most of the city's powerful citizens right inside of her home, would finally have her opportunity to turn the tables on this puffed-up little policeman. She would guarantee herself the opportunity to calmly observe him while he stood broken and publicly humiliated, all out in the open, for anyone to see. She would stand aside, coolly watching, dressed in something especially fine.

Why do men always have to kill their enemies? It's so much better to let them live, while you torment them from a distance and prolong their suffering.

She needed to urinate badly enough to feel concerned about it. This situation needed to be resolved before she was forced to put herself in the vulnerable position of having to ask to use the facilities. She tried to estimate when that would be. Thirty minutes? An hour? Say an hour, then. That single hour more or less defined her timetable for this encounter. No matter why they had dragged her here, it was crucial for her to get back out within that much time.

Keys jingled on the other side of the door. Then came the clicks in the lock. When the door opened, Elsie watched the doomed police officer walk in. He was by himself. She quickly checked his name tag. *Blackburn, then. Sergeant Randall Blackburn.* She sat quietly and kept her face impassive while he closed the door, stepped to the table, and pulled up a chair. He sat down across from her. She decided not to give him any satisfaction by speaking first. *Let him make the overture.*

The sergeant simply pulled out a torn scrap of paper with some childish handwriting penciled across it. He appeared to run his eyes over the lines again, then he set the paper down on the table and looked up at Elsie, studying her face. She felt his gaze moving around on her. Nevertheless, she fixed her eyes on the door, raised her chin, and said nothing.

But the sergeant, instead of speaking, just picked up the scrap of paper and read it over again before he finally lowered it back to the table and returned his gaze to her face, still reading her in some fashion. She cursed herself when she felt the old hot rash blushing its way across her upper chest and throat.

That was it. The business with the paper scrap appeared to be some sort of attempt on his part to provoke her. Elsie decided not to let him toy with her this way. She was going to speak first after all. So what? It meant nothing, to speak first. She set an ironclad control on her voice and prepared herself to lash out with quiet power. Then she turned to face him.

"Sergeant Blackburn, I am trying to imagine what possible circumstance could arise that would cause you to have me arrested and brought here like a criminal, when all you had to do was to send word that you wanted a meeting. *What* could be so compelling to you that your men would deny me the right to get properly dressed before leaving my home?" She held her voice down, perfectly pitched to show calm control and absolute determination.

"It doesn't matter what you have on," the sergeant quietly replied. "Think of Miss Pairo, sitting alone in a cell right now. What do you think she's wearing?" His voice was even softer than hers.

Don't take the bait! Elsie matched his technique and lowered her voice even further. "Sir, perhaps a male who wears a uniform every day cannot appreciate the social expectations placed upon a woman's manner of dress, *especially* when she mixes with the city's most powerful and influential people. On a daily basis." She wondered if that was blatant enough for this plebeian.

But he murmured his reply, absently tapping the scrap of paper against the tabletop. "None of that matters anymore."

"I *beg* your pardon! Perhaps none of it matters to you—"

She had just yelled. A real slip. But another moment passed and the sergeant didn't make any reaction. He just kept reading over that godforsaken piece of paper. Elsie felt the air going stale. Could the man smell her? Her skin crawled with the feeling of self-consciousness.

Officer Blackburn nearly whispered, without even looking at her. "Mrs. Sullivan, your husband wanted the prestige of a wife with a youthful figure. He chided you about losing weight until it became a major issue in your home."

Elsie's blood ran cold. The hot rash on her chest and throat turned to flame.

"He bought an industrial-sized scale and brought it home as an insult to you. He probably claimed that it was to 'remind' you to lose weight or something, but that doesn't matter. You knew that it was there to mock you."

Elsie tried to recapture her confidence, or even a reasonable imitation of it. She squeezed her brain for some fiery retort that would shut Blackburn up. But her mind seemed gripped in solid ice. What was happening to her?

How did he know these things?

And still he kept talking. "It was a good thing," he began, "that you had the, ah, 'arrangement' with your husband about his mistresses. Since you were aware of when they were planning to see each other next, you knew just when to shoot him, then run to her apartment while she was still on her way to meet with him. You took his key to open her door, and then planted the gun inside." He focused his gaze directly into her eyes, but she was primed for combat and did not turn away.

"I am impressed, Sergeant Blackburn. Did you get this information by reading my mind? If so, I think you need a few more lessons."

The big sergeant just sighed. He seemed to make up his mind about something before he finally spoke. "Mrs. Sullivan, have you heard of the science of reading human fingerprints to determine someone's identity?"

"Yes. I've heard of it." Elsie felt a brief flicker of triumph. She had indeed read about fingerprinting, in a recent magazine from Great Britain. She was careful not to smile too much. "As it happens, I know that there are scientists who say it is valuable for identification, but that no police departments are using it. Too cumbersome, I think they called it."

"Oh, it can be a bit messy, I suppose, what with the black powder and all. But in fact the English detectives at Scotland Yard are beginning to use it, and we've been considering it here in San Francisco. Your case is one of a dozen test cases that we are running."

She watched Sergeant Blackburn pause, probably for dramatic effect, before he added, "And your fingerprints are all over the gun we retrieved from Miss Pairo's apartment."

All of the fine hairs on Elsie's body stood up. She knew better than to speak. *A nervous mouth will betray you every time,* she could hear her mother's voice saying, giving her valuable lessons in how to lie to boys. *Keep quiet and let them wonder what you're thinking.*

She took another look at Sergeant Blackburn. He really was quite handsome, with a lovely, strong voice. She briefly wondered if she could still seduce a man like him, but immediately felt foolish for thinking about it. She forced the thought out of her mind and tried to reclaim confidence where suddenly there was none.

"I'm curious," Blackburn went on, "did you actually meet Miss Pairo just as she was coming out of the house, or did you have to wait around to catch her?"

She didn't reply. Several awkward moments went by. The two of them were alone there, after all. No windows. The door was made of solid wood. No one could see.

She knelt down in front of him and started to undo his pants.

Blackburn slipped both of his hands under her arms and lifted her to her feet. He was almost gentle, but not quite. "Use the writing tablet, there," he told her in a voice that did not invite a response. "Mrs. Sullivan, you need to write out a full confession. Put all of it down, and don't leave anything out." He regarded her for a moment, then added, "I promise you, it's for the best."

"Do you mean that?" she asked in the voice of a timid little girl, one she had always found to be tremendously effective in the bedroom. It compelled a man to show her that he wasn't angry with her.

"Mrs. Sullivan, you're under arrest for murder, now. You won't be leaving this place for a while. That's why it doesn't matter whether you are well dressed today or not."

"I can afford to post a very high bond."

"Not for murder. There is no bail." He went on to explain that as soon as she finished her confession, she was going to be redressed in the muslin coveralls of a jailhouse inmate.

As much as his words frightened her, Elsie felt sure that she caught a flash of reassurance in Sergeant Blackburn's eyes. It puzzled her for just a moment, then she realized that yes—he seemed to be saying that he could help her, if only she did as she was told. She sensed that her charms were working on him as well as ever, even in her degraded condition.

Feeling better now, she sat down to the writing tablet and picked up a pencil. When she looked up at Sergeant Blackburn and smiled, she caught him almost smiling right back, plain as anything. She began to write, then, in her studied and elegant hand, determined to please him enough to gain every possible advantage over him.

She wrote out everything: how the captain tormented her so cruelly and for so long. She emphasized that Marletta Pairo was not the subject of her malice. Rather, the younger woman was simply the natural scapegoat. The captain, of course, was the problem—a man who was simply too nasty to live. The deservedly late captain. Elsie did not doubt that she could make any reasonable person see that.

Mind over matter, the way she had always done it. So she ignored her current state of appearance and projected the idea of herself as a woman in distress. Within moments, she was transformed. While her physical appearance remained deplorable, she could tell that her presence itself became as sweet as blueberry pie. She knew that no man would do anything to harm her, when she was like this.

She concentrated on writing out her confession just as instructed, making sure to use her best penmanship. The things she was committing to the page were too scary to think about. Somehow the fears tightened her muscles and twisted at her stomach. So she kept them at bay by focusing on the challenge of writing with perfectly even letters. This served to show the policeman that she obeyed the rules, while her handwriting was still decorated with enough feminine swirls to be sexy.

Elsie Sullivan trusted that she would soon have this Sergeant Randall Blackburn curled up in the palm of her hand.

CHAPTER EIGHT

THAT EVENING

BLACKBURN WAS THE HERO of the hour, since the Sullivan widow was in the city jail, huddled with her attorney and sending out scores of frantic missives to her highly connected friends. Lieutenant Moses rewarded him by allowing him to nap in an empty cell until it was time for his night beat. After four hours of near-death slumber and half a pot of tar-like coffee, Blackburn was ready to pull one more full shift before he would finally be allowed to go back to his new apartment and get a full night's sleep.

However, once he stepped outside into the darkness and cool night air, his energy doubled. What he really wanted to do was to ignore the Barbary Coast altogether and do a little investigative work instead. The very idea picked up his pulse. Hunting down a good mystery was far more compelling than the thought of spending the night hunting down street thugs. So in silent retaliation for the brutal treatment by his supervisor, he decided to give the thugs a few hours off and pursue the mystery instead.

He turned away from City Hall's temporary station. The single advantage to walking the Barbary Coast beat was that his supervisors seldom found cause to risk themselves by going down there to check on him. Instead he headed in the opposite direction and took a walk toward the Mission Dolores, several long blocks away.

The day before, when a boy walked into the station bearing "an

urgent note for Sergeant Blackburn," the desk sergeant on duty refused to accept it unless the boy provided a return address. For
some reason, the boy refused to leave his name, but did say that he
was living at the Mission Delores, and claimed that he worked
there, guarding the place from looters at night. If he really was at the
Mission, he would be easy enough to identify. The desk sergeant
had commented that the boy had a pronounced stutter.

Blackburn still felt a pleasant buzz of surprise that the ruse
about fingerprints had actually worked on Mrs. Sullivan. With the
science being so new, she had not realized that nobody had taken
fingerprint samples from her. Most new inventions seem to be half
miracle; maybe she just thought there was some magic to it that
she did not comprehend. By the time her lawyer arrived and she
began to feel buyer's remorse, she had a long, detailed confession
written down and signed in front of several witnesses.

It would never work to back away from her confession. The current state of criminal law in San Francisco was to lean toward the
harsh side. The beleaguered population was in no mood for sob stories; every one of them had a few of their own.

Blackburn had gone into the case knowing that the city needed
to take a close look at the wife, even if they did not have enough to
justify charging her. The rush to nail Marletta Pairo felt wrong to
him as well. His failure was all but guaranteed on the assigned task.
So when the strange note arrived, he had taken it at face value and
thrown it against the wall, where amazingly, it stuck like fresh horse
flop. The easy power of it nearly took his breath away. Pure bluff
and nothing else. Even in this grim atmosphere, miracles still happened. And as far as Mrs. Sullivan's vow of putting out appeals to
high-powered friends went, well, those same people were also the
friends of Captain Harlan Sullivan—shot through the head while
he was defenseless. Mrs. Sullivan was going to have to get used to
prison food.

The kid with the note, though: He was more interesting than
some pitiful self-made widow. What was his connection to this

woman, that he could be so eerily intuitive about her? How was it that he could be dead right about all of it?

Blackburn could feel that this mystery somehow fit into the strange aura hovering over the city. It had been there ever since disaster struck. With that first shock wave, everything about the physical world came under an unstoppable destructive force. So had the more ethereal things, such as one's view of the way the world functions. In the aftermath, the strangeness of a magical clue being delivered by some ragged and anonymous boy somehow fit into the post-quake picture, right along with the ubiquitous piles of rubble. The land down near the bay shore had turned to quicksand from the sheer intensity of the great vibrations. Now everybody in the area lived in a world in which the ground itself could not be trusted to hold still, or even remain solid. So why not a boy with a magic note?

It was a fairly short walk but he made slow time, stepping among the makeshift shelters that now served as homes and businesses for the die-hard populace. Block after block, pale stalks of smoke twisted up from countless cooking fires. He cringed at the thought of another conflagration. Meanwhile, grim and determined faces peered out at him from swaths of stained blankets and ragged clothing. The city was surviving, but the eyes of its people were universally dark and hollow.

Everyone in the region shared the same invisible wound. Blackburn kept his own shoved far down, but he imagined that others could see the effects on his face as clearly as he saw it in theirs. The worst of the shaking had taken place inside of the people. It left them with the question: How far back inside of yourself do you have to retreat, to find a bit of stable ground?

Blackburn was stuck with that challenge as much as anybody else, and he felt moved to stand up for these people. This part of town was mostly a stalwart population, immigrant pioneers of hardy stock. He could see in their behavior that they remained honorable and clung to their families. No one was lying around drunk or engaging in gambling. Everybody in sight was either doing some sort of business or tending to their makeshift homes, with all but the smallest of children occupied in one handy task or another.

In spite of his admiration, he moved among them as an audience member, seldom a player. While walking his beat he was still only an observer, unless action was necessary. The act of constant observation commanded a certain distance that was grimly effective insulation against human warmth, so that walking past these tightly knit families filled him with a lonely ache. If he were off duty, it would be a perfect moment for a whiskey or two. Instead he left the hunger hanging and moved on.

When a rat the size of a house cat darted in front of him, he kicked at it without coming close. The rat disappeared in a flash of matted fur. It was finally becoming more rare to see them. The swarms that roamed the streets with impunity right after the earthquake were fading back into the broken sewer lines and scattered rubble piles. Since confrontations with humans frequently ended in death, the rats were discovering that it was easier to hide in daylight and forage in darkness. He wondered if any of them really carried the plague. If there were any victims, it seemed strange that he had heard nothing about it.

He reached the Mission Dolores well after midnight, so he bypassed the church and went straight to where the little graveyard fronted onto the road. The place was dark, with silhouettes of the larger tombstones and funerary statues defined by faint moonlight. At first the whole cemetery appeared deserted. But he stood for a moment to let his eyes adjust to the thicker darkness under wide boughs of the older trees. Smudges began to take sharper form.

There, in the very back, was the outline of a toolshed. A bright lantern was burning inside. He silently entered the graveyard and made his way back toward the shed. Once he got within a few yards, he could see a rectangle of light projected onto the ground outside the shed's door. A boy's skinny and distorted shadow passed back and forth in front of it, and a faint muttering sound drifted up from the shed. The boy seemed to be reciting or chanting, but Blackburn couldn't hear the words.

He glided forward a few more feet until he could get a good look. The kid was lanky, nearly skin and bone, but did not appear to be sickly. Twelve or thirteen years old, probably. Not shaving yet. His thick, tousled hair looked like he cut it himself and his work clothes were cut for someone else. His shoes and socks looked right for his size but the leather was worn through, enough to notice at this distance. All in all, he gave the impression of being a coiled spring wrapped in skin and hair.

He was reading aloud by the light of the single oil lamp. He paced back and forth holding a newspaper open in front of him. His voice was soft but clear, and he seldom stumbled over the bigger words or odd pronunciations. Blackburn was struck by the sight. He knew that in this time and place, illiteracy was as common as the fog. Yet somebody had seen to it that this scrappy kid thoroughly learned his ABCs.

At that point Blackburn finally realized what he was hearing— for some reason, the boy was reading from the newspaper's society pages, those fluffy stories telling all about the parties and celebrations and glittering lives of the town's noted citizens. The boy read carefully, pronouncing each word as if they were all equally important. He was so caught up in his pursuit that Blackburn got within a few feet of him without being detected.

The fog outside of Shane's toolshed was growing thick enough to slip through the open door in low wisps, but he was too engrossed in his reading to notice the cold. When he read out loud, he was somehow able to send the words straight from the page through his mouth, undisturbed. More than that, he spoke with confidence. His goal was almost fingertip close, now: to burn the sensation of speaking deeply enough into his brain that he could speak just as well when there were no pages.

The voice outside his door startled him. "Is that how you heard about the case? Reading the paper out loud?"

Shane dropped the newspaper. A gust of wind swept it away from his feet and out into the darkness. He whirled to face the speaker and saw that it was the police sergeant, Randall Blackburn, the one Shane left the note for.

And, he now realized, the last one, besides Shane, to see the Nightingale women killed where they lay.

He caught himself staring at the ground, so he forced his eyes to look up and meet Blackburn's gaze. But his mouth wouldn't move. The best he could do was to offer a wan smile and nod. It took the big sergeant a moment to catch on, then he realized that this was all the response he would get. He smiled and also nodded. And then Sergeant Blackburn just stood there, sizing Shane up with an unreadable expression. Shane thought that the sergeant seemed to be waiting for him to say something, but what?

He stepped over to an upturned flowerpot and sat on it. Sergeant Blackburn seemed to smile a bit. He reached into the shed and pulled a large pot out of his own through the doorway. He stopped outside the door, leaving the interior for Shane. Shane was taken aback; the gesture almost felt polite. Or was the cop just guarding the doorway? Blackburn flipped the big pot over and sat where they could see each other. Shane knew that the thick ceramic planter weighed more than he did, and yet the sergeant handled it like a tin washtub. It made him feel like he was made of paper himself.

It was that sense of fragility that left Shane hanging halfway in the moment and halfway back in the pantry at the Nightingale house. That was the last place that he had felt so much physical power emanating from a single person. In the Nightingale house, the madman also radiated a presence that left no doubt that you were in the company of chaos and doom. Shane's instincts told him that the cop had the strength to easily kill him, but he was just as sure that there was no such danger.

The sergeant seemed to decide something. He shook his head, then spoke up. "Well, I already know it was you who left me the note, and ordinarily I wouldn't bother you about it, except that you solved a case. Not just solved it, actually. You stopped it cold in its tracks when it was running away from me. So you can see how I might be curious." He smiled.

Was it a real smile or a trick? Shane tried to breathe slowly. *Don't think about the house. Don't even picture it.*

"All right, then. Always start with the basics. My name is Randall Blackburn. Sergeant, SFPD." He waited a moment. ". . . And you are?"

"Shane Nightingale," he answered, except that it came out "Shh-Sha-Sha-Shhane Ni-Ni-Night-Nighting-ga-ga-gale."

"Shane Nightingale, you say?"

Shane nodded.

"All right then, Shane. Now ordinarily you could address me as Sergeant Blackburn and that would be that. I'm thinking that the practical thing to do is stick with something easy. It's going to be a mouthful to use my rank, so let's just drop that and assume that you know how wildly important I am. That leaves either Randall or Blackburn. I'm thinking that Black-burn is not a good combination of sounds for you. So what about Randall? Can you just sort of slide into that one? Randall?"

Shane tried. "Raaand-Rand-Raaa . . ."

"All right. Back up a bit. Let's try Sergeant, after all. What do you say?"

"Se-Ser-Ser-Se-Ssss-Serg . . ."

"You know, I might have been too hasty discarding Blackburn. You should at least try it once or twice."

"B-B-B-lack-Black-Blackie-Blackie . . . Blackie."

The big cop laughed out loud. "Blackie? Surely not!"

"N-n-no! No. I meant B-B-Black-Blackie . . ." He sighed in frustration.

"There you go! Winner by default! So you're Shane and I'm

Blackie." He laughed again. "It's still Blackburn when you can manage it, but we'll settle for Blackie to save time, fair enough? And the reason I'm here right now, Shane, is because your note, well, it was a powerful thing today. Once you explained Mrs. Sullivan's way of thinking, I was able to go in and trick her with a phony story about a new science called fingerprinting. She caved in and confessed it all."

Shane's heartbeat refused to slow down. At any instant, the other shoe was sure to drop.

"So you see," Blackburn went on, "you broke the case."

There it was! Shane felt panic rolling through him. Shane had broken the case. Blackburn's case was broken and it was all Shane's fault. That's why he was here. Now there would be trouble. He was an idiot to write that note.

Blackburn seemed to catch his concern. "Breaking a case is a good thing, you see." He grinned. "Really, you can do it all you want."

He paused for a few more heartbeats, then went on. "But you see, that leaves me with a mystery. How does a young fellow like you, working over here at night in the cemetery at the Mission Dolores, figure out what's going on inside the mind of a grown woman you've never met who lives on the other side of town? And yet I don't see any flying broomsticks around here, or a crystal ball. Did you find out by magic? Did a little bird tell you? Did an angel light upon your shoulder and—"

"My family," he got it out all at once. "Wa-wa-watching."

". . . You learned why Mrs. Sullivan shot her husband by watching your family."

Shane sighed and shook his head.

"All right, we won't get impatient. Just have a go at it a little at a time. I've got a sandwich we can split, if it gets late." He smiled, then folded his arms and waited.

Shane realized he had to attempt an answer, even if there was far too much for him to say. His first sentence did not promise an easy task ahead. "If you, you, you, be sti-sti-still and wah-wah-watch a woman in fro-fro-frrr-front, front of a mi-mi-mirror, you'll see." He glanced over at Blackburn, but the sergeant was gazing straight at him, patiently waiting for him to form his words. He wasn't glazing over yet, the way other people did.

So Shane went on, sentence after painful sentence. Torturing himself with the effort and tormenting his listener with the time that it took. But whenever he looked at Blackburn, the sergeant was attentively listening with no trace of impatience or exasperation. It was the first time since the night that Shane escaped the burning house that anyone allowed him to speak more than a few words without interrupting him or simply walking away.

Before long, he was able to concentrate on the story he wanted to tell, and he let the struggle for the words take care of itself.

Shane spent five minutes explaining that he was an orphan raised by the friars at St. Adrian of Canterbury's Home for Delinquents and Orphans—quick to stress that he was an orphan and not a delinquent. About a year prior to the earthquake, he was adopted into the Nightingale family. These English immigrants had no extra family in the region, so they adopted Shane for a servant.

Shane spent at least ten minutes getting across that since he was more of a servant than a family member, despite taking their last name, he often came and went unnoticed. Many times, he saw Mrs. Nightingale agonize in front of the mirror about the fit of her clothing and the body that constantly betrayed her. The depth of her insecurity and preoccupation with the failings she perceived in the mirror were a real source of pain. Her husband was kind to her, and never made any complaints about her figure that Shane overheard. Even so, her frustration with herself was there for Shane to see. The lessons stuck.

Then the other day, while he practiced reading out loud, he came across the Sullivan story. Nothing about it seemed strange to him, until he read about the big scale in the house. Instantly, he could recall Mrs. Nightingale howling in frustration over her body. He couldn't actually remember what she sounded like in front of the mirror, anymore. Now all he recalled was the noises she made as death approached her. But the pain for both women was real. If Mrs. Nightingale had been inclined to sum up the cause of her anguish in the form of her husband, she might have turned on him, too.

Mrs. Sullivan had been taunted into a state of anguish by the damning presence of the heavyweight meat scale. Surely it took days, weeks, perhaps months for the effect to take hold. But like a dull arthritic ache that blossoms into fiery pain, the daily humiliation became unendurable. By the time she pulled the trigger, all she knew was that she had to make it stop.

Over an hour went by while Shane battled with the words to tell his story. The night was shifting into the chill of the deep late hours. The smell of damp bushes and grass drifted over the cemetery. Even when he was reading out loud, he never talked nonstop for that long. Yet to his surprise, throughout his story this Sergeant Randall Blackburn seemed to be in no hurry at all, as if waiting for five minutes to get a sentence or two was something that he did every day. Shane was finished with his story before he realized that he had gradually grown comfortable enough that his stutter was greatly reduced. Otherwise it might have taken him another half an hour.

Blackburn stood up and stretched, popping his joints, so Shane took the opportunity to do the same.

"All right then, Shane. I appreciate what you tell me about this woman's special sensitivity and all. And I see that you were able to sort of be a fly on the wall around your adopted house. But I have to tell you, this leap you made from one to the other, from your own experience to a murder scene in some stranger's house—I've never seen it before. Not even among adults, or among other cops. But you used it to solve this case."

"You sss-solved it. You told her about finger-pri-prints. You did it."

Blackburn looked at him and smiled. "Not much of a glory hog, are you? You know, Shane, I think you ought to take more satisfaction in this. You did a good thing. Without your help, an innocent woman would have had her life destroyed."

Shane didn't have an answer for that, since the man had no idea what a foul creature he was.

"So what do you say, then, if I come back sometime soon? Maybe we can talk over another case or two. Just to get your point of view. There's a café just reopened, not too far off. I can buy you dinner."

Shane wondered if he heard right. This police sergeant who did not realize that he and Shane were together in the Nightingale house wanted to come around to discuss police cases? He felt like a pawn in somebody else's chess game.

"I don-don-don't know."

"Won't trouble you at all. We don't have to go off anywhere, if you're busy and all. I could be here and gone in a few minutes. What do you say?"

Shane made himself smile and nod. Anything to get Blackburn out of there. Things had happened much too fast. When Blackburn turned to go, Shane felt himself speak without even thinking about it. "I'm glad you—glad that you—I'm—"

Blackburn just smiled and waved. In another heartbeat he was gone.

By that time Shane was so exhausted that he couldn't even replay the events of the night. All he knew for sure was that for the first time since the earthquake, he had spoken to someone about his former family, and that person was the man who had led his team into the Nightingale house. Shane had come far too close to revealing his awful secret.

For the rest of the night hours, his body paced quietly while his thoughts boiled. It was only once the predawn light finally began to rise that he headed over to a spot next to the Mission chapel and lay down on the ground, spent. He did not want to remain in the darkness of the shed. Even though daylight was beginning to spread across the graveyard, sleep rolled over him like a shadow.

CHAPTER NINE

HOURS LATER

TOMMIE IGNORED THE KNOCKING at his front door while he stood up on the top floor of his lovely Victorian home and gazed out over the crumbled and blackened city. The cast-iron door knocker could fairly rattle the entire house, but most people only gave it one or two raps. Tommie had made sure that the heavy swivel was poorly lubricated and uncomfortable to use.

He trusted that whoever was down there would go away soon. No doubt they were strangers. There was no family left, hallelujah, and those who were once friends of his parents had long since gotten the idea that they were not friends of his. No matter how much they admired his inheritance. To safeguard privacy, he always kept his ground floor windows so well covered that there was no way to tell from the outside whether he was home or not. It was a reliable way of getting people to leave him alone without making them too angry. Angry people get suspicious. Suspicious people intrude upon one's various pastimes.

And yet ever since the quake, these pests were often at his door. Religious witnessing teams, people canvassing for volunteers to take in displaced citizens, beggars knocking for food, for medicine, for money.

Naturally, if desperate and foolish enough, somebody could always break in. So far, nobody had been rash enough to dare. Unfortunately. That would be real icing on the cake, Tommie was certain. Still, he reminded himself that he had no need for any discontent. Because ever since the earthquake and the bizarre energies involved in the upheaval of the earth, the messages from each and every moment gave him repeated assurances that he was on the right track. He was doing good work, even though this rotting world was unlikely to ever acknowledge that, or show the slightest appreciation for it. And yet his work was vital. Everywhere he looked, there were more signs to reassure him and to urge him on.

It was a sign that he had made up his mind to elevate his work to an entirely new level only a few minutes before the earth heaved and citywide chaos gave him the power to kill at random, undetected.

It was a sign that on the same morning when he decided to switch to female victims, he should find the family of store owner Nightingale while the bastard was out.

It was a sign that the wall of flame split in two and passed his neighborhood on either side.

And it was a sign that each of his other killings since the morning of the quake was effortless to perform and easy to disguise.

He felt contented, down deep, like a cat that has just polished off a dish of cream. He had actually been able to eat several of Mrs. Allison's meals within the past few days, and even made himself take a few little naps, almost like real sleep.

There was that one thing, though. Shock and death still came too quickly for Tommie's taste. Even when he did not intend to kill right away, sometimes his victims just laid themselves right down. Or dove for the escape of death like swimmers leaping off of an ocean cliff. After a little introductory knife work, most victims became incapable of following his train of thought while he explained things to them.

There! he thought with relief. The infernal knocking had finally stopped. Another victory for patience. Let the self-righteous sisters of mercy troll for handouts somewhere else. Why should he interfere with the thinning of the herd, the very process to which he was dedicated?

He turned back to the sweeping view, northeast toward the wharves at the tip of the peninsula, and straight west out to the Pacific Ocean. Slowly, he brought his gaze downward, bringing his line of sight away from the horizon and closer to his own neighborhood. Most of the panorama was still a tableau of destruction, even though the broom-and-shovel crews were working around the clock. And then, only seven houses away from his own property, the magical ring of untouched homes began. And Tommie Kimbrough's place stood right in the middle of the safe zone.

His satisfaction was only spoiled by the sight of a giant rat waddling—waddling—along the sidewalk, like somebody's pet. It galled him to see his neighborhood invaded by vermin. Every other living thing in the area seemed to instinctively realize that if you didn't belong in Tommie's untouched neighborhood, you should stay the hell out. These seaport rodents cared nothing for any of that. *Rats may be foul,* Tommie thought with grudging admiration, *but only a fool thinks that they're stupid. A rat can survive most of the things that will kill a human being.*

A cold shiver ran up his spine and rattled his shoulders. It occurred to him that he had something in common with these marauding rats. Like him, a rat was a remarkable killing machine. But by carrying the Black Plague, rats wielded a far more massive power of death. An entire army of human soldiers might lay siege to a powerful city for many months without success, but a few infected rats could take out most of its citizens in a matter of weeks.

He felt a pang of jealousy over such power. What could be greater than the thrill of savoring his time with a victim? Answer: the thrill of truly savoring the power to cause death from a distance. Death for dozens, death for hundreds, death that took days or weeks to arrive. Death that spread like a black fog.

Then Tommie had a realization that struck him like a church bell: When you cannot conquer a source of power, *you harness it*!

"Of course," he finally spoke out loud. "Of course!" he said again, louder this time.

Tommie's eyes were wide open now. He could see the next step in his vital work. He saw it as clearly as he saw the red afternoon sun, way out there, dipping into the sea at that fateful moment and bowing to the coming darkness. Just for him.

The entire time that Blackburn sat in the headmaster's office at St. Adrian's, he felt utterly confused as to just what sort of place he was in. The name made it sound like a formal religious institution, but the place did not claim any specific church.

The headmaster droned on, accompanied by a wet swishing sound coming from a corner in the background, where a young girl of perhaps ten years studiously mopped the floor. She had close-cropped flaming red hair and a spray of freckles across her face, and her girlish energy radiated even in the act of pushing a mop.

Blackburn studied the rest of the room again, looking for anything he might have missed. There was a cloistered feel to the grounds and the buildings, but few religious symbols other than plain Christian crosses placed here and there. And yet the man behind the headmaster's desk had been introduced only as "Friar John." He dressed like a monk in spite of his secular job title. Blackburn wondered why men who were not Catholic would call themselves "friars." Or were they some new kind of Catholic? Nobody offered an explanation. He decided not to mention it, rather to wait and see if the topic arose on its own.

He had to admit that Friar John spoke in such measured tones that serenity and gentleness appeared to radiate from him. Nevertheless, Blackburn felt a wave of vaguely unpleasant sensations wash through him. At least the man was cooperative. He expressed no hesitation in telling all about the boy, Shane. Blackburn listened to every detail of the story of how Shane was adopted by the

Nightingale family a little more than a year before. It all matched the few details that the boy gave him.

It seemed clear that the central mystery of Shane's extraordinary ability was not going to be solved in this place. Friar John explained that the records told nothing of Shane's origin or anything at all of his life prior to arrival. He was said to be about four years old when he was admitted, along with a scrap of paper that only gave his first name, age, and birth date. Friar John assured him that Shane was remembered as smart and quiet, and liked well enough by the other children, even though he often seemed to work at being invisible.

Blackburn gave Friar John the sad news that the entire Nightingale family was killed in the earthquake and that now Shane was living on his own. He avoided giving an address to see if the headmaster would press him, but Friar John just nodded and explained that unless Shane got into trouble, he couldn't be forced to return. With the new influx of orphaned children from the quakes and fires, nobody was pressing for more juvenile wards. The boy had no need to fear that anyone from St. Adrian's was going to come looking for him, he said, and smiled.

Blackburn noticed that the swishing sound had stopped. He instinctively glanced over toward the girl. She was staring straight at them.

Friar John spoke in a vaguely annoyed tone, "Sergeant, this is young Mary Kathleen, with us since her crib days. Spends most of her time on punitive work assignments and never seems to learn a thing from them." He raised his voice to make sure she heard him. "I hope you never have cause to give her trouble and take her downtown!"

Mary Kathleen stifled a good-natured laugh, unperturbed.

Blackburn liked her smile, so full of swagger. The kid looked like she could box a kangaroo. "Did you know Shane?" he asked her.

"He's older," she answered. "Was he hurt in the quake?"

"Mary Kathleen," Friar John interrupted, "you are free to go for now. You can finish this up in the morning." He gave her a wan smile that Blackburn recognized as trouble. It made the girl's expression go dark.

She nodded to herself, then set the mop against the wall and walked out.

"Nice meeting you," Blackburn called after her.

She turned and flashed him a smile for just an instant, and then she was gone.

St. Adrian's policy of not allowing children off of the grounds without supervision was an invisible ball and chain for Mary Kathleen. It could never be tolerable to her. The only meaningful answer to such an awful restriction was to take solo field trips, excursions into the world that was denied to her.

Mary Kathleen knew that if she told Friar John that one of the Helpers was sneaking around to watch her bathing, she could probably get the man in trouble. But this particular Helper would do anything to keep her silent, and that was highly useful in expanding her horizons from time to time. This time the cooperative Helper covered for her while she darted out the back way and scrambled over the fence. She circled the grounds at a dead run, to reach the front entrance before Sergeant Blackburn got too far away. She was determined to follow him all the way back to wherever Shane was staying. It did not matter how long it took.

Shane "Nightingale." She wasn't used to thinking of him that way. At St. Adrian's, neither of them had a last name. It was supposed to make it easier for people to picture having you in their family. Then they could stick their last name on you without feeling guilty, since you didn't have one in the first place. If the Nightingale family was all dead, though, she wondered if he still wanted to use their stupid last name. Was he really Shane "Nightingale" anymore?

When Sergeant Blackburn finally emerged from the front gate, she was delighted to see that he wasn't climbing onto a horse or buggy. He just stretched his legs and headed off at a fast walk. She went after him, following from behind and moving at a brisk trot to keep up with his stride. The chase quickly took a toll on her. Mary Kathleen could bound like a rabbit, but she usually only needed to for a block or two, enough to evade a pursuer. For the past couple of years, anytime she sneaked out there were always a few older boys or grown men who pawed at her from shadows, pulled at her from doorways, or tried to follow her into secluded places. Then, a brief explosion of speed was the only power necessary. Now it took everything she had to keep up with the big policeman on this endurance test, block after block.

But she had clearly heard the cop tell Friar John that he just finished his night shift. Surely that meant that he would be on his way home now, didn't it? And before he went home for the day, he would stop and see Shane, wouldn't he? If the cop was all so interested in him, why wouldn't he go visit him? She kept telling herself that, while she labored to keep up with the sergeant's long strides. Her overall plan was good enough that she felt inspired.

She was a hunter and a spy, a spy disguised as a silly tomboy girl. She needed a name for herself, and therefore, something that fit the adventure. "Mary Kathleen" was unacceptable. It was the false name that St. Adrian's gave her, back when she was too young to remember. And since "Mary Kathleen" was a disguise that she had to wear at St. Adrian's in order to get from day to day, it made perfect sense for her to cast it aside and choose a special name for herself, now.

She sorted through her best words for one that might capture the feeling. A spy and a hunter were both dramatic roles, so why not use a dramatic word? Her little field trip today was a scene from a magical play, a sneak-away adventure inserted into a plain, old, ordinary day. The adventure itself, she realized, was a vignette: a separate scene in a larger play. She was in a vignette all her own. And so "Vignette" was perfect as a new name for her, a name so special that nobody else even knew it.

Vignette willed herself to be an invisible and unimportant little girl whom nobody would particularly notice or remember. In that fashion, she kept from being detected by the sergeant while she tracked him. Luckily, he apparently felt no concerns at all that there could be a small female hunter on his tail, following him up and down all these fragmented city streets.

It only took around two hours for her faith to manifest, but by then her legs were getting wobbly. During that time, the big sergeant walked all the way to the office of a newspaper called the *California Star*, and while she spied from outside the building's brand-new picture window, he stood there inside for a long time talking with a couple of other men. The men seemed to listen carefully to him, and one of them even brought out a notebook and wrote down what the cop was saying.

After that, Sergeant Blackburn left and walked a few more blocks to a ruined restaurant that was trying to get back into business. He bought a thick sandwich of some kind and walked away with it wrapped up and tucked under his arm. It looked like such a good idea that she spent the few coins in her pocket for one of her own before hurrying off to catch up with him.

The only reason she had anything at all to spend was because Friar John was careless about loose change. She would never have any money if she didn't keep making trouble and getting herself assigned the extra work duty. She had yet to come across anything outside of the orphanage that a ten-year-old girl could do to make money, except for things that made her skin crawl. The creepy Helper was bad enough. And so her cleaning duties brought a host of small opportunities to put a little jingle in her pockets.

It consumed all Vignette's energy to take the two steps necessary for every one of the sergeant's long strides, since she not only had to keep pace with his speed, she also had to dart from the cover of one object to the next. Fortunately for her, there was always something handy. All of the makeshift structures that people were putting up to live and work in made the streets look like campgrounds.

When Sergeant Blackburn eventually turned into a big adobe church called Mission Dolores and walked out two minutes later without the big sandwich, she knew that the day's hunt was successful. This time when the sergeant walked away, she remained behind.

Minutes later she was at the front gate to the cemetery, peering through the vines growing over it. There was a skinny boy sitting under a tree near the back, hungrily polishing off the sandwich that the sergeant had left for him. A breeze shifted the nearby tree branches, and sunlight through the branches lit up the boy's face so clearly that she recognized him. It was Shane, all right.

Whether Shane remembered her or not, she recalled him well enough. But for the moment, Vignette also realized that she had taken her endeavor as far as she could. Because even after the spying, the hunting, the adventure, Vignette still had no skills for confronting a boy who felt important to her for reasons that it frustrated her to try to understand.

Before she knew it, she was Mary Kathleen again. She had been gone for too long; her absence would soon be noticed. She backed away from the gate and turned toward home. If she wanted to continue having adventures, she could hardly start turning up missing at roll call, drawing concern about her whereabouts. No. Let the friars go on thinking that her only form of rebellion was to talk out loud in class.

She needed the work details to collect coins for moving around the city.

Blackburn sat in the living room of his new little basement apartment, located in one of the standing areas of town. Evening was just settling in. The restored gaslights along that particular street were already burning, so that their yellow and gold illumination played in through his ground-level windows. It was an odd view, and he had not yet gotten used to it. Tonight was his first night off since the week before the Great Earthquake struck. Even as he could feel his body automatically gearing up for a long night shift, he tried to let himself melt into the only comfortable chair he had obtained so far.

His stomach gnawed with hunger pangs. He wished that he had thought to get a sandwich for himself along with the one for Shane. But back then it had been close enough to breakfast that he didn't think about it. Now he was too tired to even bother opening a can, so he let himself sink deeper into the chair. Sleep came to claim him, sweeping his hunger aside. The boy, he thought, while warm relaxation enveloped him, was far more interesting than food anyway. Blackburn closed his eyes and let the mental notes play through his thickening thoughts.

So Shane more or less grows up in an orphanage, lives with the Nightingale family for a year, until they all die in the quake somehow. He takes refuge in a live-in job at Mission Dolores. While reading the paper aloud one day and trying to cure his stutter, he comes across an article about Captain Sullivan's murder—and right then he just "knows" that Elsie Sullivan is not the innocent widow but the perpetrator. The boy then sends a note so bizarre that Blackburn would never have considered it, if he were not already desperate for some break in the challenge that Lieutenant Moses threw down to him.

Then when Blackburn uses the information to break her and get a full confession, the boy explains his knowledge with a story that would have been long even if he could speak clearly. Something about a married woman's combination of insecurity and vanity about her appearance, when she is of an age where many other women are more attractive than she is, everywhere she goes. Something about realizing that the detail about the scale was a clear clue regarding subtle mental torture in the Sullivan household. Something about seeing the body sprawled across the scale as more than a mean coincidence, but as a staged comment, a work of sculpture made of flesh and blood.

At the age of twelve, this Shane Nightingale fellow told Blackburn about the human capacity for levels of pain and rage that most civilized people know nothing about, no matter how old they are. It made for a good story, and the boy deserved a little recognition. That day, the boys at the *California Star* had agreed. They wrote down everything Blackburn told them. The next afternoon's paper was going to run a human interest article about how Shane Nightingale, the sole survivor of his family, offered insights that solved the Sullivan case.

So far, Blackburn regarded Shane as a young fellow with a unique combination of confidence in his vision and an utter lack of confidence in himself. And so maybe this newspaper's acknowledgment would go some distance toward giving the kid back some spirit. Just watching him try to get a sentence out was painful. If a boost in self-confidence could smooth out his speech, then that would make a pretty fine reward for the kid's act as a good citizen. Once the article was out, maybe somebody at City Hall would even want to grab onto the story for political reasons and give the boy some kind of city award. Although the way Shane's eyes lit up at the sight of that big sandwich today, a decent lunch might as well have been made of gold.

The last thing Blackburn did before falling into a deep sleep was to make a mental note to take a copy of the next day's paper over to the Mission, as soon as it came out. It would be great to see some pride on the kid's face.

CHAPTER TEN

MEANWHILE

"T-O-M-M-Y . . ." Lieutenant Moses carefully printed the name.

"No, Lieutenant, it's spelled with an i-e," Tommie corrected from his place on the other side of the giant Police Roll Call Book.

Lieutenant Moses exhaled and focused a hooded glare. "You could have told me that before I started writing." He muttered while he reached for his big gum eraser and stroked the end of the line clean. Then he chanted along with himself while he formed each letter: "T-O-M-M-I-E . . ."

"Good." Tommie smiled.

Moses observed how closely Tommie Kimbrough was leaning in over the book. It made the much bigger man feel a passing desire to squash the bony upstart, just to get a spot of amusement going in an otherwise stressful day. As if it were not bad enough that he was already having to guard his own backside from every political angle, Moses had to struggle with attempting to form key relationships with arrogant mucus bags like this: one of the city's trust fund babies, *buying* his way onto the force so he could play copper. Probably to impress some female.

After donating enough to cover the cost of completely rebuilding the city's primary morgue, this civic-minded little fellow asked for nothing more than to be allowed to volunteer his time at the temporary morgue facility, where they were strapped for labor anyway. In this benefactor's free time at the morgue, he planned to draw medical sketches of anatomical parts for use in textbooks. The eager fellow had appeared wearing several thin layers of clothing, as recommended for sloppy body work, clutching a generously sized lunch pail with a tight-fitting lid to keep odors out of the food. Clearly, thought Moses, Mr. Kimbrough had done a little body work in the past.

"Have you brought any eucalyptus oil?" Moses asked. "Peppermint oil or like that?"

Mr. Kimbrough offered a modest smile and pulled out a small vial. "Eucalyptus."

"Good enough, then." All right, so maybe the guy wouldn't fall down and faint over the first mushy body. With a city broken into a million pieces, who was going to refuse his offer?

"And it's K-I-M-B-R-O-U-G-H, yes?"

"Correct. Excellent, Lieutenant." Tommie smiled again.

Excellent? Like he's doing me a favor. For an instant, he felt a flash of concern that Kimbrough might be planted there, perhaps to secretly evaluate Moses on the job. Moses knew that he would use a spy himself to keep this position, if he could. Countless other men wanted this job. So why wouldn't someone higher up, maybe someone with a friend who needs work, use a spy to watch Moses and to look for dirt? For weeks, there had been rumors all over the city about various plots to take over the government amid the chaos of the city's long recovery.

Moses wrote in "K-I-M-B-R-O-U-G-H," then noted the time and date. He closed the book. That was it, then. He would just have to see to it that little Mr. Kimbrough never got the chance to observe anything that could be used against him. "Before you go . . ."

"Yes?" Kimbrough turned back with a pleasant expression.

"Whenever you come in, you are to go only to the morgue. There's too much traffic here in the station house, so don't dally around the place. I signed you in here, today, but from now on there will be a sign-in book for you over there. No offense, but my time is pulled in other directions."

"Yes, that's fine, Lieutenant. Just as well. No need to trouble you."

"Right. And while we're talking about not troubling me, you'll make sure to keep your head down and don't bring me back any sort of difficulties in here. Agreed?"

"My presence in the morgue will be self-recorded every time I go in, sir!" Kimbrough said, like a recruit in a drill. "My head will be down at all times. Because neither of us wants any trouble. Sir." He grinned and saluted, clever as hell.

Moses studied Tommie Kimbrough's face for sarcasm and felt sure it was in there somewhere, but decided to let it pass, this time. The size of Kimbrough's donation made him practically bullet-proof, as long as he didn't rob anybody important.

Like a well-trained physician, Moses considered his first obligation as Acting Station Chief as that of first doing no harm. Therefore, the safest thing to do about this Tommie Kimbrough was to push him out the door and make it plain that the fellow could only keep Lieutenant Moses out of his way and off of his back by staying out of the station. Let him make all the strange drawings that he wanted.

Moses waved the eager artist off toward the morgue area, adding a look meant to remind Kimbrough not to make any mistakes. He observed with satisfaction that the little guy was so intimidated that he not only hurried to obey, but he even made a point of looking like he was glad to agree that yes, he would keep himself scarce.

Satisfied, Moses lumbered off in uniformed pants that were now several sizes too large for his shrinking portage. He went to see what else his people were stepping into around his partially reclaimed station. "Acting, hell," he dared to grumble out loud. "I *am* the Station Chief."

• • •

The temporary morgue was less than a block from the station, in a clearing that was formed after the collapsed building was scraped away. Workers had used rubble to construct a giant single room with a low roof and walls two feet thick. Tommie stopped just outside the morgue's large doorway. It was hung with thick canvas curtains that reached all the way to the ground. Nobody seemed to be around at the moment. He looked around and noted a worn set of wagon tracks in the ground just outside the door. The morgue team was probably out fetching more guests. He clutched his sealed lunch pail, pushed the thick curtain aside, and stepped in without bothering to look around to see if anyone was observing him.

The instant that the curtain closed behind him, the great room plunged into total darkness. The sound of thousands of buzzing flies filled his hearing, and a thick stench assaulted him. Tommie stood perfectly still for a few seconds, struggling to slow his breathing and his heart. In order to steady himself, he groped for his vial of eucalyptus oil and streaked a thick smear under his nose and into his nostrils. The room's smell did not disappear, but its power was dimmed just enough to be tolerable. He pulled several loose wooden matches from his pocket and struck one with his thumbnail.

A flare of yellow and red light filled the area around him, revealing just enough to show him that this place was perfect. Everything he needed. A series of crude stone body basins were lined up along the walls, like oversized bathtubs. Each one was large enough to place a body inside and still leave room to line the body with ice. The ice water was being efficiently drained away along thin troughs made of hastily thrown mortar, which ran down both sides of the body basin into another gutter that ran under the wall. Most of the basins were filled with bodies in various states of decomposition.

He cried out without meaning to when the flame burned him.

He lit another match with throbbing fingers. Moving along the

wall, he checked each of the bodies, just in case. During his wan-
derings, he had heard the rumors of the plague turning up after the
quake, but while most other people laughed it all off, he knew that
the stories could be true. Every single day, Chinatown received
crates unloaded from ships that brought their cargo *and* their stow-
away rats. Sooner or later, a few of them were bound to carry
plague. The city's Guiding Lights would be loath to allow it to af-
fect business in their young port city, and unless a real contagion
broke out that was too big to hide, the chaos of Chinatown could
be used to conceal all sorts of bizarre death with the city's willing
assistance.

If there weren't a plague victim in storage right now, Tommie
was confident that there would be one very soon. He used up the
rest of his wooden matches in trying to find any Chinese faces—
even one—but every body was either white, black, or one of the na-
tives. The most decomposed and truly disfigured ones didn't look
much like human beings at all, and it amazed him that in the midst
of this citywide crisis, people were still expending time and effort
on the likes of them. *Let the flies have 'em.* He passed by the last
body just as his last match burned low. There was nothing for him
here, yet. By the time the flame went out he was on his way back
outside.

Wait for it, some inner voice assured him. *It's coming. Wait for it.*

In every direction, the city was an anthill of activity and reconstruction, but the pall that hung over the morgue's grim presence
kept a bubble of avoidance for a good twenty yards in all directions.
It suited him to stand comfortably inside that dead zone, completely unnoticed by the scurrying creatures who swarmed the broken city.

Within a few minutes, the body wagon pulled back up to the
morgue with another sad stack. Tommie introduced himself and
showed his letter of permission from the Committee of Fifty, at
which the corporal in charge threw up his hands and told Tommie
to do whatever he wanted except to get in the way. Tommie made a

show of helping them unload the bodies, enough to get a close look at each corpse. These were all white, as it turned out, probably a family. He was quickly aroused at the thought of the Nightingales, and of the time spent with them that was over all too soon.

Four more wagonloads came that morning, but with nothing more interesting than severely decayed and mostly unidentifiable remains. It was not until midafternoon when the corporal and his private drove up again, looking much different than the slumped, exhausted men they had been all morning. Tommie was passing the time by smoking a thin cigarillo and practicing his smoke rings when noises of fast thumping hooves and squeaky wagon springs caught his attention. He looked up in time to see the body wagon driving in hard and fast. The men pulled to a halt and jumped down, both looking tense. They immediately huddled in animated conversation.

Tommie felt his boredom leave him, and while the two officers debated next to the wagon, he walked around to look into the back.

There was only one body. It was adult sized, but completely covered in layers and layers of cloth wrapping. The whole bundle was so thick, it looked like the corpse was swaddled inside of a heavy winter sleeping bag, bound together by an intricately tied network of knotted ropes. Somebody had gone to a lot of effort for this. Extraordinary effort.

At that moment, the corporal hurried over. His face was coated in a light sweat and he spoke in anxious tones. "Mr. Kimbrough, I understand that you got clearance, and all. And you know we been letting you alone so far, right?"

"Oh yes, Corporal. That's quite true. Is there a problem now?"

"There is a problem for sure, sir, but it's not with you. I've got to ask you *not* to even think about opening up that body there, not to draw sketches or nothing. We're about to put it under every scrap of ice we got left. There's doctors from Sacramento coming in here to look it over. Until they get here, we got to leave it be. Can you promise me you're gonna leave this feller alone?"

"It's a man, then?"

"Makes no difference. If you can't agree, then we're gonna go talk to somebody with more rank than I got."

"Certainly, Corporal. Certainly. I completely apologize. You do such important work. Want me to help carry him in?"

The corporal shook his head. "We already had to put the thing in there. No reason for you to get any closer to it."

The other man, Private Something Or Other, stepped up to help, and the two men lifted the body with exaggerated care, making sure not to touch it with anything other than their thick leather gloves. Tommie ducked inside ahead of them to light an extra lantern for the task, and they placed the body in the stone basin farthest from the others. They covered it with several half melted blocks of ice and pulled a thick tarpaulin over the entire mass.

He followed the men back outside and watched while they shook their leather gloves into a small fire pit. Then the corporal poured a generous helping of lamp oil onto the gloves and threw a match onto the pile. All three men stepped back while the flames leaped up amid an inky trail of smoke.

"Corporal," Tommie asked in his best casual voice, "where did you say that body came from?"

The corporal studied him for a moment before he took a breath and shrugged. "Chinatown."

Randall Blackburn sat at a little table in the partially restored café, across from Shane Nightingale. He had waited until they were done eating their filling lunch of heavy soup and bread before he presented Shane with the afternoon paper. Then he listened with satisfaction while the boy followed his request to read the article out loud. The story was accompanied by a generic pencil sketch of a twelve-year-old male that nobody would recognize as Shane, but his name was mentioned several times. Blackburn's acquaintance at the paper had pulled every heartstring that his editors would allow.

The writer repeated Blackburn's story about a young man adopted out of a local orphanage by the Nightingale family, of the well-regarded Nightingale Dry Goods Emporium, and who was now the family's sole survivor. Instead of dwelling on how the Nightingales were killed, it celebrated the fact that even while Shane worked for his keep at a local church, he read the *California Star* with such regularity that he noticed the article about the murder of Captain Harlan Sullivan. Based upon Shane Nightingale's astounding insight and the reporting of the *California Star*, an important clue was delivered to Sergeant Randall Blackburn of the SFPD, and a gross injustice was prevented. The true culprit was arrested and an innocent woman, wrongfully accused, set free.

" 'And now,' " Shane finished the last line in a strong voice, " 'the true perpetrator sits in police custody, after a full confession.' " He sat and stared at the page for a moment, then slowly lowered the paper to the table.

Blackburn grinned. "Now I see what you're doing with this thing of reading newspapers out loud! It's impressive. You never missed a beat."

Shane nodded and looked up long enough to show a timid smile, then quickly lowered his eyes again.

"Don't worry," Blackburn went on. "I didn't tell them which church you're working at. Otherwise all the young ladies would be sneaking down here to meet up with you."

Shane nodded a little, but this time he didn't look up at all. The boy was so clearly lacking in self-confidence that a little celebration in the newspaper had seemed like a great way to buck up his spirits. But even though Shane was able to read every word of the article and surely understood that he was being publicly applauded, he wasn't making any reaction at all.

Blackburn suddenly felt like a complete fool. Obviously, he had misjudged the boy's depth of grief over losing his new family. Had he managed to somehow make this boy feel worse?

"Well, Shane," he went on. "It's just a story. Tomorrow they'll have another one. I just thought you might like for people to know how you helped me out. You deserve it. Take some pride in it." He smiled and clapped the boy on the shoulder. "Brag on yourself a little bit. No harm in letting people know you've done something good for this city."

Shane took a deep breath and finally raised his eyes to meet Blackburn's. "Thank—thank you. I kno-kno-know you tried to he-he-he-help. But . . . I juh-juh-juh-just . . . I just . . ." He stopped and shook his head in frustration.

"That's all right," Blackburn hastened. "No need to go on about it. I should have talked to you first." He grinned. "Guess I thought the surprise might lighten your day." He handed the waiter the money for their meal and stood up. "Anyway, you keep that copy. If you want to practice reading, can't hurt you to read about yourself." He pointed at the paper. "Save it for your kids." Then he walked away and let Shane have some time to think of himself as a hero.

For Blackburn, it was uncomfortable enough to be alone with another male who was emotionally overwhelmed. And while it was less disturbing to be with a very young person in such a state, Shane was too old to dismiss as a child. He was close enough to manhood that his pain was awkward to witness, even though it also seemed unfair to expect him to show a man's stoicism and to put up the strong face.

What an age to be, Blackburn mused, old enough to see things as they are and too young to do anything about it. In comparison, his own boyhood up among the California giant redwoods was fairly idyllic, all things considered.

He realized then, that he had actually thought he might fill in a well by pouring in a bucket of water. To offer Shane this little news story as some sort of reward, expecting it to help this troubled boy, was optimistic to the point of ignorance.

• • •

As soon as the big sergeant was gone, Shane had to lower himself back into his seat at the table. His wobbly knees had nearly given him away. He was so horrified by the sergeant's news article that he had nearly blurted out his dismay, half a dozen times. It was only the blessed, goddamned stutter that saved him.

He began a slow, staggering journey back to the Mission. The cool green isolation of the Mission cemetery seemed to be the only place in the world where he could find any safety. The holy men there seldom concerned themselves with daily newspapers, and many of the city's residents could not read at all. Once he made it back to his toolshed, he could lose himself there. It was as close as he could come to crawling into a hole.

CHAPTER ELEVEN

THE FOLLOWING DAY

SHANE'S ARTICLE CAME OUT in the *California Star*, and a copy found its way into the makeshift morgue near the City Hall station. It was carried under the arm of the private from the day before, who finished reading it while sipping coffee poured from a pot hung over the fire pit. Instead of tossing the used newspaper into the flames, he pulled it into sections and then used them as protection from the cold for his hands while he carried the day's delivery of ice blocks inside. He left each section of the paper with each ice block, piling the ice with the newsprint sandwiched between to help keep the blocks from freezing together.

He left the pile under layers of burlap for Tommie to distribute over the corpses as needed, since Tommie had been pleased to volunteer to work inside. The ice was never to be allowed to melt off of the mummy-wrapped body located in the back. That particular guest got fresh ice first, no matter what. Tommie worked in earnest, and the stench of decay soon infiltrated the pores of his exposed skin and every fiber of his clothing.

No worse than a public outhouse, he cheerfully pointed out to himself. He hated those places.

Now, on Tommie's second day in the morgue, he was even permitted to make himself at home in that grim place whether or not any of the other men were around. Just him and the quiet ones.

And since this was the first time that he had found himself alone, he immediately got down to the only thing that he was actually there to accomplish.

He stepped outside into the sunlight and carefully checked his clothing. He had on full body underwear beneath a light pair of pants that he had tied tightly at the cuffs to his cotton socks. His waistline was tied where his shirt met his belt. Over that, he wore another full outfit of long pants and long sleeves that looked normal.

Just as he stepped back into the darkness of the morgue, he pulled a rolled-up piece of fabric from his pocket and shook it out. It was a fine silk cloth stitched into the shape of a large cone. He pulled the cone over his head and down to his shoulders, and then tugged a pair of thin leather gloves onto his hands. When he pushed aside the heavy canvas curtains, he carried nothing else with him but the sealed lunch pail. He moved quickly to complete his task before returning to his other duties.

To start, he removed his outer layer of clothing and set it next to the ice pile, remaining inside of his sealed suit. Then he plucked an oil lantern from a peg near the door and headed straight back to the special body basin, the one that held an icy-cool corpse that somebody in Chinatown had wrapped in far too much covering for any normal purpose.

Whoever was inside of the layered shrouds, Tommie was certain, had died of the Black Plague. He would know the truth soon enough.

When he reached the rearmost body basin, he set down the lantern and went straight to work, pulling the heavy-bladed knife from his rigged pocket and unsheathing the blade. He had spent hours sharpening it to an edge far thinner than needed, so that now as he sliced away the bottom of the body's fabric cocoon, the knife passed through the thick layers of cloth with almost no effort. At the foot, he made a perfect cut five or six inches long, separating layer after layer as he worked toward the corpse itself.

His moves were well studied. In Tommie's judgment, the best thing about independent wealth was the time it gave one for reading and reflection. Such things were paying him well in this tingly quest, providing bits of knowledge more powerful than a sidearm. He now knew, for instance, that while a rat bite could infect a human if the rat was carrying plague, the devil in the disease was that the fleas on an infected rat could also carry the plague. And not only are fleas practically invisible, they can jump several feet. Though it might be possible to successfully avoid the rats, once plague is on the loose, avoiding contact with fleas was much more difficult.

He only needed a minute of contact with the body, perhaps less. The self-sealed clothing, silk hood, and gloves would keep him safe enough, and by now any fleas that might still be on the body should have been stunned by the cold. The Chinese Oriental Rat Flea thrived on the hides of black rats, but it became inactive in the cold and it was easily destroyed by fire. Thus he felt confident that with only a few seconds of exposure, and with the immediate burning of his clothing afterward, he could dodge the disease.

As for any remaining danger, what was life without risk?

The sliced wraps finally parted to reveal the corpse's lower leg. Tommie picked up the lantern and shined it close to the opening to get a good look. *Perfect!* The purplish, blackened skin was also covered with red-and-brown circles. It made no difference if there were any fleas to carry this disease. Here, the tissue itself was infectious.

He set the lantern aside, picked up his lunch pail, unsealed the lid and reached inside. From the box, he pulled a small black rat by the tail, then took the animal firmly in his other hand. In a single, swift move, he stuffed the rat into the corpse's thick wrappings, making sure to push it all the way down to the flesh, then yanked his arm out and pinched the opening tightly shut. All he needed to do now was to place another large block of ice directly over the opening, and nobody would see anything. He moved the largest remaining ice block and set it in place to cover the opening and hold it tightly closed.

Between the rat's frenzy of fear and desire to escape, it would gnaw on the body. It would draw the plague into itself. An hour or two, he thought, should be plenty. In the meantime, he would lug more fresh ice over and completely cover the corpse, making sure the rat had nowhere else to go but into the body, which would be warmer than the ice surrounding it.

Tommie walked back toward the spot where the fresh ice sat waiting for him, stopping halfway between it and the body to set the lantern down on the floor. Then he stepped over to the pile of ice and picked up the top block, using the same section of newspaper left behind with it. It was the financial section, full of grim indicators that Tommie didn't bother to read. He carried the block back to the body and rested it against the one that already covered the slit. There were a few half-melted blocks still in place, but he thought that the corpse could use four or five more.

He went back to the ice and picked up another block, this one covered by the section of the paper that showed Shane's article. He didn't bother to look at it, just used the paper to make it easier to lift the block and carry it back to the body. When he was finished, he collected the papers, with Shane's article on the top, still not noticing the story. He carried them out to the fire pit to burn them along with his clothing after the entire job was done. He tossed a few of the papers into the pit after wadding each one. Just as he reached for the page with Shane's article, the name "Nightingale" caught his eye.

Tommie became utterly still, as unmoving as the surrounding corpses.

No.

His denial began its automatic responses—there were others with that name, unrelated others. He had seen the name before. The question could be answered in an instant. All he had to do was pick up the page and read the article.

Finally, with a slow and deep breath, he broke the spell holding him and reached forward to pick up the damp page. He held it close. There was the name, there was the article containing it, along with the drawing of the twelve-year-old boy, captioned "Shane Nightingale." The first name of "Shane" sent up another red flag. Tommie's hands grew so shaky that it annoyed him. Still, he began to decipher the smeared words on the page.

Something about the boy helping the police to solve a High Society murder. Police Sergeant Randall Blackburn tells all about this amazing boy who blah, blah, blah . . .

And then there it was. It hit him like a nail to the forehead.

"Shane Nightingale" was some throwaway kid. He wasn't really a Nightingale; he only took the name of the family who adopted him. A year earlier, he was taken in by the Nightingale family of the renowned *Nightingale Dry Goods Consortium,* all of whom had perished in the earthquake and fires, except for Shane.

"*. . . except for Shane.*"

There was one Nightingale still left. Tommie missed one.

"*. . . except for Shane.*"

Shane. The human bad penny. Tommie screamed silently in frustration, wondering how such a thing could have happened. Although even as he asked himself, he knew the only possible answer: Friar John. Somehow, for some inexplicable reason, the Headmaster had not only sold out Tommie's patronage, but he had set Tommie up for an inevitable encounter between him and the boy. Another Nightingale was out there. And because of that, *incompleteness* now marred the memory of Tommie's special work.

He took a quick look all around and confirmed that the body wagon was nowhere in sight yet, so he hustled off to the station to ask a few casual questions about this Sergeant Randall Blackburn and his special little friend.

Randall Blackburn decided to pay a second visit to the orphanage, unannounced. He went in uniform to avoid misunderstandings, but gave no other consideration to the friars. The thing that he gained from reading Shane's article in print was the realization of the huge hole in Shane's background. Whatever clue to the boy's ability that there might be, some evidence must have been left at the orphanage during the years he spent there. Blackburn wanted to get a closer look at the place itself.

He closed the distance of the last block before reaching the back gate entrance to St. Adrian's. A familiar sense of danger manifested beneath his stomach and across his shoulders.

What danger? It was a place full of kids. There were some unusual people taking care of those kids, but it was necessary work, and it was something that few others wanted to do. What danger?

His mouth instantly soured, realizing that the danger came from whatever it was that prevented a twelve-year-old boy who has been orphaned for the second time from wanting to return to the familiarity of St. Adrian's. The danger came from whatever persuaded that boy to prefer living all by himself, inside a toolshed at the back of a cemetery.

He reached the gate and saw that it was unlocked and unguarded. That made it easy enough to walk in, but seemed strange. An orphan might not desire a life alone on the street, but most delinquents would prefer it. How were they kept from running off?

He moved quietly, but made no effort to sneak around. The grounds were nicely kept and all traces of the earthquake damage had been eliminated outside. The brick buildings showed a few cracks, but nothing of real concern. Either the place was solidly constructed or the shock wave spared this part of town, another one of those strangely untouched pockets of land that existed here and there.

A cool breeze ran across the manicured grass. There was a quiet dignity to the place, but his anxiety deepened when he moved toward the main building, a long and low two-story structure. The place was full of kids, over a hundred, according to Friar John. Yet even in this close proximity, Blackburn heard nothing. The loudest sound to reach him was the rustle of the breeze in the foliage and bird calls from the upper branches.

He opened the door and stepped inside, quietly pulling it closed behind him. Everything remained quiet. He stood still for a moment, letting his ears adjust the same way his eyes adjusted to a drop in the light. Faint background sounds reached him: a scraping of a chair, a quiet set of footsteps, an indistinguishable voice. Somebody had vomited in there recently.

The bare floorboards squeaked under his weight when he moved along the hallway, passing several classrooms. A small window in each door revealed young students bent low over their desks, reading or writing. In one class, a middle-aged male was delivering an arithmetic lesson and writing on the blackboard. Every student paid strict attention.

He was still watching the class and wondering how the teachers kept such perfect order, when he flinched at the sharp sound of a mop handle falling onto the floor. He turned to see the same young girl who had been cleaning Friar John's office when he was there last. She stared at him as if he were a ghost. He started to apologize for startling her, but before he got the first word out, she spun on her heels and ran. Her speed was impressive.

Blackburn made one more pass down the hallway, focusing on the classes on the opposite side this time, but learned nothing else. He was just starting up the stairs to the second floor when he was stopped by a sharp voice coming from behind him.

"Hello, Sergeant."

There was no sound of welcome to it. Blackburn turned to see Friar John, who had managed to get close enough to breathe down his neck without giving himself away. Blackburn was equally surprised by and suspicious of the man's skills.

Moments later they were back at the door to Friar John's office. The friar had managed to whisk Blackburn there so quickly that he saw little else along the way.

"Thank you, Mary Kathleen," the friar said without bothering to turn around and confirm that she was following. "You may go back to class now."

"Can't, Friar. I'm kicked out for talking again. Supposed to mop the hall."

"All right, all right. Just go back to it, then."

She hurried back to her mop and pail without ever looking at Blackburn, which seemed odd, given her surprise on encountering him. But nothing about the place quite came into full focus for him. He followed Friar John into the office.

Vignette sneaked up to Friar John's door carrying the mop and bucket as props. She sidled up close enough to listen in without being seen. Then she silently placed the bucket and mop in position so that it might look like she was working if anybody spotted her. It was the surprise sight of the same policeman that initially frightened her, encountering him as she did, right there in the middle of a hallway that she had just been sentenced to clean. It was only moments later that she realized it was time to jump into action. His appearance at St. Adrian's was clearly fate of some sort. She knew that these were the kinds of things that she was supposed to leave up to the Lord, but she had been finding herself feeling less and less certain about what the Lord seemed to have planned for her future life. Sometimes the feelings were so strong that they overwhelmed her—whether anybody cared for that aspect of her personality or not. And that is just what began happening to her while she listened to the two men talk.

"Sergeant Blackburn, if I had anything else to tell you, I certainly would."

"I don't doubt that, sir—"

"Friar John."

"I don't doubt that, Friar John, but—"

"I even looked through his permanent file after your first visit, just in case. But there's just nothing there. Nothing useful."

"Right, but sometimes people remember things after a few days of thinking it over, so I generally like to—"

"Wander onto their premises without notice?"

"If I need to," Blackburn replied in a soft and even tone. He held Friar John's gaze until the headmaster dropped it.

"Now sir," Blackburn continued, "here's the—"

"Friar John."

"Here's the thing," Blackburn persisted. "This boy knows too much about certain kinds of very dark things. I have to see them all the time, but children aren't supposed to have any experience with them."

"I hope you are not implying that he was mistreated here!"

"I don't deal in implying things, sir. The fact is, he knows so much that besides helping me to solve a crime, he has attracted my concern. I want to know where he comes from. I want to know what has happened to him."

"Since he left, I haven't the slightest—"

"Why can't he talk? Why is his stammer so bad?"

"His stammer? Are we talking about the same boy? The Shane Nightingale I know speaks with a perfectly clear voice."

"Well that's funny, then, isn't it? Now he has a stutter that almost shuts him up entirely."

"And your guess is as good as mine, Sergeant," Friar John quietly replied.

Vignette wanted to shout. She recognized Friar John's act. Surely this big cop was too smart to fall for that, wasn't he?

"I don't mean to sound harsh, Sergeant," Friar John smiled, "but I have over a hundred children of all ages here. Some are violent, some are skilled criminals, some are little angels that people just throw away for reasons of their own. Once an orphan is adopted out, they never have to return if they don't want to. Unless they get arrested. And so I simply don't have the time to concern myself with them."

The sergeant then sat very still for a long minute, with Friar John waiting. Finally the sergeant sighed and stood up. "All right, then. But something's wrong here and I believe I'll have to follow it up until it's all sorted out."

Friar John stood, too. Vignette could tell that he looked relieved. She wondered if the sergeant noticed it. The scene held her attention so well that she nearly forgot to grab her mop and look busy when Friar John escorted the sergeant back into the hall. The friar absently waved her away, then walked the sergeant in the opposite direction.

Around the corner, Vignette dropped her mop and bucket, ran into an empty classroom and scrambled out through one of the windows. She had no way of telling where this was going, but every inch of her tingled with anticipation. Fate had her in its grip, and she was glad of it. It was about time. The job of playing Mary Kathleen had become an unlivable lie.

She sprinted across the grounds and crawled over a side fence while Sergeant Blackburn left by the front door. She knew she could catch him, and this time she intended to follow him until he went home. She needed to know where the big man lived. She could feel events pulling her out of St. Adrian's for good. Maybe she could sneak back and pick up a few of her things after nightfall, but she could never tolerate living there again. She was certain of nothing but that the life of Mary Kathleen had become a suit of clothing several sizes too small. It would never fit her again.

Tommie was only at the station for a few minutes, keeping out of Lieutenant Moses' way and overhearing just enough to learn that Sergeant Blackburn was not expected until sometime before midnight. Nobody else seemed to know anything about this Shane Nightingale creature, either.

Despite Tommie's speed, he arrived back at the morgue to see that the body wagon was already parked out front. He hurried to the canvas door and called inside, "Hello?" He heard a muffled reply and squinted toward the back to see the private standing with a lantern—right beside the infected body. Tommie felt an icy blast hit him inside.

The private waved to Tommie. "Corporal told me to come back here and work with you, make sure everybody gets properly chilled."

"You're not serious."

"That's what I would have said if I outranked him. Anyhow, I been checking over here to see how you're doing with it."

Tommie felt his heart speed up. "Uh, well, I've been working slowly. Got a spasm in my back. Makes it hard, lifting."

The private grinned. "Yeah, my back gets that way every time I lift something, too."

Tommie hurried over to him, as if to inspect his own work. His heartbeat was not slowing down.

The private gave him a leer that was half conspiratorial and half evil. "You ain't been in here having your way with the females, have you?"

Tommie gasped in shock at the thought before he could stop himself. He felt the blood drain from his face.

The private burst out laughing. "Relax, mister! I'm just playin' around. All right, so what do we got here?" The private muttered to himself for a moment while he looked over the body. Then he nodded and turned to Tommie. "I guess I can tell the corporal that you're slow, but thorough!" He laughed.

Tommie laughed.

A small squeaking sound came from the basin. The private's laugh drowned it out.

But not the second one.

The private briefly glanced at Tommie, as if Tommie might have made the noise, but just as quickly rejected that and turned to the body instead.

"Um, Private, can you come outside to the fire pit?"

The private ignored him. "You hear that just now?" He fetched the lantern and began to look all around the body basin.

"I was having trouble getting the paper to catch flame, and maybe you could—"

The squeaking repeated.

"There it is again!" the private cried. He leaned in closer to the basin and began to study the shrouds. "Almost sounds like it's coming from in there. You don't think some critter's got trapped in there?"

"No. Of course not! It's too cold. You know that as well as I do. But if you could come outside for just a minute—"

This time the squeaking went on for several seconds and both men saw the tiny movements from beneath the shrouds. "See?" yelled the triumphant private. He began quickly lifting ice blocks away from the basin.

"No Private!" cried Tommie. "There's nothing—"

"There is! It's something all right . . . What the . . . ?" He saw the sliced cloth. "Some idiot done cut into this thing! Who in hell would do that?" He tossed a suspicious glance at Tommie.

The private leaned in close to peer into the opening, just in time to see a tiny pair of rodent eyes glaring back at him, reflecting the lamp's oil flame. It was the last thing he ever saw before Tommie bashed in the back of his skull with a brick twice the size of his fist.

The private dropped dead in a heap.

Tommie stood inside the pale yellow circle of lantern light, staring down at this new and interesting problem. Finally, he broke the spell that bound him by taking a sharp breath and telling himself *first things first*. He picked up his lunch pail and set it ready with the top open, then reopened the deep cut into the thick shroud. With his gloves still protecting his hands, he quickly reached in and grabbed the rodent behind the head so that it couldn't bite, then pulled it out and dropped it back into the pail and resealed the top.

With the rat safely captive, he again held the lantern close to the slice in the shrouds and peered inside. The satisfaction brought by the sight that greeted his eyes was almost as good as an orgasm. The body had been stripped of several ounces of flesh by the rat; teeth and claw marks were plain to see. Living death was now his.

But his heart was still beating fast. Oh yes. What to do about the private's body?

The genius of desperation filled Tommie. He folded the slit in the cloth under itself so that it wasn't visible, then pulled the private's body back and lay it against the basin directly behind him. He placed the private's body face up, as if he had landed after falling backward and hitting his head on the basin's edge. To complete the picture, Tommie placed a large block of ice on top of him, as if it were in the private's arms when he fell. He swung the lantern back and forth over the scene a few times, making sure that his improvisation was convincing to the eye. Then, satisfied with that much, he carried the lantern back to the peg by the door and stepped outside.

Nobody was there, nobody approaching. All clear then. So the last thing on his list was to do a bit of acting. Another role to play, and that was fine with him. The emotional flatness of the average adult male was so restrictive and frustrating for him that containing himself in public was like trying to hold back vomit.

His hunger for an audience came naturally. He took off toward the City Hall Station, working on his expression of shock, ready to shout to any and all that the private had lost his balance while showing Tommie how to handle the ice blocks, and suffered a fatal fall. He tried to recall the private's name and got nothing, but assured himself that such a lapse would be accepted under the circumstances.

It's the worst thing I've ever seen! Tommie reminded himself to say. There was probably something else, but what? Then he got it—*Does the poor man have a wife and children?* Oh yes. People ask that. The rest was simply a matter of reciting his story so thoroughly that nobody could do anything else but believe it.

After the charade was through, he would consider what to do about Shane Nightingale, whose very existence had rudely converted Tommie's three-day triumph into nothing more than an incomplete aspiration. It galled him to have accidentally left a Nightingale to walk around free. Every moment that this boy continued to exist was and would continue to be a wrenching affront.

Suddenly Tommie realized what that little thing was, tapping at the back of his brain like a relentless woodpecker. It was the memory of Mrs. Nightingale calling out "Shane! Shane!" Since Tommie had never known old man Nightingale's first name, he had just assumed that "Shane" was it. He barely noticed at the time; the man wasn't there and his name meant nothing.

But of course she wasn't calling to her husband, because she knew that he was not there.

She called out to the boy. If she did that because she knew that Shane could somehow hear her, it meant that Shane could have been inside the house. He might have somehow concealed himself, silent and unmoving, while he listened to Tommie slaughter his adoptive family. Listened while Tommie had given of himself so freely during that entire time, so carefully explaining his reasons for each and every stabbing jab, every swiping slice, every twist of the garrote. Young Shane Nightingale had gotten a formal education in the delectable sexuality and moral triumph that there is to be had in properly justified murder. The boy was an intruder, an uninvited witness to Tommie's deepest secrets.

The smear on Tommie's work had to be removed. It was a galling mistake that called out for correction. Most important, the correction had to be done in an artful fashion, in some manner that went far beyond the mere expedience of getting away with homicide. This situation, Tommie acknowledged, was one that required his most worthy effort.

A long, screaming poem of a murder.

CHAPTER TWELVE

Lieutenant Moses was standing next to the Duty Sergeant's desk when he saw Blackburn walk into the station. It was only midafternoon.

"Sergeant Blackburn, I would expect you to be home asleep."

"Yes, sir. I just need to check—"

"You aren't going to skip work tonight, are you?"

"No. I'll be on the street by midnight."

"All right. But I don't like our men to walk around exhausted, so what do you need here?"

Blackburn lowered his voice. "Actually, what I need is a favor that only you can provide, Lieutenant."

Moses' heart skipped. He made a conscious effort to repress any show of excitement while he demurred, "I'm sure you give me too much credit."

"Not at all, sir." Blackburn dropped his voice to a near whisper. "I need access to personal property records. Specifically, anything at all that we have on the Nightingale family, of the Nightingale Dry Good Consortium, and I need to do it now."

"The Nightingale family." Moses looked interested. "That boy in the paper today?"

"Yes."

"Didn't the story say they were all killed?"

"It did."

"So the point is . . . ?"

"Sir, I just want to do something for this boy if I can, that's all. I just want to know some things, such as, was he officially adopted? Did he take the family name legally? Things like that."

Moses was not the least inclined to help the boy who helped solve the Sullivan murder—a case that wasn't supposed to be solved at all. Pressure from the widow Sullivan's high and mighty friends was raining down on him, and he knew that this was just the sort of thing that could get him replaced.

But Moses also knew something that Sergeant Blackburn did not, and that tipped the balance.

"All right," he sighed as if the favor cost him money. "Go on back and get the Keeper to locate what you want. How long is this going to take?"

"Not long, I guess. Ten minutes?"

"Good. Then you'll go straight home and get some sleep, *yes*?"

"Yes."

"Tone of voice, Sergeant—you're here to ask a favor."

"Yes, sir."

Moses had a new trick of pausing before rendering any decision whenever an underling was waiting for an answer. He used it now, allowing Blackburn to twist in the wind for a moment or two before waving him toward the relocated Record Keeping Department.

He had no fear of anything Blackburn might discover in a file that Moses had already cleaned up for inspection. The only sensitive document was the one that Moses had indirectly discovered while he was preparing to interview Mr. Tommie Kimbrough for his morgue work. He had learned within just a couple of minutes that Tommie Kimbrough had a lien against his house on file with the county, and that the lien was held by the owner of the Nightingale Dry Goods Emporium. It seemed that Kimbrough had a huge accumulation of store credit that he had run up over several years' time, but although Mr. Nightingale won a court judgment months earlier, he had only recently foreclosed on Kimbrough. Perhaps up until then he had been hoping for payment.

That record, however, was no longer available to the public. It was folded into the inside pocket of the ever baggier uniform jacket belonging to Gregory Moses.

Moses stood and watched the sergeant disappear around the corner, then he turned and shambled back to his office, where he was keeping Mr. Tommie Kimbrough himself waiting. He had been cooling his heels there for a good twenty minutes. Just to soften him up.

Hallelujah, thought Moses. Moses had a strong hunch that the foreclosure lien might be instrumental in his efforts to remain in place as Station Chief. It proved a serious vulnerability on the part of Tommie Kimbrough, who had strangely made a fat cash contribution to the SFPD at the same time that his house stood under foreclosure. The decades that Moses spent in the Record Keeping Department had sensitized him to the negotiating potential that was often contained in one's financial oddities. He was ready to deal.

Besides, this "gentleman" gives off a fishy aura, Moses thought. *Just what one might expect of a planted spy.*

Blackburn headed straight back to his new apartment, less than a mile from the station. His eyes felt sandy and his whole body ached with the need for sleep, but he felt no regret at having taken the detour. The files clearly showed that Shane had been officially adopted by the Nightingale family, as required in order to move him into their home. He legitimately had the family name as his own, and though the Nightingale family will did not list Shane as an heir, Blackburn was sure that the boy must have something coming to him. With a family business that big, it seemed certain that there should be some sort of estate left over. He resolved not to say anything to Shane about any of it until he could find out whether there was something for the boy or not.

Blackburn had spent enough of his own boyhood being happily alone that he was not particularly troubled over Shane's isolation. He just hated the idea of the boy spending the foreseeable future doing nothing more than earning each day's meals. The fact that Shane was capable of such brutal clarity of thought certainly proved that he had some sort of extraordinary talent. The boy stood out, in this city of displaced people, even though he appeared not to realize it.

If he kept the search to himself, then Shane would never miss what he had never expected. On the other hand, if it turned out that there was anything there, then Blackburn would find some way to make sure that this timid and fragile boy would receive what was due to him.

Blackburn was within a block of home. Relieved, he quickened his pace along the row of standing houses and made a beeline for his front door. There was just time for a few hours of rest before the next midnight shift of dancing with the stumblebums down along the Barbary Coast.

Not far behind Blackburn, Vignette skipped along, darting from one concealment to another. In her master spy mode, she took pains to remain undetected even by the general public. To achieve that, she made sure to behave like a stupid little girl engrossed in playing some sort of game. It caused grown-ups to dismiss her and most kids to ignore her altogether. She could outrun the others.

That was the next best thing to being invisible. As long as she never got in anybody's way, she could sense that nobody noticed her. Later, they would not remember that she was ever there at all.

Vignette slipped behind the thick pole of a gas streetlamp and peered out from behind it, just in time to see Sergeant Blackburn pull a key from his pocket and stop in front of the sunken door to a garden apartment. She ducked out of sight while he let himself in. When she heard the door pulled shut, she stepped out and pretended to tie her shoe in order to sneak a good look at the big sergeant's building.

So this was where he lived. Vignette decided that the best thing to do was to spook around the neighborhood for a while, get a feel for the whole area. And, she realized, to quickly locate any food that was looking to get stolen. She was starting to feel like she didn't weigh anything at all, as if a puff of breeze would blow her over.

First things first, then. She caught a whiff of something wonderful in the air. Not far away, somebody was doing some baking. Baked things were often set out to cool. Within moments, she was off on the trail of the luxurious smell like a hound on two legs.

"Sit down, sit down," Moses casually waved to Kimbrough. "No need for formalities with you, Mr. Kimbrough." Moses walked around his side of the desk and sat, making it a point to give Tommie a generous smile.

Tommie Kimbrough's face glistened with tiny beads of sweat— it was the worried face of an obvious spy, Moses reckoned, the tool of somebody up in the department brass. He would find out. Right now, he was in no hurry. They were on his turf.

Kimbrough realized it was his turn to speak. "Of course I'm still upset over Private, uh—over the private's death. But I'll tell you anything I can."

"As long as it's the truth, you mean," Moses interrupted with a scowl.

"What?" Tommie almost gasped the word.

Moses broke out laughing. "I'm joking with you! Please! We are among friends here, aren't we?"

Kimbrough broke into a relieved smile. "Oh. Oh! We certainly are!"

Moses made a serious face. "It is most unfortunate, however."

"Oh, absolutely! That poor man! Did he, ah, have a wife and children?"

"I didn't mean him."

"Oh." Tommie waited. When nothing happened, he added, "What did you mean?"

"The volunteer program at the morgue. There's just no way to continue it for the time being, even as badly as the help is needed there." Moses leaned forward and made sure to remove any trace of joy and triumph from his voice.

"I am so grateful for your help. It is most impressive that a man of your means would voluntarily occupy his time amid the stink of rotting bodies. I'm sure the department can relocate you to a hospital or something where you can make the same sorts of drawings."

Having accomplished what he had volunteered for, Tommie was unconcerned with the news. Now he simply needed to make sure his tracks were covered with regard to the dead private.

Moses paused and maintained his benign smile until Kimbrough realized it was his turn. "Well, Lieutenant, I'm sure that will be—"

"Because as I said, we are among friends."

"Um, yes."

"Good!" Moses pounded the desktop for emphasis. "We understand each other!" He sat staring at Kimbrough with a meaningless smile.

"So, ah, Lieutenant, should I give you my formal statement about Private, ah, Private . . ."

"The late private?"

"Yes."

"No."

"No?"

"Why would I trouble you? You wrote out a very nice statement for the duty sergeant. And after you were so kind as to spend time in my station house doing volunteer work in our city morgue, in spite of your own troubles."

"Troubles?"

"But nobody needs to know." Moses winked and gave a conspiratorial grin. He pulled the notice from his jacket and placed it on the desk. He opened it flat and turned it toward Kimbrough for easy reading, than watched Kimbrough's glance drop down onto the page. His eyes widened in surprise. All the color drained from Kimbrough's face.

"You see," Lieutenant Moses went on, "I pulled this from the files before anybody could see it. Since the quake, nobody has checked any private property details except where owners request it. And because your house was in an untouched zone, ordinarily nobody would have found it. In which case you wouldn't have needed my help at all."

He looked straight at Kimbrough again, who had now shrunken into his chair. Still, Moses was careful not to gloat while he pulled the linchpin.

"Sergeant Blackburn just happened to be rummaging through the Nightingale files today, and might have accidentally come across this dangerous document." He gave a reassuring smile. "If it had been there."

And that was it, Moses assured himself. After today, no matter how high up the ladder this little lump of shit was connected to the department brass, nobody could say that Moses failed to show Mr. Tommie Kimbrough proper respect. Even while he gave him the bum's rush out the door.

"So you see, Mr. Kimbrough, we are among friends here. Certain troublemakers could misunderstand and become very, very, very concerned as to how you made a large cash donation here while you have a foreclosure notice on your house."

Kimbrough's mouth began to move like a drowning fish. Nothing came out.

"Rest assured," Moses soothed, "a friend like me sees no reason to point out this little fact to anybody."

"I told him I would pay him!" Tommie hissed. "I kept telling him!"

"I believe you! Greedy bastard tried to break your back, didn't he?"

"Exactly! That's exactly what he tried to do."

"And if he died in the earthquake along with who-knows-how-many other people, maybe that was just the Almighty Lord taking care of things for you."

"Yes!" Kimbrough practically shouted.

"Maybe the way that things finally shook out is the *real* settling of accounts."

"It is! That's right! I knew it the moment that the quake hit. It was so strong. It had to have been *righteous* destruction!"

"Well, then!" Moses clapped his hands together and smiled yet again. "No cause for alarm, my friend." He snatched up the document and whipped it back inside his jacket. "I will keep it safe." Moses leaned in closer to Kimbrough and whispered, "Always."

"Perhaps," Kimbrough tentatively began, "I could . . . arrange to purchase that notice from you?"

"Purchase? Sir! You misunderstand. I would never try to rob a man who cannot pay his mortgage."

"I can pay it. I could pay it anytime I wanted. It's just that—"

"No! You will never have to spend a penny to assure yourself that this document is safely hidden. As long as I am Station Chief, you have my word that there is nothing to fear," he patted his jacket pocket, "from this."

Moses' impression was that the little man could not decide whether to sigh in relief or shit himself. The wheels inside his skull were turning so hard that the lieutenant could almost hear them creaking.

Kimbrough stood, offered Moses his confused thanks, and shuffled out. It was perfect. Moses never had to say anything that Kimbrough could repeat without pulling himself down at the same time. He was willing to bet that whoever was using Kimbrough would never hear another bad report about Gregory Moses from that moment forward.

"Acting Station Chief."

The term scalded him as if it was meant to imply that he was only acting *like* a station chief, and that he wasn't fooling anybody.

Except now Moses had this Kimbrough under his thumb, a man who somehow possessed both cash and connections. Now Kimbrough clearly understood that his own well-being was a direct result of how well or how poorly things went for Lieutenant Gregory Moses.

With friends like these, Moses chuckled to himself, *you don't need real ones.*

Sunset over the Pacific was spectacular when viewed from the third story of Tommie's home. He caught a glimpse through the window while he knelt to open the lid on his new glass-topped cage for the plague-infested rat. There was no time to regard the view out the window. Nature's ability to paint a pretty picture was far less compelling to him than Her ability to place the power of life and death directly into his hands.

He felt so filled with anticipation that the strain made his fingers quiver, so he kept his moves slow and deliberate until the experimental box was open and ready for the transfer.

The box was about two feet long and two feet wide, six inches high, with a solid floor and a lift-up glass top. The inside was painted solid white. Tommie donned protective leather gloves, then he opened the lunch pail and retrieved the rat. It squirmed in his grip until, with the utmost care, he released it into the white box and quickly clamped down the glass top.

The box was otherwise empty, as it had to be, for Tommie to do a foolproof check for the presence of fleas. The tiny bugs made the phenomenon of scattershot infection too dangerous. But since the rat had ingested enough of the plague victim's flesh to guarantee its own infection, he did not want or need any fleas on his rat. The white box would let him know. If he was right and the rat had no fleas, then it would be safe enough for him to handle as long as it was not allowed to bite.

Minutes passed. No fleas appeared anywhere in the box. Not a spec. He gave it some more time, just as a precaution, but nothing else showed up. It confirmed what he already knew.

Tommie had a highly effective silent killing machine under his control.

He stepped back from the box and let the rat sniff around its sterile environment. "One more hour, I think. Although I'm certain that you are clean," Tommie cooed to him. "Then you can eat, and eat, and eat."

How nice it would be, Tommie thought, if the rat could break its fast on Lieutenant Moses. *But you can't have everything,* he reminded himself.

He decided to distract himself for the night, so he whirled on down to his locked changing room and spent a few hours carefully transforming himself into a lovely female. Then Tommie walked, hips rocking provocatively from side to side, all the way down to the Barbary Coast district. The pain of the garments and shoes served to make the experience all the more real. It helped to prepare him for the kill, while he trolled the back alleys for robbers and rapists.

Such killings were less satisfying to him now. They helped to pass the time, but he knew from experience that they could never rise to the level of art. There was not enough to savor.

By eleven P.M., the fresh sourdough loaf that Vignette had managed to purloin earlier that evening sat heavy in her stomach. She wouldn't need to eat again before morning. As soon as she finished off the last of it, she crawled out from behind the bushes across from Blackburn's place, hopped to her feet and brushed herself off. The street was quiet.

She moved off in a direction that took her past one of the sergeant's windows. For a second, she caught a glimpse of him through the opened curtains. He had on a clean uniform and was strapping on his weapon belt. She already knew that he worked at night, so she was not surprised to see him preparing to leave at this hour. To her, that just meant that she had learned all she could about him, for now. After tonight, she would know where to find him if she had to.

With that, Vignette the master spy took off at a trot. Her mission for the day had been fairly easy, so far. However, the following, the spying, even stealing the food—none of that was the most difficult part. And now there was no way to avoid it any longer. It was time to face the real challenge: to find Shane and tell him what she had run away from St. Adrian's to reveal.

It was shortly after Shane had been adopted out of St. Adrian's by the Nightingale family when Vignette, in disguise as Mary Kathleen, was poking around the Headmaster's office. She spotted Shane's name on one of the files that Friar John was careless about locking up. That was when she learned the truth about how and why Shane wound up there as a four-year-old, and why his existence there was officially erased as soon as the Nightingales took him in.

But she had no intention of telling him that. She had a story that she was certain would be far better for both of them.

It took her nearly an hour to cover the distance from Sergeant Blackburn's place to the Mission Dolores. There she hurried past the wrecked remains of the newer brick church and the solid front doors of the unharmed old Mission. She stopped at the cemetery gate. The strenuous walk had kept her tension at bay so far, but when she lifted the latch and opened the gate, the screech of its rusting hinges nearly knocked her backward. Vignette had reached the moment to put all of her experience to the test. The goal today was to use her ability for something much more challenging than the little tricks she employed to make life better for herself around

St. Adrian's. Now, if only she could get Shane to believe what she intended to tell him, she would completely change her life.

Inside the gate, she squinted through the midnight blackness to the back of the cemetery. There was a toolshed back there, with a glow of lantern light coming from inside. She quietly moved into the darkened graveyard and slipped through the shadows hovering between twisted tree branches and grave markers.

She drew close enough to the shed to hear a boy's voice. Moments later she recognized it as Shane's. He was speaking at a rapid clip, but she didn't hear any replies from whoever he was talking to. Vignette tiptoed up to the door of the shed. She spotted Shane inside, pacing back and forth with a newspaper folded in one hand and a lantern in the other. Now she could see that he wasn't having a conversation, he was reading the paper out loud.

Dozens of tiny memories flooded through her, glimpses of Shane over the past several years, while they lived out their lives among a changing group of strangers. She would recognize Shane's quietly confident demeanor anywhere in the world. Now while she listened to him read with easy confidence, she could not help comparing his refined skill with her own struggles to read and write. Neither was her strong suit. She instantly admired him for it.

Somebody who could read like *that,* Vignette figured, could probably accomplish anything that she needed to get done.

CHAPTER THIRTEEN

"SHANE?"

It was a girl's voice. Whispering. Shane dropped the paper and stumbled back until he hit the wall and nearly broke the lamp. He stared toward the door, but the lantern made everything outside dissolve in blackness. Then the voice came again, from close by.

"Sorry if I startled you. You all right?" The girl stepped forward and stopped just before the doorway. She was nearly his height. Skinny as a post.

Shane recognized her as one of the girls from St. Adrian's. He couldn't think of her name, and he also couldn't think of a good reason why any of the kids from that place would be here at the Mission, well after midnight. She appeared to be by herself, but who could say whether anybody else waited for him out there?

"Who are you?" he asked her. "Who—who—who . . . ah—ah—are . . . yeh—yuh—you?"

She stared at him in surprise. "Are you all right?" She glanced down at the paper lying on the dirt floor. Shane reflexively stepped over to it and picked it up. But he didn't answer her.

"Since you asked, everybody calls me Vignette, and I'm a master spy." She gave him a "tah-dah" grin, as if that explained everything.

Shane could manage no other reply but to stare at her.

"All right, that's not what they call me at St. Adrian's. You don't remember my name, do you? That's all right. Actually, it's good. They used to call me Mary Kathleen, so that I would grow up to be a fat housewife. But now I'm Vignette—a vignette is a little story, you see?

"I ran away, Shane. Today. I'm gonna sneak back in tonight and steal my stuff, and then I'm gone from there for good."

"So nobody else sent you?" Shane tried to ask. "Suh-suh-suh-so nobuh-nobuh-nobody else seh-seh-sent you?" He felt his heartbeat beginning to slow down. If others were out there, they would have stormed in by now.

He thought that a look of sadness flashed across her face. "Shane, you didn't used to talk like that. I mean, you always got your words out just fine. And it's funny, but when you were reading just now, you didn't stutter at all. It sounded just like you. The real you. What happened?"

He gave her a look of frustration.

"Never mind, then. Too many words." She pointed at the paper. "So when you read out loud, you can talk without a problem. Is that right?"

Shane nodded, wondering why he was the one answering questions.

"Read me something."

Shane scowled at her.

"No, really. I know you can. I heard you! Come on, just a line or two."

Shane had the definite feeling that he should be insisting that she get out before one of the priests spotted her and he got into trouble. But she was a familiar face from the first place he had lived since he could remember. She knew his name. He never paid much attention to her, since she was a couple of years younger. But he remembered that whenever she passed by, there always seemed to be somebody yelling for her.

He picked up the article and began to read. " 'Police have finally put an end to the practice of looting by chasing down a secret list of suspected perpetrators—' "

"That's it!" she shouted with glee. "That's how you sound! I recognize that voice!"

He had to smile at her reaction. So he nodded and mimicked her "tah-dah" grin. He struck a mock formal pose and repeated her new name. "Vign-" He stopped himself, took a deep breath, and started again. "Vignette," he said, mimicking a stage actor.

She laughed in delight and clapped her hands. He started to laugh with her, but suddenly realized that they could easily be overheard. He jumped up, startling her as he lurched past her and grabbed the door to the shed. He pulled the door closed, turned to her, and pointed outside.

"All right," she whispered. "We'll keep it quiet here."

He nodded and sat down on the dirt floor again.

What he remembered about Vignette from when she was Mary Kathleen was that she seemed to flutter about the place like a butterfly. Once in a while, she had engaged him in conversation or some little game. He would generally play along, but he never did anything to encourage her attention. Male and female fraternization was heavily discouraged by Friar John and his Helpers. In that place, it would only draw the wrong kind of attention.

"Um, well," Vignette began, "I might as well just come out and tell you, right? I mean you must be wondering exactly why I'm here. I would be, if I were you. So here it is. I'm not, my name isn't really Mary Kathleen. I told you that, right? *They* named me that. *I* never told them to. They're not my parents. They can't name me. That's all. So I'm Vignette because I like that name and I picked it myself."

She leaned toward him. "Vignette is a master spy. I mean it. She can do things. I can, I mean. And one of the things I used to do at St. Adrian's is to get in trouble on purpose so that I would be forced to clean Friar John's office.

"That's where you can really learn things, if you pay attention.

He never tried to look at me in the shower, so I couldn't get him to give me money. Did they do that to you? Instead, sometimes I would read things that he left lying out on his desk. I'm not such a good reader, but you know, I get the gist of it.

"They know a lot about some of us, Shane. About what happened to us, I mean. Things like why we were put there, or who our families were. Did you know that?"

Shane had never asked himself whether Friar John might know anything else about him that he had not revealed. Suddenly, he couldn't imagine why he never had.

Vignette went on, "So I had what you might call a hobby, where I tried to find out where some of us came from. You know, what our stories were. And even though most of us are just found on doorways or something, sometimes the Helpers know things that they don't let on. *Extremely* interesting things."

Shane was starting to get impatient for her to get to the point. It must have shown on his face, because she sped up.

"Shane, you don't ever remember a time when I wasn't around St. Adrian's, do you? 'Cause I don't remember when you weren't there. I was only about two years old when they found me. And you were four, right?"

He nodded, wondering how she knew that.

"They didn't get us at the same time, but it was pretty close. A few days." Vignette steeled herself, then she leaped into her plan, unhesitating. *Just do it like you mean it,* she reminded herself. *The key is to talk too fast to let them think.*

"And so the file said that the notes that got left with us were done in the same handwriting. You hear me? They were done on the same sort of paper. And they think that we came from the same people! But they never tell the kids things like that, because they don't want you to know if you have a brother or a sister. It's easier to adopt everyone out, one at a time."

She looked at him with an expression of grim, cold truth. Then she made the "tah-dah" smile.

Shane's need to speak was so strong that he felt as if he would explode. He started once, and got nothing out. He stopped and gritted his teeth in frustration, then tried again. No good.

Vignette watched him in concern until he gave up and shook his head. At that point she chimed in. "Wait a minute!" She picked up Shane's notebook and handed it to him. "Here, take this. Now, just write down what you want to say, here." She giggled again with anticipation, then went on. "Okay, first write down, 'My name is Shane.'"

He had no desire for games at this hour, but he cooperated and wrote down "My name is Shane," just to make her happy.

"Good!" she whispered. "Next, if somebody asks you where you live, you might say 'I live in San Francisco,' right?"

He nodded.

"Good!" She cried out in excitement. "So write that down! You live in San Francisco!"

He cooperated, resigned to playing along. She was irritating but his loneliness had disappeared. Just as he finished that sentence, she added the last one.

"Yes! Now, just write this," she began to dictate, " 'I would never leave my sister all alone on the streets.' "

He looked up at her.

"Just write it down! I swear, I don't recall you being slow like this. 'I would never leave my sister all alone on the streets.' "

He couldn't keep from grinning while he shook his head, but he complied and wrote out the words.

"That's perfect!" she exclaimed, leaning around to look at his work. "Now, I'm going to ask you three questions, and all you have to do is read the answers right there off of your page, get it?"

Shane looked skeptical.

"No really. Try it! Here we go: What is your name?" She tapped her fingertip on the paper. He looked down at it and read—

"Shane Nightingale." His voice was clear and strong and the words came out with no effort at all. He stopped with a jolt and looked at her. When their eyes met, he laughed with astonishment before he could stop himself.

Vignette grinned from ear to ear and continued. "Okay then, and where do you live?"

Shane looked at the next words on the page and read them out loud. "I live in San Francisco."

His voice had never been stronger. He laughed out loud in sheer delight. Vignette laughed along with him, then popped up to take an exaggerated bow.

"All right, *now*," she went on with a twinkle in her eyes. "Tell me what you have to say about your sister?" She pointed at the page.

While Shane read the words, he could feel the wry smile stretching his lips. "I would never leave my sister all alone on the streets."

Vignette grinned even bigger. "I didn't think you would." She stood up, took a deep breath and brushed herself off. Shane was so dulled by amazement that she reached over and easily snatched the tablet out of his hand. She tossed it back onto the shelf and turned to him, glowing with mischievous delight.

"Now," she began, "your memory is good enough that you can still picture that page in your mind, can't you?"

In his mind's eye, he could still see the page with the three little statements written out, one by one. He nodded.

She giggled in anticipation and rubbed her hands together. "So I'm going to ask you three questions, now. And all you're going to do is *read* what you can see there on the page in your memory. Don't try to *talk*, just *read*.

"Hi. My name is Vignette. What's your name?"

"Shane Nightingale."

They both laughed to hear it work so well again.

"My, what a perfect voice you have, Mr. Nightingale. So tell me, where do you live?"

"I live in San Francisco!" he said triumphantly.

"And now, what do you have to say about your sister?"

Shane found it impossible to suppress the smile pulling at both sides of his face. "I would never leave my sister all alone on the streets."

In that moment, Shane decided that as strange as it was, it was no more strange than so many other things in recent days. But here, now, what could such a thing even mean? What did it mean, to have a sister? And what did it mean to be an older brother, knowing what he knew about himself?

At least he felt convinced that she didn't mean any harm. She was bossy, but she was so playful about it that it made him want to play along with her.

"I'm going to go back and get my stuff," she said while she teased the door open and peeked outside. She looked back at him and nodded, confirming that it was all clear out there. But before she could step out, Shane reached over to her and took her arm.

"Ah-ah-ah-are yuh-yuh-yuhhh-you—"

"Write it down!" she urged.

He scribbled his question and thrust the tablet at her.

"No, don't hand it to me—read it. Read it out loud!"

"Are you really my sister?" He read the words with ease.

She paused for a moment to look into his eyes, though she kept her thoughts away from him. *This is the test that always comes. You pass it by sticking to your story.* Light as a feather, she stepped up to him and kissed him on the cheek.

"They just didn't want us to know," she whispered. She turned and started out the door.

And then she was gone.

Shane sat quietly for a few moments, trying to digest what had happened. Someone from the orphanage had finally come looking for him, but it was not as he had feared. Nobody wanted to drag him back, or make trouble for him. The fact was, he had a real sister, a flesh and blood little sister, and she wanted to be with him.

That's perfect, he said to himself, in the voice that never stuttered. His life was broken into dozens of pieces. He lived in a

toolshed in a cemetery. And now his younger sister had manifested out of the midnight fog and just wanted to "leave her stuff"
with him.

What happens when she returns? The padres wouldn't let
them live there together. Does she go off somewhere else to sleep
every day and then drop by here for tea and cookies? How much
could she be seen around the place before the padres began to
ask questions? How much longer after that until they became
concerned?

Once they became concerned, what reason would they have to
tolerate his presence any longer? Was she there to doom them both?

But the main thing, no matter how he might try to twist and turn
it, was the promise she'd had him make.

I would never leave my sister all alone on the streets.

Whether the idea came from her or from him, he knew that he
could never turn his back on her. Not now. If she had only discovered that they were brother and sister earlier, maybe the two of
them could have even been adopted into the Nightingale home together.

Except that if they had, then it would mean that she would be
dead now, too.

Because of him.

So if this was his sister, then the timing of her discovery was
lucky for them both. Knowing that he had a family member alive
was the one bit of news that he had never prepared himself to hear.
He sat under the weight of it.

Then it hit him with a leaden thud: How would he protect her
from the secret load that he carried after his failure in the Nightingale house? He would have to make up a complete story to cover
the family's deaths. Then for the rest of their lives he would have to
remember to never slip, never drop his story. He could never allow
her to hear a word about the source of all his nightmares, or about
the knowledge that he possessed regarding things a human crea-

ture will sometimes do—things that it is best not to know too much about.

Tommie Kimbrough lay on an expensive area rug purchased on credit from the Nightingale Dry Goods Emporium, fondly gazing at his experiment. After nearly twenty-four hours, not a single dark speck showed on the pristine white interior of the glass-topped box.

But the rat had feasted on the body at the morgue, which meant that it had to be filled with the plague now. Tommie rolled slightly to get a better look at the sophisticated medical book he had purchased by mail from Great Britain for one hundred pounds sterling. He found the listing for "Bubonic Plague" and skipped down to the part that concerned him.

> . . . the most powerful form of the plague bacillus manifests as *Septicemic Plague*. In this form, it is generally transmitted to humans from the bite of infected rats. The effects develop lethality faster than any other plague form: death in a single day, from onset of symptoms. The body turns purple, then black in the death process, resulting from disseminated intravascular coagulation. This particularly virulent disease is 100 percent fatal.

Reverberations went through him in powerful waves.
One hundred percent fatal.
And they die in a day . . .
It was the manifestation of a dream. Septicemic plague. A term worthy of poetry.
Tommie's furry black guest inside the stark white box did not appear sickly in any way, and yet it suddenly was so much more than an unusual personal pet.
It was Death on four little legs. *And best of all,* Tommie mused, *this little creature works for me like the Grim Reaper works for God.*

CHAPTER FOURTEEN

RANDALL BLACKBURN STOOD at the entrance to the narrow service alley behind the Dash Theater on Pacific Street, one of the Barbary Coast brothels that came through the disaster without any serious problems. He had just been pulled by the theater manager to that very spot, where he now stood staring down at the body of The Surgeon's latest victim. What was the total? Fourteen? He was losing count.

Blackburn didn't have to make a close examination to see that the man was dead; the body lay in a pool of blood too large for anyone to lose and survive. The familiar wound was there at the back of his neck. This victim was young, twenty to twenty-five, and his body was massive. Blackburn took him for one of the dockside stevedores. The victim's pants were still fastened and there was no sign of castration, but if this killing was indeed done by The Surgeon, she would surely have placed a note on the body, leaving her individual stamp on the crime.

He paused there, steeling himself to read some taunting diatribe. Blackburn's heart was grim and heavy and he could feel his jaw set hard. There was nothing else to do but go through the pockets for identification.

Just at that moment, he felt a passing wave of embarrassment regarding the way he earned his livelihood. His mother would have a heart attack if she could see how he spent his time, and his father would be astounded that their quiet and tentative boy had grown up to fight on a daily basis with monstrous people who sometimes compared badly to wild animals. He was glad that his parents preferred to avoid the city and liked for him to come up north to visit them.

He exhaled more heavily than he had intended and stepped over to the sprawled form. And there was the note. This time it was rolled into a tiny tube and tucked between the man's lips, like a cigarette. Blackburn plucked up the tube and unrolled the slip of paper.

> *Search for me in every hour*
> *But know that you'll not find me*
> *Until I greet you at a time and place*
> *Of my own choosing*

Blackburn shook his head in disgust. The words themselves were meaningless to him and would probably prove to be useless to the investigation, but no doubt their private meaning gave The Surgeon some special thrill.

He rerolled the note and put it back exactly as it was, then stood up. There was nothing else to do here but call for a coroner's wagon and begin all the routine procedures. He saw nothing new in this crime scene to help him.

This newest murder underscored the feeling that seemed to grip most of the city now, the feeling that everything was out of control and might never get better. Since the disaster, life on the rougher side of San Francisco's streets had gone completely downhill. Nearly every time Blackburn had to arrest someone, their story of despair poured out of them. The survivors' shock and pain were so universal, and their vague charge of guilt was so pervasive, that many felt their faith shaken to the core. And some, instead of clinging to their beliefs, gave up all pretense of morality.

Like this living mockery of a "surgeon."

He hated to think of Shane Nightingale wandering around these streets alone, with no one to assure his safety. For an instant, he wondered what would happen if the boy ever ran into a monster like this one. He started to push the thought out of his head. Then it occurred to him that there was another possibility: If the boy's unusual display of deductive talent in the Sullivan case could be repeated here, he might be the only person who could help Blackburn find The Surgeon.

Vignette figured that most of the people who were up and around after midnight were not the type who would rush to her aid if something bad happened, so she moved at a constant, dogged trot all the way back to St. Adrian's. She was less than half a block from the front entrance and already looking around for an open window to crawl into, when she heard the big front door open and saw lantern light in the doorway. She pulled against a large tree trunk that was shadowed from the moon and melded her body to its dark form. An instant later, she recognized Friar John as the man carrying the lantern. He was accompanied by a scrawny and ragged-looking boy, a street urchin by the look of him.

Her heart jumped when she realized they were going to walk directly past her. There was no time for her to run off without being spotted, and outside of the shadows there was enough moonlight for Friar John to recognize her. She pushed herself tighter against the tree and willed herself to fade into the night's background. She even took a deep breath and held it while they passed.

"All right, we're on our way," she heard Friar John saying to the boy. "Now you can tell me why Mr. Kimbrough has this 'emergency,' at this hour."

"No sir, I can't."

"He always comes *here* to see me. He must have told you something about why he wasn't coming this time?"

"Nope. Don't know nothing and that's the truth," the boy assured him, perhaps eager for a tip. "Mr. Kimbrough said something about a newspaper. Don't know what he meant by it."

The name "Kimbrough" didn't mean anything to Vignette at first, but when she heard the boy mention a newspaper, the connection clicked into place. She had struggled through the article on Shane after she heard a couple of the Helpers talking about it. They were too busy swapping reminiscences of Shane at St. Adrian's to notice when she swiped the newspaper and sounded out enough of the wording to get the general idea, and then replaced it before it was missed.

And when the word "newspaper" brought Shane to mind, the rest was plain enough. This Mr. Kimbrough was a slight man with a wiry build whom she had spotted visiting Friar John on more than one occasion over the past years. They always made such a point of meeting in private behind closed doors that she made sure to push her mop close to Friar John's door one day and watched them through the keyhole. She learned only enough to know that Mr. Kimbrough was there about Shane. It made her curious enough to peek in Shane's file when Friar John was out, sounding out a few of the words until she got the main idea.

Mr. Tommie Kimbrough was Shane's older half brother. Shane was a bastard son of the father and some other woman. They just weren't letting Shane know about it. He had never even heard his own last name. When he arrived as a small boy, he had already been beaten up so badly that he was completely disoriented. He had to relearn the most basic skills. This Mr. Kimbrough made sure that Shane remained at St. Adrian's with no knowledge of his family and no contact with his brother. Something about that cruel fact twisted her insides.

He doesn't even know that he has a brother, let alone one who visits in secret. She had stored it for future use, but Shane was suddenly adopted out, one day—whisked away before she could tell him anything at all.

So Mr. Kimbrough had sent a messenger boy to order Friar John to come to him at this hour. Vignette decided that if he was not bringing any Helpers along with him, he must be going in secret. To her it was clear that this had something to do with Shane.

She would follow Friar John. But first she needed to get inside and grab her stuff, and do it quickly enough to get back out and catch up to them before she lost them. She spotted a well-located ground-floor window in the office section. It appeared to be closed, but she knew that they were seldom locked. It never seemed to occur to anyone there to protect against kids trying to get in.

Once she was out in the main hallway, which was darkened for the night, she started toward her end of the girl's dorm. But her soft leather shoes, so perfect for running along the streets, were too noisy now. She slipped them off and carried them while she tiptoed down the long row of sleeping girls to her bed.

She had left her small cigar box that held her special mementos right out on the nightstand by her bed. It was perfectly safe out in the open like that, and had been ever since the word spread around about the two black eyes she put on a girl who tried to steal it. Vignette's Helper had searched around for it and found it in the girl's things, so the girl also got in trouble with the Headmaster. After that, she could have left her box in the middle of the hall and nobody would have touched it.

But in return, she had to bathe after dinner every night for a week, using the bath area during the empty hours when no one else wanted to, so that she did not have to rush. Her Helper did not like it when she rushed. Vignette silently picked up the small cigar box that held her special mementos and set it on the bed. She removed her other pair of long pants from the hook on the wall and slipped them on right over her own, then took down her only coat and put it on. She had one dress, but she left it hanging on its peg. Instead, she picked up her shoes and the box, slipped back down the row of beds, and hurried into the main hallway. Her plan was to go out the front door at a full sprint and disappear into the night. Since she would never be back, there would be no punishment, this time, this one time.

As soon as she reached the heavy front door, she bent to slip her shoes back on and quickly tied up the laces just right for running. It was when she stood back up to reach for the door latch that she felt a huge hand close around the back of her neck.

She smelled his familiar body odor. It identified him so bluntly that she made no attempt to turn and look at his face. His grip was firm, although not as hard as when she was in real trouble.

"You're supposed to tell me when you want to go out. So I can help cover for you." His voice was deep and frighteningly gentle.

"I know! I know. I always do. It's just, tonight I had this emergency, and—"

"Oh, emergency!" He laughed and said in a little girl voice: "She had an emergency, Friar John, that's all!" Her Helper shook his head. "No, Mary Kathleen. You went and put me in a tough spot this time. 'Cause I'd lose my job for failing to report this. Think of how much risk that is. For me."

His breath always smelled of sour tobacco and stale coffee. Her stomach lurched when he breathed on her.

"Well, I was hoping that you would do me this favor, this one time, what with the emergency and all—so that I can go on in and take me a long, hot bath. You know, do it now when none of the other kids are in there. So I can take all the time I need to get clean."

He turned her around to face him and then smiled in appreciation of her negotiating skills. "Hm . . . Maybe this one time," he cooed as he released her. "You get along to that bath now. It's good to get clean."

Her brain raced. How was she to escape, with him nearly on top of her?

Then inspiration struck.

"Uh, okay. I'm just going to go put my stuff away. And take off my clothes. Then it's off to the bath."

Her Helper grinned in anticipation, and even as he did so she saw his eyes glaze over and a slack expression cross his face. He turned and headed off toward his office next door to the bathroom, the one with the little hole in the wall behind a flap. He was so eager to get his private performance that he did not mind going ahead and waiting for her to enter. She pretended to head for her bunk area until she saw him turn and step into his office. Then after a count of three, she spun around and ran back to the front door, yanked it open and flung herself through.

Mary Kathleen disappeared at the doorway of St. Adrian of Canterbury's Home for Delinquents and Orphans, never to be seen there again.

Vignette hit the front walkway at a dead run.

She only had to keep running for a few minutes before she caught sight of Friar John's lantern bobbing along up the street ahead. Relieved, she fell in half a block behind them and patiently followed until they reached the Russian Hill District. She figured that they had come two miles or more by the time they reached a fancy, three-story house inside one of the areas untouched by the fires. She could see where the flames had split in two and passed around this one particular hilltop. As if somebody had told them to.

She huddled in the cold shadows and watched while Friar John knocked at a door. When it swung open, the inner light revealed Mr. Kimbrough. He gestured for Friar John and the boy to come in, then he threw a cautious glance around the neighborhood. As soon as the door closed again, the entire front of the house went dark. She had clearly seen the lights inside while the door was open, so Mr. Kimbrough must have had heavy curtains that completely concealed any light at all from the windows. Vignette wondered why anybody would do that. A cold shiver ran up her back.

But at least she had accomplished her tasks for the day. Now she knew where Sergeant Blackburn lived and where Shane's secret brother lived, too.

With that, she tucked her cigar box a little tighter under her arm and headed off for the Mission Dolores to strengthen her position as Shane's long-lost sister. She hoped that Shane would be awake when she arrived and that he might have an idea of where they could get something to eat without paying for it. She had already burned through the sourdough loaf, but there had been no chance to check Friar John's office for spare change. Vignette already knew full well that when your pockets are empty, life runs you around on a short leash.

Tommie waved the friar and the messenger boy into his study. The boy looked nervously around, clearly not happy about being there, but he needed to hang around for his payment. Tommie was confident that the boy's hope for his coins would keep him silent for a few minutes. That was all the time Tommie needed.

"Sit down, Friar," he invited.

Friar John perched on the edge of the sofa and impatiently looked back up at him. "Well?"

Tommie could not resist an expression of mock innocence. "What?"

"*What?* Never in my life have I been summoned in the middle of the night by any but the sick and dying. I have—"

"Horseshit." Tommie kept his face blank. "The only time you get up in the middle of the night is when you want to visit one of your kiddies."

Friar John gasped in shock and jumped to his feet. "What in God's name do you—"

"Joking! Friar, I'm joking!"

"I see no humor at all in—"

"Perfect! Because I see no humor in this." He slammed down the newspaper article about Shane onto the table. Friar John leaned over, read briefly, and grew pale.

"You friars don't see a lot of newspapers, do you?"

"I saw it, as a matter of fact. What could I do?"

"Nothing, now!" Tommie shouted. "You double-crossed me. You were *never* supposed to adopt him out. Never! What the hell have I been paying you for all these years?"

"Your payments don't keep our doors open, Mr. Kimbrough! And you are actually quite casual about making them. Our expenses are unimaginable! The Nightingales offered a very generous fee for Shane. I have to think of the other children!"

"Not before you think about *me,* you don't! I had *dealings* with that family, you understand? And I never knew anything about Shane being adopted out! To them? To the Nightingales? Are you crazy?"

"You haven't been to see us for over a year!"

"So what? The checks keep coming, don't they?"

"No they do not. You are very irregular about—"

"Everybody gets paid eventually! Everybody! What, you're a friar with no patience?" He leaned in closer and dropped his voice. "I realize, now, that Mr. Nightingale started pushing me to take things on credit right after you adopted Shane out to him. Lots of things. Expensive things. It was almost as if he knew my weakness. Almost as if someone told him how to ensnare me, create a big debt, win a suit, take my home. Take my home from me. You sold that boy to Nightingale and then told Nightingale how to use my weakness against me to *steal my home.*"

Friar John's face turned pale.

Tommie abruptly turned to the messenger boy. "You don't need to see what I'm about to do to him," he said, nodding toward Friar John. And with that, he snatched up a cast-iron statuette and swung it so hard that the top of the boy's head was crushed under the force of the blow. Bits of brain and blood streaked a flare across the wall behind him. The boy's limp body fell to one side.

"God Almighty!" Friar John shouted, staggering backward in shock. He did not move far enough away to save himself.

Tommie took two quick steps closer and then swung again. This time he used less force, so that Friar John only fell unconscious, to be saved for later.

"That's it?" Shane quietly asked, though the words took him longer. He stood looking at the cigar box that she held out to him.

"Well," she began, then shrugged. Before Shane could react, she unbuttoned her pants and pulled them down, only to reveal another pair underneath. She held out the spare pair along with the box.

Shane exhaled with a smile and took the pants and the box. He stepped to the wall and put the box up on the top shelf. He hung her pants from one of the tool pegs, turned to her, and smiled.

She smiled back. "See? You can keep my stuff here. There's no way anybody can tell it belongs to me," she said. "And those pants would probably fit you. You can wear them, if you want. Give them back, though."

Shane tried to reply, "That's all right. People donate clothes here. They let me pick from it, sometimes. I can probably get you another shirt." But he stalled on the third word and bogged down.

"Wait!" Vignette clapped her hands in glee. "This is when you do it. This is when you write it down first, then read it back to me."

Shane grabbed his writing pad and pencil and quickly scrawled the words, then held up the pad with a self-conscious grin and read out loud:

"That's all right. People donate clothes here. They let me pick from it, sometimes. I can probably get you another shirt." He laughed and shook his head. He had not even stumbled.

"Good!" replied Vignette. "Then I can always keep one set of clothes clean. See? It's good for me to have a brother already." She thought for a second and quickly added, "And don't you worry, having a sister out here will be good for you, too."

He grinned and sat on the dirt floor, made a motion of writing in the air with his finger.

"How?" he asked. The word came out strong and clear.

"I saw that!" she said. "I saw you do that! You wrote inside of your mind and then you read what you could see. Right?"

He gave her a conspiratorial smile and nodded.

"That could work all the time, you know? I mean, if you could learn to make that a habit." Her face lit up. "Hey! We worked that one out together, didn't we? So there you have it. You first big blessing from having a sister! Isn't that right?"

He seemed to concentrate on the air for a moment, and finally answered, "Right. But you still can't—can't—stay here. They'll cah-catch us."

Her face fell. "I know. You don't have to tell me that."

He concentrated again. "Do you know our last name?"

"Uh, no. No. I thought we could just use yours."

He turned to her in surprise, thought for a moment, then realized that he liked the feel of the idea. He nodded. "But you can't be alone out—out—here. Where will you lih-live?"

This time her voice was much smaller, nearly a whisper. "Oh, I don't know yet. They would never let a boy and girl stay together here. Usually, anyway. But what about family? They wouldn't think that anything was wrong with that, would they? Why would they? Even holy men come from families with girls, don't they?"

Shane laughed and nodded.

"We could just go straight to them and say we're long-lost family who just found each other after the Great Earthquake. I can work, you know! I can work like the dickens. All I ever did at that stupid place was work."

". . . Yeah. I know."

"Besides," she softly went on, "Catholics really like big families, don't they? We're just family, that's all."

She studied Shane's face while he looked back at her with a resigned smile. Finally, he got to his feet, brushed himself off, and picked up one of the two sleeping blankets that were folded on the shelf. He tossed the other to her.

"Tomorrow," he managed to say. "We can tell them. Tonight, if—if—if they come . . ." He gestured toward the outdoors with his blanket.

"You'll sleep out there tonight in case anyone would find us before they knew you were my brother?"

Shane nodded, then his face darkened with a strange sort of sadness. He rested one hand on her shoulder, but no words came out.

She whispered, "You would take care of me though, right? They'll see that it's only right for you to do that, won't they?"

Shane concentrated for a moment, then looked Vignette straight in the face. "They will. Or we'll both leave."

Shane silently held her gaze. Finally he grinned and pretended to punch her in the arm, then went out to sleep in the open cemetery, leaving her the lantern and his other blanket.

Vignette stood near the doorway and looked out into the darkness. It was as if everything she had ever learned had prepared her for this day. She wrapped herself up in the blanket like a giant woolen hug, and lay down on the cool dirt floor. In her circumstances it was as good as a beautiful feather bed. She fell into the untroubled sleep of victory.

Out in the graveyard, Shane made his way back to the grave next to the Mission wall.

A sister. He had a sister. He was a brother. The strangeness of his life continued to amaze him. Somehow, he was being given some sort of a second chance. Life was asking him if he had learned anything at all from his failure and humiliation. Gratitude and exaltation overwhelmed him. He was ready to dare anyone in the world to ever try to scare him so badly that he would fail to help his sister. Not this time. Never again.

It was the first time since the Nightingale horrors that he allowed himself to fall asleep before it was light outside.

CHAPTER FIFTEEN

FRIAR JOHN'S BODY LAY UNCONSCIOUS, but the pain began to pull him upward, like a drowned body returning to the surface. Part of his awareness tried to keep him from rising any closer, but that same part of him sensed with growing concern that the harder he tried to stay unconscious, the faster he was waking up.

After he opened his eyes, Friar John realized that he was lying stretched out on his back with his hands securely bound behind him and pinned beneath him. He was looking up toward the ceiling. Expensive stamped copper sheets. Where was he?

Then all of his senses became alert, and the pain hit him with such terrible force that Friar John shrieked in agony and terror. He screamed from his bowels to the top of his skull, and only then did he become aware that his mouth was jammed full of cloth and that the gag was tied down. His screams were stifled there, except for a few small bleats that made it through his nose.

He finally raised his head an inch. It was just enough to get a look around, but the pain waves were rolling through him with such ferocious power that he forgot what he was looking for. Panic swept him. Only the feel of the rope around his neck kept him still. He tilted his head just enough to look down at himself. He was rolled up in several layers of heavy fabric, roped shut. It was tied off tightly at his neck, leaving his head sticking out and the rest of him completely covered. His feet were tied together inside the wrapping, which was pinched tight below the soles of his shoes and tied off. That rope was stretched across the floor to a large eyebolt that appeared to have been sunk into the wooden floor just for that purpose. A few bits of sawdust still lined the hole.

The pain rolled through him over and over, timed to every heartbeat. His screams stayed bottled up inside of him, and with his mouth completely sealed, most of his energy had to go into breathing through his swollen nostrils. He already knew that the rope holding his neck was tied off somewhere behind him, probably to another eyebolt like the one beneath his feet. But the pain took everything else away from him, making him forget everything except trying to wriggle and squirm out from under it, kicking at it, flailing his whole body all around inside of the heavy fabric cocoon.

Then he remembered. Tommie Kimbrough. Friar John had rolled the dice and hoped to collect the Nightingales' outrageously high fee without letting Kimbrough know about Shane's adoption. Using Kimbrough's reckless financial habits against him was supposed to be Friar John's own private joke, one for him to enjoy for years to come, a revenge upon Tommie for all of his harassing visits, his late payments, and his surly, abusive attitude.

There was no reason for the plan not to work perfectly—all those years, and Kimbrough never once asked to see Shane. He always just took Friar John's word about where Shane was and what Shane was doing and how his health happened to be. Friar John's only solemn duty was to immediately summon Kimbrough if Shane ever gave any indication that he remembered anything of his life before St. Adrian's. But Shane never had, not a word. Friar John had felt certain that he never would.

He could have told Kimbrough that Shane had gotten sick and died. Maybe he should have. But who could predict a thing like that news article? What were the odds, in a city whose population was only estimated and where feral children of all ages roamed? Everything should have worked perfectly well.

Then his recent memory cleared. He recalled seeing Kimbrough attack the boy, striking him over the head. The blow killed the boy on the spot. Then he remembered Kimbrough turning on him. That explained the pain in his head, then. But what about this other pain in his leg?

The pain flared again. Hard. He tried to pull away, but the teeth only gnawed harder.

Teeth—animal—biting—biting—biting—

Friar John screamed into his gag. He screamed over and over, in pain and sheer horror at the realization that something was trapped inside the wrapping with him. And it was eating him alive.

He felt the four little paws scramble over his midsection and knew then that this thing chewing on him was a full-sized rat. The harder he tried to squirm away from the teeth, the more frightened and aggressive the rodent became. Teeth that could eat through cabin walls now took out the trapped animal's frustration on Friar John's mortal coil.

His wounds were soaked with the black rat's saliva, laced with the potent strain of the Black Plague. Friar John was only aware of the terror and revulsion; there was nothing to let him know that the blinding speed of bacterial replication had already gotten well under way in his bloodstream, before he had even regained consciousness.

He tried to throw his upper body into a seated position, but his struggles yanked the rope more tightly around his neck. He felt it grab hard and tight, and it snapped him back down to the floor with such force that he cracked the back of his head. After that, the rope never eased its grip, even once he stopped moving. Now his swollen nostrils had to pull air in through his garroted windpipe, while the cloth wadding packed his tongue down tighter than the dirt around a casket. He struggled to breathe, pulling in thin wisps of air and shuddering with broken sobs on every exhale. His eyes were still focused up at the copper ceiling when Tommie Kimbrough stepped into view, glaring down at him.

Tommie pulled a chair next to Friar John's prostrated form and sat comfortably, fitting a factory-rolled cigarette into an ivory cigarette holder. He settled back and lit it with a long opera match. After he puffed out a smoke ring, he paused to let the ring grow wide, then blew a thin stream of smoke straight through it without disturbing the smoke ring itself.

Only then did he turn back, but by then Friar John was losing himself to the pain again and forgetting why Kimbrough was even there. When the rat took a violently aggressive bite and Friar John felt a chunk of his flesh torn away, his useless screams buried themselves in his wadded gag while his entire body convulsed.

Tommie stood back and patiently waited for Friar John to quiet down. He bent over and preened in front of a mirror for a while, but it became obvious that the headmaster was going to be useless for conversation as long as the screaming continued. Tommie glanced at the grandfather clock. Almost six. Barely daylight, but Friar John had already been out cold and feeding the rat for over three hours.

That was plenty of time for this phase of the experiment.

So Tommie reached down and pulled the slipknot around Kimbrough's neck and peeled back the thick fabric of last winter's drapes. He rolled the layers down past the groin area to reveal his special friend, wrapped in a little harness made of rawhide strips and tied to Kimbrough's leg by a short cord—with nowhere to go and nothing to do but eat.

Tommie was amused by the way that Friar John watched him with blazing intensity while he snatched up the rat and dropped it into a nearby glass-topped box. He had shown Friar John where his pain came from, but that was all right. It didn't tell the real story.

There was nothing to be done about the real story now, anyway. Instead he poured the rest of his bourbon into the wound and ignored the fresh screams while he stuffed it with a wad of rags and bound it up just tight enough to keep up a gentle pressure. There would be no bleeding to death here.

With that thought, Tommie realized that he was quite possibly missing an opportunity. Why worry about keeping Friar John's plight a secret from him now? Why not tell him? Let him burn up his last few hours on Earth in the maximum state of terror. Who in all the world deserved it more? Because of Friar John's betrayal, it was Shane who flawed Tommie's finest hour of justifiable revenge. Friar John had sold Tommie out for money. He was Judas, with his thirty pieces of silver.

Tommie focused on Friar John's terror-bugged eyes while he pulled the heavy fabric back into place and tied it snug at the neckline. When he was all done, he spoke but did not deign to look at Friar John.

"The most important thing about this experience for each of us, Friar John, is that we *savor* it." He thought a moment, then laughed. "On second thought, it's important that *I* savor it. You? You can choose for yourself." He gestured over to the box. "You think the bites hurt? They're nothing, Friar John. The bites are nothing! It's what they *do* that matters. So let me spare you the suspense—you'll be dead by this time tomorrow."

Friar John made a little whimpering sound and tried to shrink from him.

"What's that?" Tommie asked. "Oh, no, you misunderstand. I'm not going to be the one who kills you! No, sir. Not at all. I am merely hosting your experience." He pulled his chair a bit closer.

"Let's start with symptoms. Ordinarily, you would already be feeling a nagging little tingle of sickness worming its way into you. You know the feeling, yes? Something is gnawing at you, but you still think you can just tough it out. Right? Your mouth should be getting dry by now, but you probably can't tell, with all that cloth stuffing. And your eyeballs. You know that feverish feeling, when your eyes feel like they're too big for the sockets? The way it hurts just to turn your eyes one way or another? Oo! Tell me when you get that. Or better yet, don't tell me and I'll try to guess."

Friar John slumped in despair and tried to turn his head away from Tommie. Tommie picked up a rag and used it to protect his hand while he reached down and grabbed Friar John's face and turned it back to him. The uncontrollable noises from his victim sounded like a cross between sobbing and strangulation.

"No, you probably haven't noticed your eyes yet, because your head still throbs from that thumping I had to give you, just to get you calmed down and ready to receive." He smiled in satisfaction.

"But that's all right. Receive you did, and what you received is now growing inside of you." Tommie broke into the silly voice that he used for cute toddlers. "You are a garden, Friar John. Did you know that?" He dropped the voice and continued.

"But here's the thing—you'll *really* know that the Devil is coming for you when the pain starts in your gut. Sharp pain, according to my research. A few hours after that, your blood pressure will drop so low that you'll start feeling dizzy. Too dizzy to stand. Even when you lie flat, you'll still keep getting dizzier and dizzier. Finally, when you can't hold on to this world anymore, you'll have to let go. And right up until that last instant, the pain in your gut will be like a stoked fire. Problem is, after you're so dizzy that you just can't help but puke yourself right on out of your body, I am afraid you'll be going straight to Hell. Frightfully sorry. You know what for, though, yes? Oh, don't look at me that way. Of course you do."

He leaned in close to whisper to Friar John with sensual intimacy. "So since we only have a day or so, I propose we share in this whole experience. And if you agree, why then I promise you that every step of the way—" He let out an involuntary laugh. "It will be just as new to me as it is to you!"

He picked up his knife and began to sharpen it on a pocket-sized whetting stone. He slowly brought the blade and stone to a point just under Friar John's nose.

"Now," Tommie began, "you little trouser-cough of a man. Let's see if we can find a reason for me not to slowly carve away your entire face like pulling a fat tick off a dog."

Friar John launched into another fierce set of convulsions, which Tommie watched without comment for a few moments before he continued. "You would prefer that I not, then. So for the sin of double-crossing me, adopting Shane out despite having accepted my money for years to safeguard him, you will tell me where I can find him today."

He brought the knife edge to within a millimeter of Friar John's right eyeball and tested the edge with his thumb. "This thing could peel the skin off a gnat."

He reached behind Friar John's head and pulled the release knot. The gag fell out of his mouth. For a few moments, the headmaster could only gasp and wheeze. Tommie gave him a glass of whiskey and allowed him to drain it. Why not? The condemned man and his last drink, Tommie thought.

"You could tell me now, or I can reintroduce our rodent friend."

"Mr. Kimbrough," the headmaster gasped. "In the name of God!"

"I did not ask you where to find God, Friar John. I asked you where to find Shane."

"Mr. Kimbrough, I'll do whatever you say! Please! Let me out!"

"So I'm going to have to get the rat again, then?"

"No! No! God! I'll tell you! I mean I don't know, but— He didn't tell me exactly where, he just said that Shane is living at one of the Missions. Here in the city."

"Who said that?"

"A policeman. A sergeant. Name of Blackburn. He's with the City Hall Station. He's the one who knows, not me! I don't know! He never told me! I would tell you! I swear on the Blessed Virgin Moth—"

Tommie clubbed him over the head with the same heavy statuette. In the hush that followed, he stepped back and took a breath of relief. The silence was sweet. He replaced the gag cloths and quickly tied the wad back in place, before Friar John could shake off the effects of the blow.

"I'm afraid that you're too noisy to leave without a gag, and I have a vital errand. I'll be back in a few hours at the most. Now, this is very important, so listen carefully: I want you to pay close attention to your symptoms as they come over you, so that we can talk all about it when I get back. No memory problems allowed, now, all right? I'll be pressing for clear answers, so stay awake and pay attention." He poked Friar John in the scalp a few times with the tip of the blade, just for emphasis.

"I'll take those grunts for acquiescence."

Tommie stood up and gave Friar John's bindings a once-over to assure that there would be no escape. Then with a cheerful wave, he left him bound up in his thick fabric cocoon while he went upstairs to get dressed.

Late that morning, Shane and Vignette began working side by side near the front of the long carry-away line. Rumor had it that the padres were tired of all the physical labor of toting away the crumbled remains of the big modern church, and more laborers were needed to handle the ant-like task of carrying off a large building, brick by brick, while avoiding damage to the older one next to it. Shane was not under any pressure to work there because of his night schedule, but nobody was going to turn him away if he felt like joining in.

Vignette had on the larger of her two pairs of pants, plus a thick and baggy shirt. With her short-cropped hair, she looked as much like a boy as Shane did. Nobody questioned her presence there, as long as she kept working. It was not a time and place where a person's identity mattered, so long as they could stay sober and work like a mule. The job paid nothing in wages, but there would be soup, bread, and coffee waiting for the hungry workers at lunchtime. That slim promise alone had been enough to replace every one of the exhausted padres with someone who, months before, would never have considered doing such work.

The food line was already being constructed, and now the workers could catch whiffs of the meal that was about to open up for them. They worked at top speed without realizing they were doing it. Shane and Vignette were caught up in the rhythm of the line as they passed bricks back down the line toward the debris bins. Shane had spent the last several passes with his eyes fixed in space, imagining words written in block letters. When he could see them clearly enough, he read them out loud to Vignette while he handed her a brick. "Don't stop until everybody else does."

She handed the brick to the man behind her and turned back to Shane while he took another brick from the man in front of him. "What if we're the last ones there and they run out of food?"

He shook his head, but gestured for her to wait. They passed four more bricks back down the line before he could respond. "They won't," he told her. "I know people here." He smiled.

One of the cooks blew a big lunch whistle and all the workers dropped their tools. They had just enough restraint left to avoid stampeding the table, so Shane and Vignette made it there among the first arrivals. They were as hypnotized by the sight and smell of the meal as everyone else while they picked up empty tin dinner plates, bowls, and eating utensils, then began to move down the long table while the cooks doled out servings. The line compacted down into a tightening mass and they felt themselves pushed along by the gathering force of everyone's hungry anticipation.

"Shane!" called out an adult male voice. "I'm proud of you for working today, but when will you sleep?"

Shane turned from the food table to see portly Father Juan Carlos standing behind him. Father Juan Carlos had the look of a man who wanted to cut in line and get his lunch with minimal delay.

"Oh! Fah-Fah-Fah-Father. Hi." He made a gesture by holding his thumb and forefinger close together. "Juh-just a lit—just a little."

"Ah!" Father Juan Carlos smiled, looking around, enjoying the view from that part of the line. "And who is your friend?" he politely inquired.

"Vignette," Shane stupidly began. Fortunately his stutter only let him blurt out, "Vin-Vin-"

"Vinny," Vignette interrupted with a masculine scowl. "We're brothers. Just found each other. After the quake and all. Everybody else bought the farm. All of them."

"Ah! *Brothers!*" cried Father Juan Carlos as if a miracle had unfolded. He looked around with an expression that invited all to witness. "You were separated by the terrible earthquake, and you have discovered each other once again at the Mission Dolores!" He called out to everyone within earshot. "Isn't that wonderful?"

Everyone within earshot agreed, with all the enthusiasm of hungry people impatient for a meal. More than one grumbled about there being a line.

"Two young *muchachos*," Father Juan Carlos rhapsodized. "*Hermanos,* who both thought that they were alone in the world, but the Lord looked after them!" He was much too grateful for being in the company of this miraculous occurrence to worry about miniscule things like lines and places in them.

Vinny piped up in a boyish voice, loud enough to be heard by everyone in the area. "Thank you, Father. But since we saved your place in line for you, why don't you get in here and grab a plate?"

"Oh!" replied the happy friar without missing a beat. "That's right! I suppose I should. And thank you again, *chico.*"

"It's our pleasure, Father. We'll be seeing you around, since we're both living out in the shed and guarding the cemetery at night and all. Looters, you know. If we even see one, we'll set off a ruckus they'll hear for miles!"

Shane shot Vignette a panicked look, convinced she was about to say something that would draw the wrong attention to them. He was ready to move into the streets with her if he had to, but he hated the idea of letting that happen.

"Oh. Really?" Father Juan Carlos replied. "Both? Then you've gotten permission—" He paused. "Yes. Well then. I'll see you at mass, no?" He smiled and lost interest in them, loading up his bowl and plate.

"Yes, Father. Both of us. We do everything together."

"*Bueno,* then," the hungry friar replied, eyeing his ample lunch. He smiled around at the nearby workers. "Thank you everyone. Blessings upon you." He continued to smile while he walked off with his food.

Shane paid close attention to a number of the workers, who seemed to accept Shane and Vignette as just a couple of brothers who lived out in the cemetery, seemingly with permission. Something told him that as long as he and Vignette kept quiet and didn't cause any trouble, rumor could serve them as well as fact.

CHAPTER SIXTEEN

THE LATE MAY MORNING AIR was misty cold, ignoring summer. Tommie had eaten nothing at all for over two days to achieve maximum inner purity. At this point he was feeling lighter than air, filled by an unusual sort of electrical charge. He walked all the way to the City Hall Station from his place up on Russian Hill, just to burn off some energy. In contrast to the morning's frosty temperatures, his body radiated heat like a powerful gaslight. He could feel himself glowing.

By the time he entered the station house and found his way to Lieutenant Gregory Moses, Tommie was prepared to overwhelm that shrinking lieutenant and quietly coerce him to tell everything he knew about the surviving boy Shane—and about his connection to Sergeant Randall Blackburn, one of the lieutenant's own men.

Tommie knew for a fact that whatever scraps of willpower remained in the lieutenant's semi-corpulent form would quickly dissolve in Tommie's presence. Afterward, Lieutenant Moses would feel proud to have been of service to one of his betters.

Moses had to wonder just how much of a fool that they thought him to be, these faceless higher-ups in the Department brass, that they would send Tommie Kimbrough to test him yet again. Their low opinion of his intelligence grieved him far more than whatever it was that they were doing to try to take away his position and give it to their nephew, or their bartender, or anybody they might owe a favor. He was astonished that anyone who knew him would judge him to be such a fool. Did they have no idea of the kind of mental skills necessary to run the Record Keeping Department?

And yet here it was. He was being presented with this little popinjay of a man and some mad plan to persuade Moses to give out information about Sergeant Blackburn and that Shane kid. The one from the newspaper. Moses threw a glance up at the only other occupant in his office: some attorney sniffing around for answers to a few questions. Moses left him to continue waiting while he dealt with Kimbrough.

"Oh, I'm afraid that Sergeant Blackburn is most likely home asleep at this hour, Mr. Kimbrough." He smiled a smile of kindness. "He works a midnight shift, you see."

"No, Lieutenant, as I just said, I don't need to speak with him right now. But, well, you know how much I support the work of our police."

"Oh yes."

"And after reading the article, I just couldn't stop wondering about how the sergeant met the boy. Or about whatever has happened to the boy since then."

"It's only been a few days."

"A lot can happen in a few days, Lieutenant."

Moses briefly noticed that Kimbrough seemed to be trying to glare at him with a strange intensity.

"I'm afraid that I wouldn't be able to tell you," Moses replied, modifying his smile to one of mere professional courtesy. "Not that I know anything to tell. If you want to come back at around eleven-thirty tonight, maybe you can catch him before he goes back on duty. See if he's willing to talk to you."

Moses watched Tommie's face darken and fought the urge to taunt him.

"Lieutenant Moses," Kimbrough began, "I'm only taking this personal and direct route because I know how busy our city leaders are with the reconstruction efforts, and I hate to bother them for favors just because they are willing to do them for me. It seems unfair to take advantage of my inheritance in that way."

Moses could no longer keep his contempt bottled. "Oh, really? Your inheritance? Must be a real tribulation to have that much money."

"It's a civic obligation, the way I see it."

"An obligation! Like the obligation to pay your bills."

"Exactly."

"Such as the mortgage bills on your house. That sort of thing, yes?"

Kimbrough's face darkened again. This time he took a pause before he said anything. When he finally spoke, it was done softly and in measured tones. "I wonder if the lieutenant has reconsidered my offer to buy that foreclosure notice?"

"Absolutely unnecessary! Save your money, sir." He leaned close to him and whispered, "Your secret is safe with me."

Moses picked up the big Duty Roster and started going over names. A moment later he looked up again, as if he were surprised to see Tommie Kimbrough still in front of his desk. He gave him one more vague smile and then dropped his eyes and went back to work on the roster. By the time he looked up again a minute or two later, Kimbrough was gone.

Moses worked for another ten or fifteen minutes before Randall Blackburn came walking out of the rear office area.

"All right, Lieutenant. That's it on all the paperwork for this latest one. Maybe now we can get some funding for extra detectives to track this maniac down."

"No money for that now, Sergeant, we've been down that road. Meanwhile, this gentleman over here has been waiting for the last thirty minutes, just to see you."

The attorney stood up and extended his hand. He was a tense-looking young man with a suit that was perhaps a size too small. "Gabriel Towels, Sergeant. Esquire."

"Mr. Towels, I'm way overdue to go home and sleep."

"Yes sir. I'll just—" He looked around as if there must be spies. "Can we talk somewhere private?"

"Use the office," Moses told them with a wave. "Time to make a few rounds." He walked out and left the two men alone.

Blackburn sighed. "All right, Mr. Towels, if we could just—"

"The article about Shane Nightingale—"

"That again?"

"What do you mean?"

"Never mind. What about it?"

"Sergeant, I represent the Great Republic Insurance Company, and part of my duty is to locate benefactors of our policies in the wake of the earthquake and resulting fires."

"Good. And you have a check for me?"

Towels ignored that. "Until the article, we had no idea that anyone in the Nightingale family survived. Nobody filed any claims, even though Mr. Nightingale owned three apartment buildings. Though his business was not covered, they had to have fire insurance under the law, and therefore were insured.

"We are not one of those companies who are trying to avoid their obligations to clients, Sergeant. We owe the Nightingale family twenty-seven thousand, five hundred, seventy dollars, and forty-two cents."

"Forty-two cents."

"We're very thorough."

"You're looking for Shane Nightingale so you can give him money?"

"Yes. And he does not need to be a named heir to claim the money, as long as nobody else in the family survives to step ahead of him."

"Shane's rich, then? That money is his?"

"Well, not rich. Perhaps someday, if he invests well. But the point is, we can have a check in his hands within a few days, as soon as he signs the papers."

Blackburn felt an idiot grin spread from ear to ear. He was about to watch Shane Nightingale's life turn around on a dime and speed off in a whole new direction. For once, he was going to see a deserving kid get an honest break, and maybe change his whole life for the better.

He clapped Attorney Towels on the shoulders, accepted his business card and promised to bring Shane in to see him right away. Then he was out the door and on his way to the Mission Dolores, full of glee at the chance to be the bearer of this news.

While he hurried along, he once again failed to notice that he was being followed. And since the chaotic atmosphere of reconstruction was everywhere, offering a thousand points of distraction to disguise another's presence, Tommie Kimbrough discreetly tagged along.

Blackburn and his secret tail reached the old Mission in less than fifteen minutes. He went in and excitedly checked around for Shane, who was nowhere to be found. But when he peeked into the rear toolshed, he saw that Shane's meager belongings were still in there. So it seemed that Shane was missing out on his daytime sleep, too.

Oh, well, he told himself. *The money will still be there tomorrow.*

He decided to stop by again after his shift, early the next morning. Then he headed home to catch a few hours of sleep.

This time there was nobody waiting to follow him. Tommie was already on his way back to Russian Hill, now that he knew exactly where to find the person who had spoiled his perfect crime.

Shane worked to keep up with Vignette while they jostled and pressed their way through the crowded outdoor marketplace. Even though she was two years younger, she seemed to have some sort of motor inside. Her legs kept pumping away while his grew heavy.

Vignette also seemed to make it a point to keep him laughing just hard enough that he could rarely get in a full breath. She threw him questions that only required short answers, then gave him a second or two to respond. After that, if he still wasn't ready to answer, she began chanting random letters and numbers while he fought to keep up his concentration.

Every time she managed to make him stumble, they both laughed together. The thing that kept them on the same wave was that they both sensed how quickly Shane's ability was growing because of this little game. It tickled because it worked. Shane felt himself flooded with emotions of gratitude that he had not felt since the day of his adoption.

Finally, she whipped into an alleyway and grabbed his sleeve when he passed. A second later she had pulled him into the shadows underneath a stairway.

"Look!" she beamed. She opened up her baggy shirt to pull out a loaf of bread and a large cooked turkey leg. Shane's jaw dropped.

"Where did you geh-geh-geh-"

"You were right behind me!" she interrupted. "Where do you think I got it?" She put her face right up in front of his and bugged her eyes out at him.

Shane broke out laughing. The combination of her lively innocence, her street smarts, and her warmth was completely overwhelming. And now, to see her casually demonstrate her mastery of petty theft, the whole picture of her that resulted twisted his funny bone until he had to let go and laugh.

"You're feeling guilty, right?" She prodded him and giggled. "You think we should give it back, don't you?" She tore the loaf in half, then pulled a chunk of turkey off of the leg and handed it to him, along with his half of the bread.

He took it, bit off a mouthful of bread and followed with a large bite of the turkey leg. Then he nodded and said, "You're right. Let's give it back." But all that came out was "You're rihh, leth givih—" followed by a cloud of bread crumbs and turkey bits.

They both screamed with laughter. The sense of relief while the laughter poured out of him was so deep and so strong that all he could do was ride along with it. Shane realized that laughing to death would not be a bad way to go; he just hated the thought of missing out on more time with his sister.

The early afternoon light was blocked out of Randall Blackburn's little garden apartment by thick drapes. He had been forced to accept the first place he could find because of the severe housing shortage, but he was grateful to have somewhere to go after work that was private and quiet. The artificial twilight inside was restful, giving the place a quiet feel that was the complete antithesis of his working life. On most days at this time, he lay sound asleep after the prior night's shift. He slept on this day, also, but there was no peace in it. Images of his wife haunted him, as they sometimes did. She appeared to him holding their swaddled newborn daughter in such a way that he could not see the baby's face. It was the same as always.

He had let the grim surgeon talk him into not viewing the dead newborn's remains. What was there to see? they asked him. The infant had died in childbirth, shortly after the mother succumbed to blood loss.

And so he never got to see their baby. As often as his wife's image came to him, the one thing that never varied was that she held their new baby so tightly that he could see nothing. He knew that the baby was a girl; someone had told him, but he had not even seen her in his dreams. No matter how many times his wife and baby visited his sleep, he never got a glimpse of his daughter's face.

Blackburn sat up with a gasp, still reeling with dizziness. He focused his eyes on the blanket and made himself take deep, even breaths until the room began to hold still and his head cleared. The heavy curtains rustled slightly at the open windows and the breeze gradually cleared the cobwebs from his brain.

He checked his watch; it was barely afternoon, too early to get up for work. Dropping back onto the mattress, he closed his eyes with a deep sigh. He felt stirred up inside, with the sort of emotional hangover that sometimes hit him after having to break up a married couple in the middle of a vicious fight.

He spent a few moments wondering what it was that had awakened him like that, leaving him sweating and so upset. But the images and words were already fading. Sleep began to pull at him. He closed his eyes and took a couple of deep breaths, and then he was out again.

Not long after sundown, Tommie paced back and forth across the floor of his study, angrily stepping over Friar John's prostrate form each time. He had already tied his victim down once again by the feet and neck, but Friar John was so far gone now that the restraints were a ridiculous overstatement. Tommie was astounded by the speed of this infection. Friar John's face had already turned several shades of red, purple, and black. His eyes were blank. He only moved when he convulsed with yet another sharp gut pain.

Tommie tried yelling into Friar John's ear again, hoping to force some awareness back into him. "I trusted you and I *confided* in you that I have this difficulty with money. Parting with it is more painful for me than it is for you working morons. But all my bills get paid, eventually. It really is no one else's concern. And yet you used that against me. How did you persuade the Nightingales to adopt Shane, in particular? Did you offer incentives to encourage them not to take some other child?"

He turned and kicked Friar John in the ribs and got a satisfying grunt of shock and pain out of him. Friar John's eyes popped open and focused on Tommie, who was delighted to see that he was conscious again.

"Oh! Back with us, then? Lovely! They say many dying people often experience a final few moments of energy and clarity before they expire. How fortunate that this is also the case with you.

"You are dying of the plague. You were supposed to be my experiment and I was going to record every aspect of your death, but the disease, as you may have noticed, has turned out to be far too strong for my needs. Much too quick. Too quick." He pulled out his heavy-bladed knife and admired its edge.

"This knife, however, is a highly controllable instrument. Simple and effective. Some things, it seems, need no improving. I should have trusted it to deal with you. I could have spent days carving my initials over every square inch of your body, keeping you gloriously alive *and conscious* the entire time! Think of that! *Think* of it!"

Whether or not it was that image which did it, Friar John's eyes glazed over again. This time, he continued sinking. He seemed to melt into the floor and shrink within his cocoon.

"No!" Tommie cried. "Not yet, damn it!"

But as if to spite him at the last, Friar John completed the act of dying without paying any regard to Tommie's demands. The last air wheezed out of his stilled lungs in that familiar death rattle that Tommie knew always signaled an end to his special recreations.

He stomped the floor. "It's too soon!" Yet even as he spoke the words, he began moving toward the side door leading to his garage and stable. He knew it would take half an hour to hook up the buggy.

All this work, Tommie lamented. The time and effort and personal risk that he expended—all of it wasted. The strain was so powerfully toxic that it killed within hours, and it rendered a victim unconscious long before that. The weapon was too powerful, period. This vile germ was hardly slower than using a shotgun.

The only priceless moment was the look on Friar John's face when Tommie bludgeoned the boy to death in his presence. The sweetest things never last. Tommie was discovering that terror was much better than pain for motivating a victim. It was certainly more entertaining for him.

After all of this, it was not going to be enough to merely kill The Bastard. Tommie needed to terrorize him first, then utterly destroy him. His simple existence was a claim on Tommie's wealth. The destruction of his father's bastard son would be an exorcism.

CHAPTER SEVENTEEN

LATER THAT DAY

RANDALL BLACKBURN PICKED HIS WAY along the broken side-walk. Every step carried him past crowded temporary dwellings and lean-to tents that served to replace the buildings of the Barbary Coast district. The neighborhood had been decimated when the fires swept through. Citizens' committees clamored for changes to the district, and a sea change of public image for the entire district seemed inevitable.

Strangely, little had changed so far. Familiar faces swirled all around him in the darkness, popping in and out of the lantern light and the campfire shadows. True denizens of the bottom-dwelling existence had gravitated back to the old Barbary Coast area like homing pigeons. No matter what happened to the real estate itself, the location, location, location, was still near the ships. The ships brought cargo, and many times the cargo included alcohol. Sailors needed somewhere to blow off steam and get rid of their pesky money. And so it continued to propel an ongoing dark party that randomly rotated through the neighborhood.

Blackburn was the lone, wandering force of order for the district, the cold point of contact where the law's carriage wheels met the cobblestone. At least until the eventual day when the powers that be finished the neighborhood's transformation.

But tonight he felt his energy sagging even though he had several hours left to go. The destruction of nearly everything all around him seemed to be a lesson that his efforts on behalf of justice were wasted in the law. The civic powers that controlled him and paid his wages could be dethroned with a single shaking of the earth, but the low criminals displayed a resistance to change that rivaled rats and roaches. The Barbary Coast denizens triumphed at the art of survival by learning to live off of garbage.

In a small tent less than ten yards away, he caught a clear view of some poker player turning over the table, grabbing up the pot and fleeing into the darkness. It took another second or two before Blackburn noticed that his own feet were not moving. He was perfectly capable, but in that brief moment of decision, it was the same petty thief who had fled from him a thousand times before. Easy to chase down, difficult to beat into submission, time-consuming to arrest, and pointless to rehabilitate. They were chipping away at Blackburn's life, one street fight at a time.

He watched for another moment while the thief fled with the howling players hot behind him, then he turned and walked away. "Bastards," he muttered.

Bastards. He walked away with blinders on and left them to work out their own difficulties. What was he doing? In the days before the quake, his self-delusion was much easier to maintain amid the red-lighted windows, loud piano music, and raucous laughter of the Barbary Coast's fake hotels. The doomed women in their gowns and layered makeup looked so much better under the tinted gaslights of the old dance hall atmosphere. Now, most women's desperation was plain in their ragged appearance and their aggressive, angry manner. Makeup was seldom seen. Quick contact in its most base form was all that their clients could expect.

Blackburn bumped into them in the shadows under stairways, stepped over them rutting like pigs in back alleys, arrested them when they did it out in full view, and ignored them on any other occasion. Nothing stopped it. The word was out, hanging over the city like a dark cloud, worming its way into the brains of anyone with nothing else to anchor down their life.

His energy dropped again. It was hard to walk. It felt useless. He stepped into a lean-to "bar" with two small tables, both occupied, and rapped his nightstick on the nearest one. The two men seated there promptly got up and hustled away. He sat down and motioned for the barkeep to bring him a beer, then he turned his back to the outside world and asked himself once again what the hell he was doing.

Yet here he still was, on the Barbary Coast beat.

This is what they think of you.

His disgust and resentment burned so deeply that the beer glass was empty before he knew it. His parents had not brought him up to risk himself in this way. How would he explain it to them, when he could no longer explain it to himself? As a "guardian of society," who was he actually protecting?

His original goal of working his way up to the rank of detective seemed like a bad joke to him, now. Chasing down thieves and arresting wife beaters was never going to bring him the sort of action that moves an officer up the ranks. His beat could kill him at the drop of a hat, but it wasn't going to get him any glory.

And of course, somebody up there knew that. As for the city mucky-mucks he took orders from, reports were coming into City Hall of officials whose mansions were not covered for earthquake damage, so they set fire to their own homes, which all had fire insurance as required under the law. Entire insurance companies were now teetering on the brink of bankruptcy while these hogs were helping to collapse the system so that they could build themselves bigger mansions next time.

What was he doing? Life had slapped him to the ground so hard during his rookie year that it had been hard not to take it as a direct repudiation from God. In a single day, his wife and infant daughter disappeared, leaving him haunted by the sense that if he had chosen some other line of work, their deaths would not have happened. And yet after almost ten years of burying his grief and his rage in his dedication to his work, this is where it put him: seated in a nasty, smoke-stained tent that served as a temporary tavern of the crudest possible nature, drinking alcohol on duty, right out in the open among the very people he patrolled every night.

And so what?

It was still dark out while Tommie drove his one-horse rig up to the northern tip of the San Francisco peninsula. He steered the big draft animal down the rutted road leading to the rocky shoreline. The Pacific Ocean flowed into the San Francisco Bay through the narrow Golden Gate, and Tommie was parked near the narrowest part of the strait. The opposite shore lay less than a mile away, swallowed in the darkness and the fog. A relentless current of six or seven miles an hour swept everything before it into the bay when tides were rising, and then back out to the open sea when they drained back out.

With a little push, any floating object would either join the rush toward the bayside shoreline or disappear out to sea over the western horizon, all depending on the direction of the tides. At several points during the drive up, Tommie had found himself debating whether there was more merit in letting a body disappear at sea or causing a bold statement to wash up onto any of the Bay's public beaches.

He appreciated the value of secrecy, living as he did behind veils of it, but he was repeatedly swamped by the giddy sensations that rushed through him when he pictured the unsuspecting beachgoers who might encounter his handiwork and vomit on the spot.

Humor won the internal debate.

He would dispose of the body while the tide was coming in, guaranteeing that Friar John would have himself one final opportunity to present his naked carcass to the view of small children.

Whatever was left of him by then, Tommie cackled. Given the cold seawater and nibbly fishes, he was still going to castrate his victim, but this time he would use Mother Nature instead of a heavy-bladed knife.

The darkened sea break was deserted at that hour, and he had no problem in avoiding detection while he parked the buggy and stepped around to the back. He grabbed Friar John's carcass by the ropes and pulled the fabric cocoon out and onto the ground. The water's edge was only a few yards away at that point, but to get the body there he would have to traverse a row of jagged boulders and fist-sized rocks.

Tommie was wiry and fit, but he was smaller than his passenger by a good six inches in height and by thirty or forty pounds. There was no way to carry the load over that terrain. He would have to drag the cocoon by its ropes. That was just as well. To carry the thing any distance involved far too much close contact, given the virulence of the disease. There was surely no good reason to touch the thing. So Tommie put his strength into it and dragged his burden across the rocks, yard by gasping yard, until he was nearly at the water's edge.

He squinted at the ground by the faint starlight and saw that the water was receding, but it was barely down from the high water mark. This tide would be headed back out to sea for hours and hours before it turned back through the Golden Gate and into the Bay. If he pushed the carcass in now, it would sail off and be lost to history. And a very funny joke would go untold.

Tommie wedged the cocoon tightly between two large rocks, where it would safely remain until the rising tide returned. Then the power of Nature herself would pry it loose and send it on its way. With just a bit of luck, the friar would be swept into the Bay and beached somewhere. Tommie sliced open the cocoon, so that Friar John could bid the world farewell in all of his bloated and rotting repulsiveness, pink and purple and red and black. It would be his very last opportunity to personally show the world what he had really looked like inside, all along.

Blackburn quit his shift at four A.M. for the first time in his life, feeling well assured that nobody would ever find out. His mood improved as soon as he walked away from his beat and started for the Mission Dolores. It was such a relief to be headed away from the human swamp of drunks and muggers and on his way to deliver good news to a deserving kid, he didn't even feel anxious about how things might turn out—until he had the Mission's cemetery gate in sight.

He stopped there, when the questions hit him. How was he going to do this? Build the boy up to it and spring it gently? Give it to him straight and let him decide whether or not to be upset on his own? How much protection did a young fellow that age need, anyway?

He quietly opened the gate and gently closed it behind him. He felt no urge to rush into things, now that he was there. He glided through the darkness toward the toolshed at the back of the property. When he drew closer, he saw that a lantern was shining inside the shed. The door was pulled open to allow a beam of light to fall onto the ground outside. In the shadows of the outer wall next to the door, he saw Shane sitting with another small person. The other one had the appearance of a skinny boy, but there was femininity to the posture and movements. She employed a theatrical array of gestures when she spoke, and the pair seemed to be engrossed in conversation.

They spoke quietly, whether out of respect for the dead or the fear of disturbing the resident priests. He realized that there was no reason to stand in the darkness and eavesdrop on them, the way his habits told him to do. So he continued toward them and only heard a few lines before they noticed his approach.

"Shane?" Blackburn called out. Both kids immediately whipped around to face him. He got close enough to offer a reassuring smile and wave. "It's just me, Shane—Sergeant Blackburn. How are you doing?" He saw the girl regard him with mild curiosity, but Shane had that same trapped animal look again, even though he tried to hide it.

Both of them stood up, waiting for him to let them know what was going on. He decided to just plunge in and let the chips fall.

"I'm, ah, actually here with some news, Shane. It concerns you. And it's good news, too."

Shane looked as if he was wracking his brain for what sort of good news a police officer was likely to bring him. Blackburn realized that he wouldn't care to be approached that way himself, so he decided to jump to it.

"All right. This is it, then. Hold on to your hat." He took a deep breath before continuing. "You know, the interesting thing is that we've got whole insurance companies that are going into bankruptcy now. You know what that means? It means to fail. To go broke. Because so many people are coming up with every trick they can think of to make a claim that they've got no right to. But you, Shane, you never went to City Hall to check, and you never went to some attorney to look into it, and you sure never talked to the insurance company people. They told me." Blackburn gave him an admiring smile. "You're a bit young to deal with insurance people, but this gentleman here"—he handed Shane the business card for Attorney Gabriel Towels—"is a lawyer for the insurance company that covered Mr. Nightingale's other properties."

"Prop-properties?" Shane asked, uncomprehending.

"A couple of apartment buildings, a few other things. Anyway these people have figured it all out down to the last penny, and this man told me that you have a lot of money waiting for you. We aren't talking about the kind of money that you go out and spend on a party or a bunch of clothing or things like that, either, Shane. This is enough to change your life all around. Now, he said it's not enough to make you rich forever, but it's enough to take care of you, if you're careful with it."

The girl leaned to Shane and whispered, "See it and read it." Blackburn recognized her now as one of the kids from the orphanage.

Shane stared into space for a second, then turned to Blackburn. "There must be some mistake."

Blackburn noticed that Shane did not falter, but decided not to mention it.

"Well, don't say that so fast," the girl cautioned. She glanced over at Blackburn and gave a little sigh, then smiled at him. "I saw you in the office because I used to get in trouble on purpose, just so they would make me clean in there and I could look for our files."

"Excuse me?" he asked. "I don't know what that means."

"I'm Shane's sister. They called me Mary Kathleen when I met you, but my real name is Vignette. And I finally found our file, the one for Shane and me, that proves we're brother and sister. They were never going to tell us! Can you believe that? All so that they could adopt us out easier. You know, without a lot of kicking and screaming."

"Ah. That's why you're here then."

". . . Obviously."

"Good. All right. Good then. Now Shane, you need to go over and see that man as soon as you can. If you want to go later this afternoon after we've both had a chance to catch some sleep, I'll come by and go with you."

"Would that be soon enough?" Vignette asked, concerned. "Maybe we should get something to eat and go on over as soon as they open up."

Blackburn laughed. "You can, but I bet it's a good idea to have an adult with you who's on your side."

"Are you sure about this?" Shane quietly asked. He kept reading in his mind's eye. "Are these people sure this is right?"

"City records prove you were formally adopted by the Nightingales."

"I mo-mostly worked for them."

"Doesn't matter, they gave you their name. You're legally a Nightingale and this money is your family estate."

"A family estate." Vignette repeated the words with solemn wonder. "*A family estate.* I think those are the most beautiful words I ever heard."

"Sergeant Black-Black-"

"Just don't say Blackie."

Shane laughed and relaxed a little. "Sergeant, they would never leave me money."

"Right. Interesting part, that. They don't have a will saying that you can or can't have it, or that anybody else can, either. Maybe it burned up with the house. That wouldn't be a problem if the family had survived. But after the disaster, you *are* the Nightingale family, Shane. You're it. And so it just doesn't matter what anybody else wanted, anymore."

He tried to make his own vision appear inside their minds. "You could go to school. A great private school. You can both go. You can have decent lives."

Shane's face suddenly lit up so that it nearly glowed. His eyes darted back and forth for a moment, then he concentrated and asked, "I can share it with my sister, right?"

"I'm pretty sure that you can, pal." He clapped him on the shoulder and shook his hand. "Congratulations. Things are going to change."

Shane stepped back to the toolshed and sat back against the wall, reeling. He rubbed his forehead with his palm, but this time he made no effort to speak.

Blackburn turned to the girl, Vignette, as she wanted to be called. She smiled at him, then turned away and dreamily looked up into the sky. The impact of the news made her shudder, even though her arms were wrapped around herself. Her teeth chattered while she stepped over to Shane and sat beside him.

"It's like we just got permission to stay alive, Shane." She squinted into the thought and nodded with a smile. "It's a sign. I think it makes a lot of sense."

Shane stared at his watch hanging on the wall, then turned to Blackburn and cleared his throat. "Do you think we could meet here at four o'clock this afternoon? I mean, would you come, Sergeant Blackburn?"

Blackburn noticed that this time Shane got through two entire sentences without stuttering at all.

Tommie felt strangely out of place while he drove his rig up the road leading to St. Adrian's. He nearly always walked when he was in full dress and makeup, risking the beat cops for the joy of attracting predators. Here, sitting high up in the buggy seat in full splendor as an ersatz female, he felt uncomfortably exposed. The hour was now very late, the sea fog was thick. There was scant traffic on the streets at this hour, so he drove along in reasonable isolation.

When the first destination approached, he pulled the draft horse to a stop across from the main offices of the orphanage. The gas lines to light the streetlamps had not been reconnected yet in this neighborhood, so there was only faint moonlight to betray him. And in the moonlight, Tommie knew that he appeared to the world as a mere silhouette.

The office windows were all dark. There was no one to look out and see the well-dressed lady getting down from her buggy. No one would have been alarmed if they had. They might notice that she carried an oil lantern, but that was to be expected for a woman alone in this darkened neighborhood. Nothing to arouse suspicion at all. She walked briskly toward the offices, moving with a feminine sway that developed into a little skip. She became suspicious only when she used her forward momentum to swing the oil lamp in a wide arc and hurl it forward with shocking power.

The lamp flew straight through the glass of one of the windows and shattered inside, spraying oil in all directions. There was a pause of about two seconds before a low wave of flame appeared, rising from the office floor. It quickly became big enough to expand under its own power, moving to consume every record in the office files—every document telling anything about a bastard who now went by the name of Shane Nightingale. Tommie knew that the housing area was in another building, so all of the kids would survive to join the bucket brigade before the fire crews arrived to stand around and help watch the place burn.

Tommie sauntered back to the buggy and climbed in. When he glanced back toward the offices, the fire was already growing. But it would be several minutes before it became apparent to observers and visible through the fog. There was plenty of time to vacate the vicinity and get over to the Mission Dolores, to be mistaken for a grieving lady who has come to visit a grave, perhaps also to pray at the beautiful Mission altar. And what kind of person disturbs a small, grieving woman in a graveyard?

With Friar John out of the picture and the orphanage records destroyed, The Bastard's history had been eliminated. And now "Shane Nightingale" had just been moved one step closer to not existing at all.

CHAPTER EIGHTEEN

VIGNETTE WAS RELIEVED that the morning sun was finally beginning to cook off the fog. Ever since Sergeant Blackburn left, she and Shane were so excited that they expended their extra energy with a long stream of boring physical chores. The work helped to relax the nerves, but it barely relieved the stunned sense of disbelief that gripped both of them. Vignette could see how deeply affected Shane was, even though he worked so hard to keep his reaction to himself. She felt grateful that he had accepted her so completely. He embraced her as his sister, to the point that his first thought on hearing about his good fortune was to bring her into it.

She had come to him with such blind hope in her heart, and Shane had actually showed himself to be the extraordinary young man whom she needed him to be. For the first time, it was safe to finally let go and love someone, a boy especially—a boy who would not go away, a boy who would not hurt her, a boy who cared about what happened to her every day.

For about an hour, they had both been using the Mission's long-straw brooms to clean the walkways and all of the grave tops. Shane had told her how he made it a point of doing something every day that the padres could easily see, to demonstrate his value to them. Vignette's pragmatic side grasped that. She wore a good inch off of the broom's bristles.

Shane also cautioned her to avoid disturbing any mourners who might come through after sunrise. Sometimes they liked to stop in to leave flowers at the grave and pray undisturbed. So far they had the place to themselves, except for a single lady standing off in the shadows in a far corner. Vignette could not tell which grave the woman was visiting, but she seemed to be deep in prayer. Shane was so used to visitors passing through that he ignored her altogether. Vignette was glad for that. Every adult they had to interact with had the power to give them some kind of trouble or grief. If this adult wanted to be left alone, that was good. One less thing.

Vignette worked away, making sure Shane noticed that she was not one to shrink from a little effort. She sneaked glances at him whenever she got the chance, half expecting him to turn to her and begin his explanation of why he really could not accept her. Instead, he just kept working, and she felt a rush of such love and gratitude for him. It felt like it was probably the next best thing to romance and surely a thousand times safer. It was a space that she could occupy, a place where she could live.

A few morning birds were singing in the branches overhead, but the only sound in the cemetery was the whisking of the brooms over the stone and mortar surfaces. With a slight echo to the air, she and Shane barely had to do more than whisper to hear each other.

"I'm almost finished over here," she announced.

"Me, too. Just about. Cou-cou-cou—"

"Read it first."

"Couple of minutes." He laughed and shook his head.

"All right, then. After that, why can't we both sleep in the shed? They know we're family, and all."

She saw Shane stop sweeping for a moment, then he shrugged and said, "No, since they know us now, I think . . ." He paused, then continued. "I think we just show them we're honest and we work hard."

Vignette laughed out loud.

"What's so—"

"You're talking about how to keep your cleanup job! You just got rich!" She laughed out loud and whirled with the broom, but Shane grabbed her shoulder and brought her to a halt.

"Vignette. We heard a story. That's all. We don't have any money yet."

He held her gaze until she lowered hers. She wanted to argue. It hurt to be rebuked by her own brother. But she also saw that it was foolish to celebrate something before you even know if it is true.

But what if it is true? the inner voice repeated. *What if it is?*

What if there were no monster in the closet, this time? What if shadows were only shadows? What if everything worked out just right? It felt as if every cell in her body wanted to believe that.

"But," Shane began, smiling, "wouldn't it be something if that money was really there?"

They both smiled at the sheer joy of the idea. It was enough to break the spell of the job. Shane collected their brooms and went to drop them back inside the Mission's custodial closet, tactfully leaving Vignette free to go ahead and climb into her sleeping blanket. She stepped into the dark shed, ready to remove her pants and shirt and hang them up. It struck her that everything was working out so much better than she had dared to hope.

A strong forearm snapped around from behind her and caught her around the neck. The arm was thin but had animal strength. Before Vignette could make a sound, she was lifted up by the neck so that her toes barely brushed the floor. She must have done something to infuriate Shane, and he had attacked her. It made no sense, but it fit her experience. Old skills kicked in—the arm was reaching around her over her right shoulder, so she instinctively turned her head to the left to take the pressure off of her windpipe. When she did, she got a peripheral look at her assailant.

It was the woman from the cemetery.

Vignette was so used to having grown-ups mad at her that she wasn't particularly shocked by the fact that one was attacking her;

she just couldn't imagine what she had done to make this woman so angry. Both of Vignette's hands were clasped around the arm, which was wedged under her chin. She struggled for air under the vise grip. Finally she felt the woman place her lips close to Vignette's ear, just before she spoke in a husky whisper.

"I like turning the boys into girls. But I've always done it after they were dead—small courtesy of the trade. In your case, I'm going to float you out to sea, up at the Golden Gate. You'll still be alive *after* I do it!"

Vignette's strangled voice came out in a broken rasp, "I'm already a girl!"

She heard a grunt of surprise. The pressure eased on her throat. Then the crazy woman grasped both of Vignette's shoulders in an iron clutch and turned her face into the light. When the woman spoke this time, there was no more whisper. It sounded more like a man.

"Who the hell are you?" the voice demanded.

"Vignette."

"Oh . . . 'Vignette.' My goodness. Royalty. If you're a girl, why is your hair chopped so short?"

"They always cut it off for punishment."

"What are you doing!" Shane's voice boomed from the doorway. He sounded more like a man, too. Not old like a man, but dangerous like one.

Vignette and the intruder both spun around. Shane stood outlined in the doorway, staring at the crazy woman with an intensity that Vignette had never seen before. He looked like he could turn into a wolf. She never wanted anybody to look at her like that.

"I said what do you want?" Shane snarled. His entire body was shivering in fear, but his fists were clenched and his face was red with rage.

"Ah, Shane," the woman said, as if they were at a tea. She turned to Vignette with an apologetic little grin. "Sorry. It was the short hair. Tsk! You must have really been a bad girl!"

While the woman was talking, Shane hurried over to Vignette and planted himself in front of her, blocking the woman. He dropped his hot gaze onto Vignette and barked a single order. "Run!"

Everything about the way he said it forced Vignette's muscles into motion. She was out the door and speeding through the grave-yard toward the front gate before she even realized that she had decided to obey him. The springs of her legs fully unwound and sent her flying past the tombstones while the growing whoosh of runner's wind filled her ears. The adrenaline of survival blasted through her. She maintained that speed all the way off of the Mission grounds, across the road, down the block, around the corner, and several more blocks before she grew tired enough to slow to a normal trot.

She thought about looking for a cop, but wondered what she was supposed to tell him that would get him to help Shane and not the crazy woman. Vignette could not remember a time when she had ever thought of adults as being anything other than unpre-dictable and dangerous. Police could be just as crazy as any other adult, except they also had the power to put you in jail. What then? She had to do something.

She considered going back to the Mission, but everything about that felt wrong, and Shane's order left no room for it. She needed to trust that he was bigger, older, and as she saw during that mo-ment there in the toolshed doorway, he carried a reservoir of anger that gave him a disturbing kind of power. Surely, she told herself, he could either deal with that nasty woman or outrun her.

It was at that moment when Vignette realized that there was one adult they could trust, and that her feet had been heading in the di-rection of Sergeant Randall Blackburn's place ever since she left the Mission.

CHAPTER NINETEEN

IT TOOK SHANE A WHILE to wake up. After a long struggle with his senses, he finally realized that he was actually seeing something, but barely. There was general darkness with only faint illumination. He was facing into a broken and jumbled version of what should have been a ceiling. He knew that he must be underneath one of the city's many collapsed buildings that had not yet been re-claimed.

His attention focused on a long, hard source of pain that was running up the length of his back. He finally realized that he was bound to a wide construction beam by several windings of thick rope. The rope was pulled so tight that it caused the beam to dig into his skin. His feet were just touching the floor, on tiptoe, and his ankles were bound to the beam with another turn of rope.

The pain in his head was intense and unrelenting, impossible to ignore. Something had struck him, propelled by a deathly solid force. The blow could have just as easily killed him. So he was alive, then. Wasn't he?

He could see that there was a source of faint light coming from the floor, just out of reach of his vision, but he could barely lower his head far enough to look. His line of sight caught just enough to see a workman's oil lamp perched on the floor, which threw a dim yellow-orange glow and cast a patchwork of jagged shadows overhead. A few broken pieces of signs with Chinese characters on them were enough to give away the location. Since all of China-town was swept by the fires, this artificial dungeon only existed be-cause the building was mostly stone and masonry.

The throbbing in his head was so awful that every heartbeat sent another sharp stab into him. He winced at the worst ones. Some-thing terrible was happening to him. But every time he squeezed his memory for an answer, for details of any kind, he only got deeper pains.

Shane finally became aware of another presence in the room; there was the sound of a slight foot scuff along the broken floor. Somebody nearby took a deep breath. Then he felt somebody's body warmth loom in close to him, and it felt as if somebody's face hovered just underneath his chin, right up near his throat. He could feel a slight, hot breath glancing off of his skin.

"Shane." It was an adult voice, but young. "Do you know me?"

It was with that second phrase that Shane was overwhelmed by a singular stab of fear shooting through him.

That voice . . .

There were only a few words. It was impossible to be sure, but that voice . . . At that moment, Shane saw the face of a strange-looking woman rise up into his view. Her makeup was badly smeared, and when she brought her eyes close to his, her breath was hot and sour.

"Do you know me?" she asked again. But to Shane's astonish-ment, this time the words sounded as if they were spoken by the same young male.

The woman reached both arms upward over her head and grasped handfuls of her own hair, as if to pull it out. But instead, it came off as a wig, which she raised up to arm's length, instantly be-coming a short-haired young man in smeared makeup.

This time he looked Shane directly in the eyes. "I said, do you know me?"

With those six words, Shane did know. His body knew before his brain did, and his bladder emptied down his pant leg and over his shoes.

"I've nev-nev-I've never— I've never—"

"Stop! In that case, my friend, it seems extraordinary that you tried to club me over the head with a hand shovel this morning, forcing me to defend myself. Because if you don't know me, then you have no reason to try to kill me, do you?

"No, there'll be no easy death for you. Because I know what you are now, Shane. I see it clearly. You are sent to torment me in this life. I tried to be rid of you, but then some treasonous bastard arranges for you to be in one of the few places where you could reappear in my life like a stubborn weed.

"So, big things to come for you! Things that work best while you're still alive, too!" He was pacing while he spoke now, feeling his own rhythm.

Shane tried to recapture the rage he had earlier that day, when he first found this maniac there in the toolshed, menacing his sister Vignette. But the magic power was gone now, like evaporated water. Without Vignette there to give him reason to stand and fight, the power for such a thing felt far beyond his reach.

That icy knot of dread in his stomach began to suck the life from the rest of him. He felt the old powerlessness rapidly coming over him, bringing the same invisible monster that held him so petrified and useless in the Nightingale house.

"Do you remember my name?" asked the man in a dress.

"I don't— I don't know your na-na-"

"Oh, I think you do. You used to, Shane. You used to say it."

"I don't—"

"The name is Tommie. T-O-M-M-I-E. You can say it."

"Tommie," Shane repeated. And that's when a whiff of the old magic wafted under his nose.

He did not stutter at all in saying the name, because he was only mimicking what he had just heard. So the word came out loud and clear. And a little rush of strength and confidence followed from the sound of his own voice speaking without faltering. The sense of helplessness over his frustration paled next to his need to strike out at this killer in some way. He concentrated on the next words he wanted to say, so they would also come out strong and clear.

"In the Nightingale house, you never once told them your name. Why? Were you ashamed? Was that it?"

Through the haze of pain that blurred his thinking, Shane saw Tommie snap around to stare at him in shock. Now there was no doubting it, for either of them. Each one was face-to-face with the only other living person who knew what actually happened inside of the Nightingale house.

"Ashamed?" Tommie spoke the word as though he had never heard it before. "I was the living embodiment of Judgment Day! I dished out nothing that this family hadn't earned! Don't tell me about them being some sort of innocent family, either. They were willing to take *my house* for themselves."

He showed Shane a cynical grin. "And shame on you for telling the newspapers that the Nightingales all died in the earthquake . . ."

"I never told the paper anything," he said in a low, steady voice, imitating someone who is not afraid. "Somebody else told them those things."

Tommie leaned toward him and stuck his face within inches of Shane's. "Then where did they *get* the story from, eh, Shane? Somebody got it from you, at some point, didn't they? Do we *have* to talk to each other as if we are stupid?"

But Shane had already seen it—Tommie was late with his reply. He had faltered. Shane felt another rush of confidence, enough to allow himself to actually feel how much rage was boiling away inside of him. The rage gave him a place to put his fear, and the power of all that fear expanded so quickly that he could feel new strength exploding through him. He moved to build up his confidence a little more by letting Tommie know that he remembered the insanity at the Nightingale house.

"You did every evil thing, to those women," Shane said. "Except for—except for—the main thing that—" He fumbled for the right term, but all he had ever heard were the nasty street words. "The thing that men and women do together. That's the only crime you didn't do. But it wasn't because of your conscience, right?"

Shane had the last word out before he realized that he had spoken all those words without a hint of a stammer. Tommie seemed to notice, too; he flashed a nervous glance at Shane. And in that one moment, Tommie Kimbrough looked nothing at all like a cocky killer.

The moment did not last.

Blackburn was a light sleeper under most circumstances, and he could not help but hear the knocking at his front door. But since he was only a couple of hours into sleeping and had a full shift coming that night, he lay still in hopes that the noise would stop.

It did not. A light, rapid set of knocks came, then a slight pause, then another burst. Incessant, like a woodpecker. Who could it be? The idea of a visitor never crossed his mind. Most likely a neighbor, he groused. Some little difficulty that they wanted him to sort out, having heard that a policeman lived there.

"Oh, what the hell." He sat up, climbed out of bed and picked up his robe, which he donned on his way to the door. As soon as he had it tied, he reached forward and pulled the door open. A girl stood there, panting hard. Choppy red hair, dressed like a boy.

"Hi." She smoothed out the front of her shirt.

"Oh, I remember you. Shane's sister. Um—"

"Vignette."

"Vignette. Are you all right? Because I was sleeping, and—"

"Shane is in trouble."

She shot him a look so earnest that he snapped out of the remaining fog of sleep. "All right, Vignette. Try to keep it simple and just tell me what's going on."

"This woman came to the cemetery. We never saw her before.

For a long time she just stood by a grave, praying. We thought she was praying. But when Shane took the brooms back inside, I was in the toolshed because we wanted to go to sleep, but she sneaked up behind me and grabbed me around by the back of the neck."

Blackburn was taking in every word now, and it struck him that Vignette was describing all this in a strange voice. Her calmness had an eerie feel.

"She wasn't that much bigger than me, but she was strong. Her arm around my neck was thin, but she could grip like a man."

"A man?" Blackburn felt his pulse step up a few beats. "What makes you say that? Just because she had strong arms?"

"Not just that. She was strong all over. She leaned back and lifted me up off of the ground so that even my toes couldn't touch it, and I was—my throat was squeezed in her arm and so I had to turn my head just to be able to breathe and she held me up in the air like nothing."

"Do you have any idea why she would—"

"She thought that I was Shane! See? Because she just sneaked up behind me and all my hair got chopped off last month and I have the clothes on so that, you know, she actually thought I was him. And she said she was going to turn me into a girl and then throw me out in the ocean up at the Golden Gate. She said that she liked to turn boys into girls."

"Turn boys into girls? What do you think she meant by that?"

"She said she used to do it after they were dead, but that now she was going to do it while I was still alive, except that I told her I was a girl and that's when she realized that I wasn't Shane, which is when Shane showed up and scared her off. You should have seen it! Then he yelled at me and he said to run and get out of there. So I did. And he didn't say anything else, you know, like where I was supposed to go or what he wanted me to do or anything. So I came here. Actually, it's more like my feet came here and just took me along."

"This woman thought that you were Shane. And she wants to turn Shane into a girl. Did you see a knife? A really large one?"

"No, but still. You see why I came here."

"Wait right there," Blackburn replied, with the dread already working its way through him. He darted back inside and threw on civilian clothing, strapped on his service revolver and tucked a pair of cuffs into his back pocket. Then he hurried back outside. "Let's go," he told her while he walked out into the street.

He sensed her following along behind him while he waved down a passing two-seater buggy and showed them his badge. "This is an emergency. Can you drive us to the Mission Dolores?"

The policeman's badge was enough for the driver to instantly agree. Blackburn lifted Vignette into the cab and jumped in after her. In less than five minutes, they were at the Mission and the two-seater was clattering away into the distance. Blackburn insisted that Vignette wait outside the main gate, then hurried through it, across the graveyard and all the way back to the toolshed. No one was around, and he strained his ears for any sounds. The silence was near perfect, tinged only by the scraping of crickets and light rushes of breeze through the upper branches. Was she still here?

There was every reason to believe that this woman could be The Surgeon. The small frame, the reference to castration. But here? So far away from the waterfront where she had always struck before. And striking out at children?

Blackburn felt his own anxiety slow everything down so that the time it took him to cross the width of the cemetery felt longer than the ride to the Mission. All along the footpath, he listened for any sound that might give something away, until he was nearly at the closed door of the shed. Still there were no sounds of struggle from inside. No voices.

He reached forward with his left hand while resting the right hand on his gun, then grasped the door handle in a firm grip and yanked the door open.

Nothing. He peered in, his eyes adjusted a bit—still nothing. The shed and its contents appeared undisturbed. The sleeping blankets were still stacked on the wall shelf. The tools were not in disarray.

He was thankful to also see that there was no blood anywhere and no sign of physical struggle. But that left him with nothing. After scanning around in all directions, he stepped back onto the walkway and headed toward the front gate. He needed to find out what else Vignette remembered. And for now, he planned to keep her with him as much as possible. Despite circumstances, she was still safer with him than on her own, knocking about in the city.

It was time to head for the station house. This mad killer could no longer be dismissed. Whatever drove The Surgeon to her grisly work had now turned its hunger onto innocent citizens, wandering inland far from the waterfront dives, even going after children. Blackburn had seen far too much of this monster's handiwork to be able to tolerate the idea of Shane being captive in her company.

He had to convince Lieutenant Moses that the station must issue enough resources to hunt this killer down, and to get The Surgeon off of San Francisco's streets *before the day was out*.

He knew there was no chance that Shane would live any longer than that.

Lieutenant Moses had lost so much weight that he was wearing brand-new uniform pants and a retailored shirt for the first time. Unhappily, now that he was a few hours into his long shift, he had to accept the possibility that he had been optimistic in donning the new pants. From the waist down, he felt like he was trapped in a pipe. Even when he stood as straight as possible, the crotch seam dug into him with a persistence that made him mildly nauseous. When he tried to bend over to pick up anything, his own trousers gave him a silent kick to the scrotum.

Moses felt all the more foolish for it, knowing that he brought all of it on himself. Events of the night before saturated his judgment. He had simply felt so relieved and confident while he was getting dressed for work that morning when he pulled out the new outfit—which he had not planned to wear for another two to three weeks—that sheer euphoria had clouded his judgment. But still, still, his first sexual experience in many years had been an overwhelming personal event, just short of spiritual ecstasy. And with that glow fresh upon him when he arose, it had felt natural to commemorate the occasion with the new outfit.

The night before, he had taken a quiet, predawn stroll through the prisoners' cells on both the male and female sides, just to personally see to it that everything was shipshape. The men were either all asleep or smart enough to fake sleeping until he passed through. Then he headed for the women's side.

There was just the one woman in custody.

Her section was sealed off, as was the men's, so that no night guard was needed at the entry. He stepped inside, and out of professional consideration for the prisoner, very quietly pulled the door closed and locked it for proper security.

He had to stop at the door for a moment. His breathing was fast and shallow and he felt mildly dizzy. The sensations swimming through him felt better than anything he had ever experienced. He drank them up, and absorbed the wonderful swirls of pleasure cascading through him.

Before he knew it, and certainly before he had taken a moment to think it over and perhaps ask himself if he had a plan, he was standing at the cell of prisoner Elsie Sullivan, who awaited trial for murder without bail. She had spent most of her stay huddling with her bevy of attorneys and uptown sympathizers. Moses felt nothing against the woman personally, but her presence in his jail did make things politically difficult for him. All the investigators knew she was guilty, but she had certain civic bigwigs in her personal circle who did not want to accept that.

In the darkness, Moses could only hope that he was not staring down at the sleeping form of his own destruction: a proud woman who might be inclined to punish him for her stay in his jail after she was cleared. Nevertheless, he was captivated by the sheer sexual pleasure of being so close to her. She lay helpless before him, trapped behind thick iron bars.

Another sexual thrill fired through him. At the same instant, he caught a faint whiff of Mrs. Sullivan's aroma, and the two sensations combined to buckle his knees. In moments, Moses was kneeling right next to the bars, and then the bars were all that separated him from her sleeping form. Her face was only a few inches from his.

Moses knew how dangerous it was to risk having one of his own men walk in, discovering the lieutenant on his knees next to her. But the simple scent of her skin held him in chains. He closed his eyes to the danger of discovery and concentrated on separating out the smells of her hair, her skin, her breath. He leaned his ample cheek into the cool iron bars to get as close as possible.

Over recent days, Moses had stolen glances at her on more than one occasion, whenever he could find business that would pass him close to her cell. He felt like he could willingly chop off his own legs for the chance to rub his face over every square inch of her body, just one time.

He flinched when Elsie Sullivan turned in her sleep until she was flat on her back, but her eyes remained closed. He relaxed, then studied her breasts beneath the fabric of her gown for a moment, before he glanced at her face and realized that her eyes were now open. And that she was staring straight up at him.

He froze. A moment passed. Then another. When finally she spoke, her voice was soft, conspiratorial.

"Well, you're going to have a hard time explaining why you're on your knees, there, aren't you, Lieutenant?"

He leaped to his feet with all of the speed that his newer and slimmer form could display. "No! No, I—I was just checking—just looking around for that damned thing. Where is it?"

"Psst!" she hissed to him with a coy little smile.

It was magical, Moses thought, the way that she metamorphosed into a playful kitten right before his eyes.

"Don't worry," she whispered. "It's all right with me. I'm glad for the company." She smiled and sat up, leaning against the bars so that she was close enough to touch. Moses realized that if he still had his cheek pressed to the bars, he would feel her skin against his own.

For the next whirlwind hour, it was all so easy. Gregory Moses had never known that he could be so witty, so entertaining. And when things got a bit quiet, he impressed both of them with his deeper, philosophical side. Elsie Sullivan was utterly captivated, and she even lowered herself before him and confessed that if she had ever been lucky enough to find such a man as Gregory Moses in her own life, things would surely have gone much differently for her.

Moses could see her point. It broke his heart to think of how a ravishing creature like this—who, it turned out, was not at all like the stuffy and removed person that he would have guessed her to be—had been unfairly driven into this dungeon.

When she reached through the bars to work her magic with her hands, Moses fell into a trance unlike anything he had ever known. She guided him through every movement with the delightful nastiness of a secret best friend. It only took a few moments for a lifetime of sexual repression to explode out of him. Lieutenant Moses cried out without meaning to. He was so lost in ecstasy that he could not have stopped it if the entire Committee of Fifty had walked into the cell block.

Everything that happened afterward seemed only natural, to him. After all, why on earth would he let this delightful woman rot away inside that dingy jail cell? Did Moses obtain his current position in order to gain power that he did not bother to use? Not that he could recall.

Within hours, he found a sympathetic judge who wrote up a bail order, in an amount just high enough to sound harsh if word got out. Within two hours of that, the attorney for the lovely Widow Sullivan had posted bond and escorted his client back to her large and tastefully beautified home.

Gregory Moses was transformed. He experienced levels of confidence in his manhood such as he had never known. He felt them when he woke up that morning, and throughout the early part of the day, up until the new pants began to get the best of him. He had yet to solve the new pants problem when the two new detectives Gibbon and Mummery came stomping into the station with such an annoying display of laughter and brash confidence that he made a mental note to punish them later.

The two detectives were also accompanied by two uniformed officers, men Moses recognized. He was just about to point out to them that this was *precisely* the sort of casual attitude that he did not tolerate under his watch, when Detective Gibbon loudly announced that Lieutenant Moses was under arrest. Moses was charged with committing an assault of a sexual manner upon the Widow Elsie Sullivan while she was under police custody. Moses noticed that Detective Mummery just stood by, giggling into his uniform glove.

Detective Gibbon called for the two uniformed officers to handcuff Lieutenant Moses—right there inside of his own station—and prepared to lead him away while the rank and file drifted in to watch. Moses was so stunned that he could only gasp for air. Speech had not come back to him yet. His head swam. He was so traumatized that he barely noticed when Sergeant Randall Blackburn stepped to the front of the crowd of onlookers. The sergeant also had some kid with him, a boy, it looked like. Maybe a girl.

"Lieutenant Moses—?" Blackburn began, but Detective Mummery stepped forward with a sneer and raised his hand. "The lieutenant is under arrest, Sergeant Blackburn. Have to ask you to step back."

Moses watched Blackburn comply, but the sergeant looked confused and stared at Moses. As soon as Moses saw the surprise on his face, he knew that Blackburn had no part in this.

But of course, Moses realized; it made sense that Blackburn was no part of any plot. The man was a sergeant. No, this variation on hell came from somebody much higher up in the structure, somebody who could order the arrest of a Station Chief.

In the next instant, the answer leaped up before him.

Tommie Kimbrough. The son of a bitch must have betrayed him! He used his fancy contacts to get some sort of false confession from the Widow Sullivan. The little fellow had thumbed his nose at Moses, and even dared to ignore the fact that Moses knew all about the foreclosure notice. Kimbrough was daring Moses to move against him.

A rush of anger filled him until there was no room left for fear. Every muscle cell in his body twitched for the chance to spring, but bound up as he was, the only weapon left to him was verbal. So while the officers escorted him across the station floor and toward the stairs leading down to the jail, he craned his head around until he could see Sergeant Blackburn, who stood aghast.

"Sergeant!" Moses hollered. "I found a foreclosure notice on Tommie Kimbrough. It fell out of the file on the Nightingale family!" The officers kept pulling Moses along. He was nearly at the door. There was only time to get out one last line.

"Nightingale foreclosed on Kimbrough's house, and a few days later *they were all dead!*"

The stairway door slammed at that point, cutting off the sight of Sergeant Blackburn's astonished face, staring helplessly. He had to assume that Blackburn heard enough. If the fellow was worth half of what people estimated, he was going to drop everything and make sure to find out anything he could about Tommie Kimbrough.

Moses felt some measure of satisfaction in knowing that Kimbrough would never walk away from his betrayal with a smile on his face, but he also realized with dawning dismay that he had just committed his final act as the Acting Station Chief. The wild ride that began with the collapse of City Hall on the morning of the Great Earthquake was over, just as his fears had always projected. All that sacrificed sleep, never a day off. For nothing. New thin clothes. For nothing.

The ability to look at himself in a mirror without feeling his heart sink was gone.

Blackburn stood amid the chaos on the station house floor and saw that everyone was captivated with the hot gossip about Lieutenant Moses. He glanced down at the girl Vignette, and as soon as their eyes met, they both shared the obvious question. How, amid a broken command structure, was he supposed to get clearance to round up a group of beat cops and detectives and spread them out in an organized manhunt for Tommie Kimbrough and Shane Nightingale?

Vignette tapped him on the arm and motioned for him to bend close to her. When he did, she put her mouth next to his ear and whispered, "I know where Mr. Kimbrough lives. I followed Friar John there when Mr. Kimbrough sent for him. It was late at night."

Blackburn considered that. The headmaster of St. Adrian's had been summoned in the middle of the night to the home of Tommie Kimbrough?

He took Vignette's hand, turned around and walked out of the station house.

The early afternoon streets were busy up on fabulous Russian Hill. Ice wagons, coal wagons, fish wagons, meat wagons, commerce makers, and pleasure seekers passed their horse-drawn carriages within inches of one another and gave resentful room to the rare automobile banging and smoking its way up the hills. Blackburn's street sense told him that at this hour on a busy day, a policeman and a little girl could walk up to a lovely three-story Victorian residence and appear to be making a simple house call. Charity work, perhaps.

The front door was set far enough off of the street that no one other than Vignette saw when he took a casual look all around, and then rammed his shoulder into the door so hard that the lock immediately gave way and the door swung open. A moment later, they were inside. He pushed the door closed and set it back on the latch to conceal its damage from the other side.

The curtains were drawn and the house was dark. They both stood at the door for a moment to let their eyes adjust. There was a claustrophobic feeling to the air that seemed out of place in the big house until his eyes adjusted well enough for him to see the details.

There was a lot to see.

There was three times as much furniture as the place needed, and several times as many lamps, statues, and wall ornaments. On top of the furnishings themselves was what appeared to be years of accumulation of paper trash of every sort. Years' worth of newspapers were stacked in bundles and tied with rope. The bundles were piled up to shoulder height all along the walls. The whole place smelled of musty paper.

His eyesight was finally able to resolve thin trails cleared through the piles of junk. Each trail had a specific purpose and led to a chair, a sofa, a shelf. "Wait here," he told Vignette. Then he moved off down the trash trail that led to the stairway.

"All right," she replied, following him anyway a few feet behind. He ignored the fact that she disobeyed him, and they moved up the stairs to the third floor, climbing between rows of books and bundles of newspapers that lined both sides. He planned to begin searching from the top down, but the surprise sight on the top floor simplified his task. With the exception of a few storage closets stuffed with linens, most of it was completely bare with plain wood floors. The walls were lined with mirrors. One of those new vacuum sweeping machines was parked in a corner.

There was a horizontal ballet bar mounted on freestanding supports in the middle of the room, obviously designed so that the person using it would get a full view from every angle. Apparently, Mr. Kimbrough thoroughly enjoyed the sight of his own reflection. Blackburn turned and went back down to the second floor with Vignette shadowing him.

The view there was much more like the downstairs area; excessive levels of furnishings and knickknacks stuffed every bit of open space. Trails were carved through the mass to allow access to a bathroom, a sitting room with barely enough space for one person to sit, and a bedroom so stuffed with unnecessary items that even half of the bed was piled high, leaving only the other half for sleeping.

His interest peaked when he tried the knob on the final unopened door on that floor and found it locked. Unlike the other glass knobs throughout the house, this one was made of delicately carved ivory. The doorplate appeared to be gold.

He took a step back and kicked the door open, noticing that Vignette barely flinched.

"Hold it now, what's all this?" the words popped out of him on their own. He stood in the doorway of what appeared to be the boudoir of a whorehouse madam. Red velvet was draped everywhere, and even the wallpaper was embossed with red-and-gold fleur-de-lis patterns. This room was neither barren nor packed. A single chaise longue occupied one end of the room with a lamp and reading table. On the other end was an elaborate dressing table fit for a Broadway actress and piled with an array of makeup items and half a dozen colorful female wigs. Next to the mirror stood a rack of elaborate dresses and walking outfits, with the appropriate shoes lined up below.

Turn boys into girls . . . And these were, no doubt, the same outfits that would be described by witnesses who saw a "small-boned woman" near the crime scenes around the Barbary Coast. He turned to see Vignette staring up at him.

"All right, now," he whispered. "You have to see everything? Look around inside of here and meet The Surgeon."

"I've heard about her. You think I don't know anything? She's some crazy killer lady."

"Right. Except it turns out, here, that she's a man after all. A man who dresses like a woman. That's what all this is. Right here is where Mr. Tommie Kimbrough has been turning himself into The Surgeon. And whatever it was that he was talking about doing up at the Golden Gate, it looks like he might be already headed out that way."

"And he's got Shane," Vignette quietly added.

CHAPTER TWENTY

AFTER SHANE GAVE HIMSELF up for dead, he was amazed to feel himself gripped by the utter fearlessness of his rage. An absolute transformation began taking place inside of him. Because of it, his fervent wish to reclaim the bold stance that he was able to make for Vignette not only came true, it arrived as a sum multiplied.

All of the anger that he had barely sensed within himself in the past now overflowed and demanded release. His lifelong concern about how anyone else might perceive him receded into his memory and dissolved there. Every part of him that formed while he was playing the good orphan to encourage his adoption out of St. Adrian's vanished, while the parts of him that were so concerned about being the perfect adoptee for the Nightingale family disappeared.

The shame that caused Shane's speech to stutter also left him, and the voice that boomed out of him was nothing that he recognized as his own.

"God damn you, you bastard! God damn you into Hell! I swear I'll kill you! I will kill you!"

Tommie backhanded him across the mouth with such force that Shane was knocked into momentary silence. It left his head ringing.

"Who are *you* calling a bastard?" Tommie hissed. "You don't know what the hell you're talking about!" He paused to pace back and forth, practicing his breathing. Finally he made himself calm and continued.

"I'm the *real son,* you miserable larva! I'm the real heir! You're just my father's little 'oops,' some son of a whore that Daddy was careless enough to impregnate!"

"There, you see?" Shane shot back. "You are out of your mind! I don't have anything in common with you! You think that I'm your bro—"

Tommie struck him again. Harder this time. The room swam and Shane's vision blurred.

"You will *not* use that word! I do *not* think you are my brother! That's the whole *point,* you stinking idiot! You are a piece of garbage that our father and his slut left behind. She would have kept you in her shitty little world and no harm would have been done! It's all you ever deserved anyway! What have you ever done to earn anything, any privilege? Who the hell are you?"

Shane just stared at him. He had been forced into silence, but the rage still fueled him, demanding release.

Tommie sneered. "Oh, not feeling so talkative, now? You were quite the little tough guy there for a few seconds, weren't you? You never would have known anything about this, and I never would have known anything about you, if my parents—*my* parents— hadn't found me naked with a couple of the neighborhood boys. Is that justice? Is that the way for me to find out I have a bastard son of a bitch for a half brother, and that I am then completely disinherited in his favor, just because of who I am?"

"You are getting crazier by the minute, mister."

"My, aren't we confident? What happened to your stu-stu-stutter, bastard boy?"

"It decided to leave so I could tell you that you are going to rot in Hell."

"The bastard boy is a fortune-teller! He knows my future!"

"That's right."

"You don't look that powerful, under the circumstances. Hadn't you noticed?"

"You're the one who didn't notice. You didn't notice me in the Nightingale house. And I heard everything. For a day and a half, I heard it all."

Tommie's triumphant look faltered for just an instant, but he quickly restored it. Shane went on anyway.

"So what about our half sister, Vignette? Did she have the same mother as I did?"

Tommie looked at him, puzzled, then just shook his head. "You'll be glad to know that the father who intended all your life to leave his bastard in poverty is dead. And so is the bitch who was willing to throw me away, her own son, just because I was different. Different from them. They killed each other."

"You killed them."

There was a long pause. Shane could not see what Tommie was doing. Finally, from a corner behind him, he heard Tommie's voice. "You don't know that."

"Oh, I know it. Because I know you. I listened to your pathetic babbling for all that time. And after a while, I could tell that half of the time, you didn't know whether you were talking out loud or not. Sometimes one of them would answer you when you said something, and it would surprise you. Because you didn't know that you said anything out loud."

Tommie focused a stare on him as if he were a lab specimen. "Interesting, you're still not stuttering." He gave Shane a pouty smile and a little wink. "Shane, Shane. Were you faking it all along? A fake stu-stu-stutter? Why? To get girls, perhaps?" He whispered conspiratorially, "I know you're at that age . . ."

Shane ignored the question. What difference would the answer make? Despite the fear gnawing at him, his rage still focused his attention like a sunbeam through a magnifying glass. He knew that he had the power to turn that burning ray onto Tommie Kimbrough. And he knew the exact combination of words to make it happen.

Shane took a deep breath and once again squeezed every muscle in his body to keep his voice from faltering. He looked straight into Tommie's eyes and held his gaze.

"I have to empty you out."

This time Tommie could not conceal his shock. Shane saw the blood rush to Tommie's face. And off in the back of Shane's mind, a part of him wondered how a man who has slaughtered innocent people as a source of joy could still have the ability to blush at all.

Tommie made an incredulous little giggling sound, then asked, "You're going to do what?"

"You know what it means. I heard you say it. I heard you tell all about it. It's just something you were thinking out loud. Without even knowing you were talking! But I heard it. Even after they were all dead and I knew for sure that you had nobody to talk to, you kept right on arguing with your demons. I listened. I was inside of your head."

Tommie leaped forward and flashed his heavy-bladed knife directly under Shane's nose. "Shut up! Shut the fucking hell up!"

"You started that way with each one. 'I have to empty you out.' Three times, I heard you say that. And with Mrs. Nightingale, the first one, you even made her guess what it meant to say 'I have to empty you out.' She wasn't that frightened at first, was she?"

"I didn't want her frightened at first. I wanted to experience her intact personality. I wanted to hear her speak while she was still thinking that she would bluster her way out of everything. She thought that she still had a life to defend."

"And you used your knife. Little cuts. Little cuts, hour after hour, until you dissolved her into a babbling, grown-up baby."

"That's the part I love. Watching all of their haughty pride dissolve, their opinions, their judgments, their rejections. Everything that makes one a unique creation eventually collapses into the sameness of infantile shrieks and babbling. And that, my friend, is triumph."

"Over who?"

"Whom," he corrected. "Over whom. And what do you mean?"

"Well, that's what confuses me. Because while you were killing Mrs. Nightingale, you kept talking to her like she was your father. Telling her how you're just as much a man as she is, only you didn't mean her, you meant your father. And you hate your father for rejecting his only son for some silly little game with a bunch of boys. Only you weren't killing him this time, because you already killed him the first time.

"And Amy, the older daughter. Did you know that you were talking out loud when you started pretending that she was your mother, and bawling her out for not keeping her husband at home so that he couldn't sire a bastard son? Did you think that you were just alone and safe inside of your head?"

Tommie did not reply, but he slowly turned to face Shane. All the pretext of civility fell from his face. His eyes seemed to sink back into his head.

"Now I know exactly how I'll do it. I'll leave you tied to that beam and haul you out to the Golden Gate *before* I go to work on you. If I start here, I may not be able to stop myself and you'll bleed out before we get you into the water.

"And then, just before you and your beam go into the water, I'm going to treat you to exactly one hundred little slices from your head to your toes. Your blood in the water will draw sharks from incredible distances. And there are plenty of them lurking around the mouth of the Bay. I trust they will eat you slowly, because of the beam, you know. Surely it will slow down their rate of consumption so that you can savor the experience of being eaten alive at sea. Eh?"

Shane leveled his gaze. "You killed your mother and father for money."

"I killed them for throwing my life away!"

"And the younger girl, Carolyn. Even while you were dancing her all around the room, you kept telling her to stay away from you, to stay out of your life. At the time, I didn't know that you were talking to me. Through her, you've killed me once already, haven't you?"

With that, Tommie paused for a long moment and studied Shane's face.

"But you killed yourself all those years ago, back when you killed them," Shane added. "Ever since then, you've just been walking around with a dead thing where your soul should be."

"How poetic," said Tommie. He snatched up a writing pen, dipped it in an ink bottle, and announced, "I have this custom, just this little thing I do. Sort of a trademark, lately." He picked up a small notebook, opened it and dictated to himself while he wrote:

"Even if The Last Nightingale could be revived, how would it tolerate the cure? Knowing that Life merely awaits to devour it again . . ."

He read it over silently two or three times, then happily exclaimed, "It will work perfectly for your suicide note, little bastard brother!" He dropped the notebook into a large section of oilskin. He folded it snugly inside and tied it with thick twine.

"There. Waterproof. Good enough so that the note will still be readable when they find it on your body. In case there's anything left of you to wash up on shore. Not bloody likely, the sharks and whatnot. A hundred little cuts. So forth."

Tommie tucked the oilskin envelope into his coat pocket, then reached down into some box that Shane could not see. When he stood, he produced a thick muslin potato sack. He stepped up to Shane and raised the sack overhead, then Tommie let his mask of civilization fall away again. This time his dead-eyed face melted into the expression of a man so nauseated by his own existence that he could never be at peace with the outside world.

A moment later, the bag swooped down over Shane's head and everything went pitch black. He felt Tommie's hands pulling the bag all the way down over his shoulders, and a rope was tied around his shoulders and chest, keeping the sack in place. Next he felt the thick board that bashed him across the side of his head, but only for an instant before unconsciousness overtook him.

Twilight was rapidly dropping into darkness while the horse-drawn taxi clipped along at a brisk trot on its way back to the Mission Dolores. Vignette struggled to grasp the rapid turn of events. As usual when she let herself get caught up in the business of grown-ups, she soon found herself stuck between shouting men without being able to figure out what the problem was. Sergeant Blackburn had raced her away from Tommie Kimbrough's house and back to the station to get more men to go capture him. But everybody was all excited about the fat man in charge who was arrested that day. She stood mute around the angry adults, but felt only disgust for the policemen yelling at the sergeant. Nobody would help him because there was no boss around to give orders.

Now he had her in this cab, forcing her to return to the Mission to wait all alone in that stupid toolshed without Shane—because of course nobody could let a girl go along to catch a murderer. Worst of all, the sergeant seemed to be able to completely shake off her best attempts to manipulate him by trying to appear too scared to go back alone.

He just smiled at her. "You have to wait where it's safe, Vignette."

"Shane's out there. If he can be there, I can be there!"

The sergeant laughed out loud at that, and he didn't bother to argue with her. She was glad to see him laugh, since his face seemed so tired and worried. Maybe it was safe to ask him.

"Why wouldn't the other cops help us?"

"It's called command confusion."

"They didn't seem confused."

He laughed again, a little. "Well they all seemed crystal clear about not wanting to be of any help."

This was good, Vignette thought. She had him talking and he

seemed to be feeling friendlier at the moment. Maybe if she could keep this up . . .

"If I was with you, I could still wait in the taxi, but if either of you got hurt, then as soon as you got back I could start helping to bandage you up while we run for a doctor! You can't argue with that!"

"Got me there. I can't argue."

"So can I come?"

"No."

They rounded the corner and pulled up next to the Mission. She flashed him her very best look of betrayal and hurt, but he just put his hand on her shoulder and smiled.

"I want you to wait here so I know you're safe, because if I have to worry about you I might not be able to do my best to help Shane."

"If we're together, we can look in two different directions at the same time!"

"Vignette, this man is madness itself." He lifted her down and put her at the curb. "I have to go."

The sense of worry and fear were too much for her. She turned and ran back into the cemetery, to at least be around the place where her brother lived.

Once she was gone, the cabbie turned in his seat and asked, "What now, sir?"

"Well that's the thing, actually," Blackburn replied. "I need this carriage to drive up to the Golden Gate. I'm on the trail of a man who I believe has killed a couple of dozen people so far. I expect to find him up there tonight, because he has one more victim to kill there."

"You mean *that's* what the little girl was talking about? A real killer? Some sort of maniac killer? And you're going after him?"

"Yes indeed. In fact, it looks like I'm all that there is, at the moment."

"Sir, there's no light at all up there! Can't see your ass, if you don't mind me sayin' so. Fog covers moonlight, starlight, all of it."

"I believe you. That's why I'm prepared to offer you double your rate all the way out there and back tonight."

"Very generous, sir. But I can't possibly risk my horse in that—"

"I'll triple your rate."

"Triple now? Triple? Sir, you'll be down twenty dollars that way."

Blackburn pulled a twenty-dollar bill from his pocket, leaving himself with nothing but a few coins. "I have to go right now. You can either take the money to drive me up there, or you can take the money for renting your rig to me, and I'll drive myself. But I'm telling you," Blackburn said, "I could sure use one more man along with me, tonight."

"What, to go after this maniac?"

Minutes later, Blackburn sat alone in the rented hack, steering his way up to the Navy Presidio, a huge expanse of preserved land that fronted onto the strait of the Golden Gate. The search would require as much luck as skill, since there was plenty of deserted and rocky shoreline where the Pacific Ocean poured into the San Francisco Bay.

Just as the cabby warned, the lack of light became a real obstacle at the northern tip of the peninsula. There were no structures and no lights anywhere. The air smelled of incoming rain, and the early arriving clouds sucked up any moonlight before it hit the earth.

He slowed the horse to a brisk walk and proceeded toward the shoreline. The sound of the wind was in his ears, topped by the clip-clop of the horse's gait. He strained to hear any trace of voices, any noise that might tip off another person's presence. Nothing came back to him. He slowed the horse to a gentle walk, letting it stumble along the rutted road at the only safe speed.

Even then, there was no sound in the air to guide him. Just the rushing wind and the big animal's steps. After a few more moments, he caught the first faint sounds of surf on the distant rocks.

He leaned into each crash of each wave, straining to hear a voice in the pause between them. There was nothing, still nothing, just wind and waves and horse hooves in darkness so thick that it held his vision down to a few yards in any direction.

Fear twisted his stomach and tightened his jaw. His muscled body felt the lack of sleep and the night all around him seemed impossibly huge. He wished that in such times he had some kind of abiding religious faith to sustain him. But it still seemed to him that God had ripped his family away in one icy blow, telling him that his ambition as a family man was denied. His heart had frozen to the spot, that day. Now he couldn't pray anymore for the same reason that he couldn't just start another family again, as people used to advise him. Back when they still did.

While he drove slowly through the night, he still had a bitter taste in his mouth about the casual disrespect from the officers hanging around the station. There was no Station Chief to direct traffic; discipline was gone. So there was nothing else to do but venture out to the Presidio alone and see if there wasn't some way that he could ruin The Surgeon's plans for the night. His frustration mounted at the slow pace while he drove the horse forward. It felt as if the elements conspired to slow him down.

Soon the sounds of the sea became the dominant noise, combined with the rushing of the sea winds, the clatter of the buggy wheels on the rutted road, and the steady clop of the horse's walk. There was too much ambient noise for him to hear any signs of other people. He wondered how this was going to do any good.

In the seaward distance on his right-hand side, he could just make out the flashes from the rotating beam of the big gas-powered marine searchlight. That fixed his current location near the narrowest part of the Golden Gate passage.

The chill in the air seeped through his light jacket and an involuntary shiver rippled through him. At this point the mist hovering over the ocean water was dense enough to steal the last hint of light from the sky. He pulled the carriage to a halt and tied back the reins. It was quieter, then. He felt encouraged that he might hear something this way. He would just have to carry out the rest of the search on foot.

Shane was in and out of consciousness throughout the rugged ride to the north shore in Tommie's horse-drawn wagon. He remained bound to the beam by several turns of thick rope. Time after time, he rolled back up to the surface of awareness, and it would occur to him that he could work his way out of the ropes, if only he could gather his strength and focus his energy. But that same strength flowed back out of him every time, and he sank back into the dark nothingness.

When enough time passed that he could come back to the surface and stay, the thing that roused him was a sharp drop in temperature and the sensation of cold wind blowing across his body. He shivered uncontrollably, while clouds of spray flew through the air on wave blasts that sounded like cannons. He rolled his eyelids up and found the strength to hold them open. There was almost nothing to see in the darkness and fog. But in the background there was a slow and rhythmic pulse of light that had to be coming from one of the searchlights along the shoreline leading into the bay.

Shane was instantly wide awake and panting with fear when he realized that the monster was making good on his threat to kill him at the Golden Gate.

Now he felt the beam dragged backward a few feet. Then the head end of the beam was tilted up and rested on a rock, so that it held him up at an angle. A few seconds later, the next searchlight strobe flashed across the feral grin on Tommie Kimbrough's face, hovering right over him. All traces of his dress and makeup were gone.

"I developed a whole new expertise in handling rats with the plague," Tommie said, "just for you. I was going to wait until you died that terrible death, then haul your carcass out here and push it into the surf."

Shane knew that his only chance of survival in this desolate place was to distract Tommie long enough to allow him to wriggle free of the bindings and make a run for it. With luck, he might disappear in the thick darkness.

"You think I don't remember anything before being at St. Adrian's," Shane began. "But you're wrong."

"Horseshit." Tommie pulled out his heavy-bladed knife and began testing the edge.

" 'I have to empty you out.' I know why you say that."

"I'm going to start your hundred slices with small cuts, just enough to let you taste the blade for a while. After the first fifty or so, we'll go ahead and float you on out into the water. Before I push you off, well, I'll do the deep ones then. Those are the ones that will bring the sharks, you know."

"It's what our father said to you. After he caught you with the boys. He tried to whip you until everything sinful got knocked out of you. You think I don't remember?"

Tommie stared at him. When the searchlight flashed again, his face looked as cold as a fish. "Maybe the current will carry you on out to sea," he replied. "Maybe it will sweep you into the bay. But most likely, the sharks will devour you within a few hours. Or a few minutes, even."

"They tried to make you out to be garbage! They tried to take away your future and throw away your life, even though you weren't hurting anybody. He tried to beat you until there was nothing left inside of you. So now you do it to the others because you're still trying to make our father and your mother stop!"

"*Shut up!*" Tommie screamed it at the top of his lungs, raising his knife high overhead and tensing to thrust it deep into Shane. Just before his arm began the downward stab, Shane pulled his arms from behind, tore the rope from around his neck with his right hand and simultaneously blocked the stabbing motion with his left. He sat up just as Tommie stabbed downward again, this time driving the knife deep into the beam.

Tommie's plan to begin with the small cuts seemed to have left him. As he struggled to pull the knife free of the beam, Shane kicked for his life against the ropes at his ankles until his feet finally pulled free. He tucked into a defensive ball just as Tommie thrust at him again, and an inch of the blade caught in his thigh. The pain made him scream into Tommie's face, but his survival instinct flooded him with strength.

He jumped away from the beam with the fiery wound burning in his leg and screamed a howl of rage. He screamed knowing that nobody else could hear him out there, but that Tommie was the only audience that he needed for his utter revulsion at the creature that his so-called brother had become. It was likely the last sound that he would make in his life and he was leaving no doubt about where he stood. The little boy who had shuddered helpless in the kitchen cupboard now faced the killer bare-handed and poured every ounce of his life force into defiance.

It kept him from realizing what happened for a second or two after a single gunshot was fired from somewhere nearby. Tommie grunted with surprise when the bullet whizzed by inches from his head. He swore while he spun on his heels and sprinted in the opposite direction, vanishing in the inky blackness. When the search beam swung by again, there was no trace of The Surgeon.

Shane staggered under his own weight and fell to his knees in the rocky sand. He was so drained and exhausted that he barely flinched when a sharp scuffing sound came from the beach next to him and Randall Blackburn appeared at his side. For an instant he wondered if he was dreaming again, but he felt Blackburn's strong hands clutch him.

"Are you all right?" Blackburn asked.

"He stabbed my leg. I can't chase him."

"*Chase him?* Listen to me. You don't go anywhere. I mean it, Shane. Stay right here. I've got a buggy up on the road but you'll never find it alone, especially not bleeding like that."

"All right. I know."

"I mean it!"

"I know."

Shane felt Blackburn give him a reassuring squeeze on the shoulders, then he heard the big sergeant stand up and run off in the direction that Tommie had just fled in, along the waterline toward the big signal light. His footsteps were surprisingly fast. They only receded in the distance for a few moments before they were gone among the sounds of the ocean.

Shane huddled on the ground and wrapped his arms around his knees to conserve his warmth. There was no way to tell what was happening with Blackburn, or when he might return. And the thought of Tommie somehow getting the best of the big policeman and showing up back there once again was too awful to contemplate. He could only huddle and wait. In between the periodic sweeps of the distant searchlight beam, it was as dark as the bottom of a well.

CHAPTER TWENTY-ONE

RANDALL BLACKBURN SPRINTED across the rocky sand into the opaque night. The flashes from the sweeping navigational beam gave him brief glimpses of his surroundings, barely enough to keep his direction oriented. He fell to the ground several times, abrading the skin on his palms and his knees and sending him scrambling to recover his pistol. He lost valuable seconds with every stop, and the resistance of the night and the terrain made him growl in frustration. He could only hope that Kimbrough was having the same difficulty, that somehow he would not continue to have the Devil's own luck as he had done for so long around the Barbary Coast.

The thin strip of sand beach ran out near the narrowest part of the strait. Blackburn stopped, using the sweeping beam to look for alternate routes. But all of the land leading away from Golden Gate point was so flat that he knew Tommie would be visible in the beam if he fled in that direction. Blackburn decided that his quarry must have continued over the rocky shoreline that was formed by a long stretch of seawall boulders. They were the size of elephants, with jagged fragments of smaller rocks filling the spaces between.

Blackburn jumped to the top of the first one, immediately caught his foot on a patch of slime and went down face forward between the big rocks. He struck the fragmented stones with a series of impacts. A fiery burst shot through him when he felt the ribs on his right side crack and separate, jabbing his flesh from within. He screamed with pain, but his voice barely carried over the sounds of the surf. When he was able to climb to his feet, he felt as if he had a spear tip lodged in his side.

On any other occasion, in pursuit of any other fugitive, this would be the point where the chase was abandoned for another day, even though he still had five shots left in his pistol. He was no longer sure that his right arm could hold steady enough to aim and fire.

But this quarry was The Surgeon. Nothing could blur the terrible joy that the man took in his crimes—Blackburn had encountered his demonic leavings time and time again. The Surgeon was attempting to kill Shane Nightingale at the moment that Blackburn managed to creep up on them. It was their shouting match that lured his attention along that strip of beach, and he knew that if he had arrived a few seconds later it would have been for nothing.

So he pulled himself to the top of the next boulder, waited for a flash from the searchlight, then leaped to the next one. This time his footing held. He managed to make it from rock to rock without falling again, by timing his movement to the light beam. Each time it flashed by, he checked out his next potential landing spot on the top of the next rock. He also kept tuned to the rocks out in front of him, and after his first six or seven leaps, he caught a glint of reflection about twenty yards ahead. The search beam had caught the wet leather of Tommie Kimbrough's long coat and reflected off of it, giving Blackburn a sure fix on his position.

He felt his heartbeat jump into high speed and pump him with so much adrenaline that he barely noticed his broken ribs. He threw himself into a reckless pursuit and double-timed it to make two leaps per light flash. That closed the distance by at least half, but by then the rocks ran out again and there was another stretch of a narrow, rocky beach. He was close enough to hear Tommie's footsteps speed up on the flat ground. That was going to end it. His injuries would never permit him to catch the athletic killer in a sprinting contest.

He staggered to a halt, gasping, and managed to raise his gun by holding up his right arm with his left hand. He pointed the barrel in Tommie Kimbrough's general direction and waited for the next searchlight flash. When it came, he saw that The Surgeon was surprisingly close. He adjusted his aim in the flash of the light beam, then fired into the inky darkness where Tommie Kimbrough had just been. There was no way to tell if the shot found its mark. But now that he was back on a flat strip of beach, Blackburn was able to keep walking forward in the dark until the next pass of the beam. It finally arrived and swept the strip of rocky sand.

The beach was empty.

"Nooo!" Blackburn bellowed. He spun in all directions, but there was nothing to see. When the beam made its next pass, he saw with certainty that Tommie had not headed back inland. Minutes dragged. In order to scan the landscape, he was forced to wait for each new sweep and take one direction at a time. Finally, he turned out to face open water and waited for the next flash.

And then at last, there it was: the brief reflection of light off of the wet leather of Tommie's long coat. He was not far offshore, perhaps twenty-five yards, attempting to quietly drift off into the bay on the rising tide. He had escaped notice so far by not breaking the surface with his arms or legs.

Blackburn realized that with the current rising, Tommie could simply float his way right into the great Bay and then swim for any random landing point along miles of shoreline. Anyone who could outrun Blackburn across a beach lined with slippery boulders could manage to do that much.

There was no chance of swimming out to catch him, with broken ribs. The Surgeon was making his escape, right out there in front of him. Blackburn's frustration was worse than the pain.

In desperation, he dropped to the ground and kneeled on his right leg while keeping his left foot flat, so that he could use his left knee to stabilize his shooting hand. Then he aimed in the general direction of Tommie Kimbrough's escape path and waited for the next flash. When the beam swept by, he got a solid fix on the coat's reflection and emptied five shots. He saw the second shot hit home just before the light went by, and felt sure that the third one would have also hit the mark. The last two were well-aimed guesses.

The next pass of the beam showed nothing but black water. He waited and watched for another pass, then another, and another. Then he caught the crucial glimpse, only a few yards from where Blackburn aimed his shots; the low, floating body rolled slowly in the current. He watched it for three more sweeps, growing more convinced with each one that he was looking at a floating carcass.

A flash of white foam exploded next to the body and the long leather coat spun violently in the water. Something out there had just taken the first bite.

The infamous "Surgeon" had become his own final victim.

When Blackburn heard a footstep behind him, he whirled with all the speed that his fading strength allowed, wondering if Kimbrough had an accomplice. He was ready to go down using the empty pistol as a fighting club, but when he tried to raise his right arm, the pain was so sharp and intense that he lost his balance.

Shane grabbed him in time to keep him from falling to the ground. "Did you get him?"

"What? Yeah. I told you to stay back there."

"I heard the shots. But are you sure?"

"Positive! I said 'stay there,' as plain as—"

"No! Are you sure you got him?"

"Look out there, wait for the next flash."

A moment later, the beam swept across the water. The water was calm and the rising tide was bare.

"You see him out there anywhere?"

"No."

"Well, I saw him out there. Big as life, with something already gnawing on his carcass and ruining his nice leather coat."

Shane strained his eyes to penetrate the darkness, hoping for any glimpse of Tommie Kimbrough's body, any confirmation that the killer was gone. He kept it up for a minute before he finally nodded and exhaled. "All right, then."

Blackburn sat down on the rocky shoreline with him. "He'll likely wash up somewhere close by. If there's anything left."

What Shane would have loved to do, given the chance, would be to use his bare hands to tamp down the earth on top of Tommie Kimbrough's grave until it was as hard as stone. He turned to Blackburn.

"My leg is still bleeding, and you don't look so good."

Blackburn smiled when he noticed that Shane wasn't stuttering at all anymore, but under the circumstances he saw no reason to bring it up. He felt himself growing woozy enough to swallow his pride and let the kid help him to his feet. Then he placed his good left arm around Shane's shoulder and guided both of them on a slow trek back to his rented taxi.

Vignette paced back and forth in the moonlit spaces between the cemetery trees, walking fast, digging her heels in with every step and spinning so hard on the turns that her knee joints hurt. Still nothing slowed her down. The powerlessness of the moment was sheer torment. She needed the sense of focus that the violent pacing gave her.

Vignette tried not to hate being a girl, to loathe being small, to detest being young. But those were all the qualities that prevented her from being of any use in helping Shane. She could not lose him. She could not. She could never let the world give her a dream come true of a big brother—even if she had to goose the world pretty hard on several occasions to make it happen—and then have him taken away again, just like that.

At some point in whatever it was that she was doing, she caught a flicker of shadow from the front area of the cemetery, up by the main gate. The flicker happened again, showing that it wasn't a shadow, but a silhouetted form.

Somebody was walking into the graveyard. One person, alone. Not a woman, but someone in pants and a shirt, someone with short hair like Shane's. Someone was walking like Shane walked, hurrying toward her, covering the last few steps to her with a beaming smile. When he put his arms around her without a single word, hugging her just right, not too strong, she had more joy and exaltation shooting through her than she could stand without breaking into pieces.

She hugged him back, gripping him hard, as hard as she could, trying to prevent herself from waking up and finding that Shane had turned into her pillow.

At last, he stepped back, put one arm around her shoulder and began to walk her toward the shed. She noticed that he was standing up very straight. He seemed taller.

"Would have got here sooner, but I had to drop off the taxi at the City Hall Station and get bandaged up over this cut on my leg. Sergeant Blackburn looked like he got kicked by a horse. His ribs are wrapped up tight. He's sleeping at the station. The taxi man drove me here."

"What the hell happened?"

"I'll tell you in the morning."

"In the morning?! Who cut you, Shane? Was it that crazy guy? How did you fight him off?"

"Vignette. I promise. Let me sleep and I'll tell you tomorrow. We have to go see that lawyer, you know. We should sleep."

"Do you mean to say that it's all right to just go in there now and go to sleep? It's safe to do that?"

He looked her straight in the eye. "That's what I'm saying. Sergeant Blackburn shot him and he sank into the ocean. Sharks got him."

He opened the shed and stepped inside. "Even though he got pretty banged up, Sergeant Blackburn's still coming by tomorrow." He went inside and lit the oil lantern. "He's going to stick up for us." He grabbed up both sleeping blankets, passed her one and tossed the other over his shoulder.

She unfolded it and wrapped it around herself before lying down. "How are you doing that?"

"What?"

"*Talking*, Shane. Are you reading it first? Is that how you're doing it?"

"Well . . ."

". . . *Well?*"

A wide grin spread across his face. "I'm getting faster, aren't I?"

Late the next afternoon, Randall Blackburn stood ramrod stiff under his rib bindings. From his place on one side of Attorney Towels's massive desk, he watched Shane sign on the dotted line on the final insurance form. Blackburn signed it next, as Shane's guardian and witness, making the transaction legal. And with that, he watched Shane Nightingale take possession of a bank account totaling close to twenty-eight thousand dollars of the Nightingale family estate.

It struck Blackburn that Shane looked like he would be sick at any moment. He wondered if it were just nerves. Whatever was going on in the boy's head, he did not look particularly happy or relieved to be taking possession of this money.

Vignette had quietly taken a chair and let everybody go about their business, and it was clear that her reaction was the opposite; she was fighting to control her excitement. The energy of it radiated out from her. Seeing her that way made it all the more strange not to see something like that from Shane.

A few minutes later Blackburn escorted Shane and Vignette out of the building. When he spotted a small café that had reopened a few doors down the street, he guided the kids to it and pulled them inside. He waited until they were seated alone at a small table in the back, then pulled a folded newspaper from his coat pocket and set it on the table. At first, he left the paper there unopened.

"So," he began, "I guess nobody can blame you for being over-whelmed."

"I'm not. Maybe I am. I'm just— I don't know."

"Well *I* know!" Vignette chimed in. "You had to fight for your life and you talked a crazy man out of killing you and today you got all this money." She gave a short laugh. "I'm surprised you didn't faint yet! We're getting some food here though, is that right?"

"In a minute," Blackburn assured her. "Why don't you look at the menu and pick out what you want?" He picked a menu up off of the table and handed it to her. She took it, but held on to it as if the menu itself could bite.

Blackburn turned to Shane and lowered his voice. "Shane," he began, "you now have every reason in the world to begin a new life with your sister, and to do it as if you both plan to grow up and make a good accounting of yourselves."

He opened the paper and pointed to the afternoon's headline, and there it all was: how the body of Tommie Kimbrough of Russian Hill had only been in the water for a few hours before the tricky currents swirled it up onto a public beach a few miles away. There was very little of Mr. Kimbrough left, but part of the torso seemed to have been protected by the leather coat, which was recovered. He was identified by the wallet in the inside pocket. There was also a note wrapped in oilskin. It was assumed to be the guilty farewell of a killer who could no longer abide his sense of remorse. The identity of The Surgeon was now known.

"That note was supposed to be for me," Shane said. "He was going to put it in my pocket before he pushed me out into the water, so people would think it was my suicide note."

"Suits me, the way it turned out. Cuts down on paperwork." Blackburn stared at him. "This ends it for you. You see?"

"See what?"

"Now you know it for sure. He's gone and you don't have to go around looking over your shoulder. You're free. So you don't have to spend any money running from him. You just need to use your money to build a future for both of you."

Shane looked from Blackburn to Vignette with a rueful smile. "You want to know a secret?" Shane asked. "He said we were half brothers. Me and him. He said we had the same father. He said that he was the one who gave me away to St. Adrian's after he got away with killing his parents—our parents—my father—the same—"

"Read it back," Vignette interjected.

He ignored her and added, "Which means that my father was Vignette's father, too."

Blackburn thought that Vignette went pale when she heard that, but there was already too much else for him to think about.

Shane put a consoling hand on Vignette's shoulder. "I asked him to tell me what your real name was back then, but he just looked at me."

"Oh. You mean my name? I like Vignette. I don't care what they called me back when I was *born*. It's not my name *now*. At St. Adrian's they called me Mary Kathleen but that's not my name anymore, either. Nope. We can forget all about that one."

At that moment, a realization hit Blackburn so hard that he whistled through his teeth and clapped his hands together. The other two gawked at him.

"Shane!" he began, "that's it!" He laughed. "This is amazing! Listen to me—here's the best way in the world to get back at that maniac. If we can get our hands on the birth records, you and your sister will stand to inherit the Kimbrough estate. Even his house!"

Once again, Shane's reaction seemed to come out of the blue. "No!" He jumped up from the table, eyes wide. "I don't want anything of his!"

"That's right!" Vignette quickly agreed. "Not from anybody like that."

Blackburn started to object, but Shane cut him off.

"To hell with him," he said.

"Yeah!" she agreed again.

"Those people weren't my family. I don't want anything of theirs."

"Neither do I," Vignette nodded. "We would just have to be *reminded* all the time. We don't even want to look at the birth records!"

"What?" Shane turned to her.

". . . Why be reminded?"

"Oh. Good point."

Blackburn felt things slipping out of control. "Shane," he began, "I know you have a lot of reason to be just as angry as hell about all of this, but I have to stop you for just a second here. We are probably talking about a great deal of money. That amount you have now is enough to get you started in life, it can get you both the right schooling, but it won't support you."

"What's wrong with that? I never wanted to grow up and just sit around, anyway."

"What's the right schooling?" Vignette interrupted.

"Oh, you know," Blackburn smiled, "one where the teachers are so good that you actually learn to read and write without any problem."

Vignette blushed and closed the menu.

"Shane, how did you get so good with the written word?"

Shane shook his head. "If you stay quiet and read, they leave you alone."

"Staying quiet hurts too much," Vignette muttered.

"Well, I don't know if you were aware that there was a fire at St. Adrian's. Only in the offices. None of the kids were hurt. But tomorrow, the department's going to announce that they think Friar John was in there and that the flames consumed him."

He sat back and gave the kids a moment to react. Neither one said a word. They both sat silently looking forward as if waiting for somebody to speak.

He nodded and spoke under his breath, "All right. No love lost."

He shifted in his seat and cleared his throat. "But as for the two of you, this is the thing—you can't come into this much money without people noticing. And there are plenty of adults who will steal from a kid without hesitating. That's why I signed off on the forms as your guardian. It wasn't just so you could get your money. Because I know that unless you're protected, it will all disappear."

"We could live with you!" Vignette enthused.

Blackburn and Shane both turned to stare at her. There was an awkward pause.

"Actually, that's just what I planned to talk to you about. Both of you. I've saved most of my salary for a long time, and well—I can get a place big enough for us. You don't have to stay, you're not my prisoners or anything, but somebody's got to look out for things while you two finish growing up. I guess I'm volunteering to do that, here."

"That sounds great!" Vignette immediately responded.

Shane just stared with his mouth slightly open.

Blackburn went on. "We'll get you both into a good school."

"Shane could go to school first, if one of us needs to stay home."

Blackburn smiled at her and quietly asked, "What's your favorite thing on the menu?"

Vignette just scowled at him and pushed it aside. Shane snorted at that and said, "You better get used to it. If I'm going, you're going."

"And you'll both have to learn how to cook. We'll take turns."

"What if we can't learn how?" Vignette asked.

"Then I expect that I won't be able to learn how, either, and the three of us will be eating a lot of garbage." Shane and Vignette both laughed and groaned.

"All right now, let's order something to eat." Blackburn grinned. "Shane, read Vignette the choices. Then I have to get a taxi and lay up at home for a few days. It'll be a while before I can do all this, let alone walk a beat. If I took a punch now I'd be in trouble."

"Let us come with you," Vignette pleaded.

Shane brightened up at that, adding, "We'll stay and take care of you."

"We don't even need to go back there," Vignette said.

"Well, I have to get my watch."

"I'll go! You're too tired."

"I can do it, Vignette."

"Maybe, but so can I. And right now I bet I can run faster than you and get back quicker, too!"

Vignette and Shane played at arguing the point before deciding to go together, while Blackburn smiled and shook his head. The sound of their request had caught him completely off guard, but it felt like the first pass of rain over a desert. Even though he had known that the issue was going to come up, he felt an equal mix of excitement and fear at hearing it. But he was also completely unprepared to feel his heart break open at the beautiful sound of two young voices telling him that his company was something they actually wanted.

"I guess you're better off there than in a toolshed." He turned to Shane. "We'll have time to talk, too. I've got some other crimes on the books that you just might see into, like you did with the Sullivans. Like the way you handled Kimbrough. The way that you can see certain things, it seems natural for you to do this work." He grinned and clapped him on the shoulder. "You can be my 'apprentice' and help me clear some cases."

Shane's face darkened. "Maybe. You know, sometime."

Blackburn let it go. "All right, then. But we're going to have to fill out a lot more forms to do this. So Vignette, what last name will you be using?"

"Well, I tell you one thing for sure, you can forget Kimbrough. I don't care what that guy said."

"Same for me," Shane agreed.

Vignette turned to Shane. "So you're keeping Nightingale, then?"

"I think so. I mean, sure." He thought for a moment, then added, "I need to. I need to carry the name."

Vignette nodded and turned to Blackburn. "We'll be using Nightingale, then."

Shane glanced at her, then smiled and nodded at Blackburn.

Later, on the taxi ride back to the little garden apartment that Randall Blackburn would soon exchange for a house with three bedrooms, he thought back to his late wife Jeanette and the daughter he never got to know. It amazed him to think of how powerfully the heart of a young man can break over the loss of the love of his life.

For almost ten years, he had locked his grief inside and hidden in his work, trying to make the need for a family leave him, trying to insulate himself against ever feeling such agony again. He had succeeded in feeling nothing but a lot of isolation and loneliness. In spite of that, it seemed as natural as breathing for him to reverse direction and take these two young ones under his wing. He could already see that there was going to be nothing easy about it, and he could hardly wait to get started.

THE END

DOSSIER

The Last Nightingale

ANTHONY FLACCO

A MILLION TINY SLAPS TO THE HEAD

THE FIRST KNOWN investigative procedure that can accurately be called a "criminal profile" is frequently attributed to Dr. Thomas Bond in the late 1880s. The London physician was called in to examine the body of Mary Kelly, one of Jack the Ripper's more savagely disposed victims. Initially, Dr. Bond was only asked to determine whether or not the victim's remains indicated that the perpetrator had any surgical skill, but the doctor was so horrified by the intensity of the crime that he stayed on to reconstruct the event and develop a speculative description of the killer. This approach was so unprecedented that there was not even a name for this new system of thinking about the relationship between an individual personality and a specific crime. However, in spite of the apparent novelty, the insights that Dr. Bond employed are all, at their essence, part and parcel of the timeless human capacity for wisdom. The same quest drives the appreciation for the psychological aspects of crime fiction. Avid readers of crime fiction have eyes honed for the vagaries of human personality.

Dr. Bond based his work upon (a) inferences taken from the crime scene; (b) the condition of the victim's body; and (c) the random nature of the crime. History tells us that Bond's work did nothing to reveal the identity of The Ripper. Nevertheless, in terms of engendering a whole new way of thinking about the psychology of crime, it was and still is a wellspring that serves anyone who searches for greater understanding of human behavior by accumulating insights into its most deviant forms.

Since the methodology of profiling is one that guides an investigator to a deeper and more three-dimensional view of an unknown subject, those same tools are equally effective in deepening the way in which crime fiction is written. This is part of what makes it so appealing to contemporary readers.

The more commonly known aspects of the field of criminal profiling have entered the Western world's zeitgeist to the extent that the general public now possesses a language for delving more deeply into motive and into personal point of view in the telling of a story than it has at any time in our past. Today, a well-considered characterization of a criminal profiler will show a flawed individual with feet of clay, perhaps in many ways little different from the quarry.

Perhaps largely due to the effects of TV and film, most people today realize that the reputation for "dark arts" being behind the methodology of modern profilers is simply the result of the startled amazement that often greets a good profiler's conclusions. The prosaic reality is that the professional profiler merely employs a system of thought created to help investigators think unthinkable things while they do intolerable work, and yet remain focused on their goals and their job functions. The patterns that a profiler is trained to study are the result of thousands of bits of information accumulated over generations of law enforcement experience regarding how criminal behavior tends to work.

The skilled profiler questions how the given criminal behavior (as indicated by the crime scene) *served* the perpetrator during the commission of the crime. Just as important, the profiler asks how such needs in the perpetrator may have been caused in the first place. Writers of crime fiction have learned to answer these questions also, because modern readers of crime fiction are far more sophisticated about criminal psychology.

Unfortunately, at the same time that public awareness of the profiling field has grown, the use of the word "profiling" in the media has sometimes taken on a churlish political tone. It's not difficult to see why. Today, that word has been distorted until it covers a range of meanings. It might refer to the specific field of behavioral analysis taught at the FBI academy, or instead to the use of over-broad physical descriptions for targeting a certain group, or it might even describe the sparking point for spontaneous outbursts of stranger-on-stranger violence. Whether or not these uses of the word are accurate in any given example, as an aggregate they have imparted a politically incorrect aroma to the word profiling that the core concept does not deserve. The fact that certain people or media organizations misuse any term or topic does not diminish its value in more earnest and capable hands.

So let's assume that today, those capable hands belong to you, reader. Let's hunt for the meaning of the idea of "profiling" as it applies to you and to me, regardless of what the folks at Quantico are teaching their recruits. And why not? You are a reader of mysteries, ready to pursue the answer to a puzzle through a menagerie of dark fantasies, are you not? Thus you may be "profiled" enough to deduce that you employ a number of skills in your reading and in your daily life that you would also be employing if you were to profile someone in the most educated use of the term. Scientific profiling simply provides an experimentally verified structure for utilizing natural insights into human behavior. You, reader of mystery fiction, a born profiler, may have figured that out already.

The old-school name for it was "learning to be a solid judge of character," or words to that effect. But the skill set starts about as far down the mammalian chain as you care to go. You can pick any single example among all the conscious creatures and still be assured that if that creature gets rudely slapped in the side of the head every time it turns to the right, it will eventually adopt a movement pattern that consists primarily of left-hand turns.

It is self-evident that all living things must be *expected* to choose behaviors that increase their chances of survival, which they will understand to be those things that help them avoid pain. Pain itself is our most powerful message of *Don't Do That.*

So let's not. Instead, let us assume that there is a constructive purpose to be made of the million little slaps to the head that events and people give us, every day of our lives, and try turning to the left for a while, just to see if anything improves. Profiling, then, is the logical extension of that fundamental survival behavior. While the insights provided by good crime profiling are impressive, the results that those same insights can offer to our personal lives are desirable and real.

The very process of living among others of our civilization will guarantee the constant abrasion of cross-purposes and misunderstandings, but we define our social selves by how we deal with such things. At the same time, those daily conflicts teach us countless mini-lessons about others that we file away, without even thinking about it. They become part of the individual database that we each possess—our private shorthand for making quick decisions under pressure. In the making of those decisions, the countless little flashes of memory work together, with the goal of refining our ability to handle passing challenges with a minimum of pain or danger.

That is why, although we must acknowledge that any given group of four or five large and rowdy young men lounging against the corner of an alley are *not necessarily* drunk and dangerous, no reasonable person would condemn another individual for crossing the street to pass. If the men really are just a few guys hanging out on a corner and not a threat, then they won't take offense just because someone quietly avoids them. They will realize that the stranger is simply being cautious. Therefore, those who do cross to the other side and safely pass by can legitimately congratulate themselves; they may not have formed a criminal profile *per se,* but their natural profiling abilities may well have saved them from an unpleasant, dangerous, or lethal experience.

The problem with profiling, then, is (1) it works; and (2) it is too easy for the general ideas of profiling to be "borrowed," without having to also acquire the knowledge and skill to properly and fairly apply the principles to the work. We think of young black male defendants insisting that they were pulled over by the police on a charge of nothing more than Driving While Black, or Hispanic citizens caught up in a sweep of illegal immigrants. In such cases, we know that it is reasonable to at least consider the possibility of bigotry, otherwise such accusations would fade into the same background static produced at any courthouse full of defendants. Whether or not the arrests had anything to do with bigotry or deliberate persecution, when suspects are incarcerated due to errant attempts at profiling, many emerge from the experience deeply shaken and permanently outraged.

Nothing changes the fact that in the wrong hands, stereotyping that is inaccurately *called* profiling can be used as a tool of bigotry, and that any tool can be turned into a weapon. The fact that the profiler's tools are powerful should only assure that they are handled with care. There is too much of value there, to avoid it. In our daily lives, profiling skills allow us to extend our universal right to avoid pain or danger by employing our experiences to help predict future actions. *A million tiny slaps to the head*—each one a single bit of the data used to sort out the angels from the demons, the talkers from the doers, the safety from the danger.

The commonsense elements of wisdom, old as civilization, are plain to see in the standardized thinking of professional criminal profilers. Consider the fundamental concept behind modern profiling in the United States, today: the categories of Organized versus Disorganized crimes. These terms can pertain to the crime scene itself as well as to the perpetrator(s), and the FBI teaches this fundamental division of crimes and crime scenes to its trainees. Under this system of observation and conclusion, our unknown perpetrator or perpetrators immediately give away a great deal about themselves, simply by leaving the crime scene in a state that must inevitably fall into one category or the other. The result is a delineation that not only works for crime investigation, but one that is the logical extension of insights that ordinary people have used for centuries to spot potential trouble with others.

THE DISORGANIZED CRIMINAL

When these emotionally driven types go through a crime scene in a frenzy, they reveal a lack of self-control that is fundamental to who they are. These killers will be careless about potential evidence while they are lost in the act of the crime, while the sensations of the moment overwhelm any concern for consequence. That trait will also extend throughout their lives. Once captured, this person's physical and social life will undoubtedly reflect an inability to sustain normal habits and a sociable disposition. These perpetrators are generally shown to be persons of lesser intellect, or those whose lives are not dominated by the use of their mind. They can seldom provide a credible character witness who will speak up for them.

Disorganized killers tend to live in a personal state that makes them comparatively easy to spot. They generally do not blend well in polite society. If they do get away from the crime scene, often it is because they break and run, then wander tramp-like for days, weeks, or longer, between places where a desperate person on the run might hide for a day or two. They often go so far off the grid that conventional means of tracking them are useless, making them much harder to locate than other suspects.

Meanwhile, back in ordinary life, we all employ the rudiments of the same insights every day. They are simply more basic versions of those same insights that prompt profilers to expect that a Disorganized crime scene indicates a perpetrator who will display a marked lack of discipline and self-control throughout the rest of his non-crime life. We know that if friends or relatives begin to detach, to become emotionally unpredictable, to let their personal appearance slide, that we are watching someone's stability crumble. The wild beast that anyone can become under the right combination of stressors will loom closer to the surface as their personal stability collapses. We need no police training to feel deep concern for any loved one who begins to show signs of deterioration in attitude, in conduct. We see such things and hear internal warning sirens going off in the background.

THE ORGANIZED CRIMINAL

An Organized crime scene may not display obvious signs of "organization" as we think of it around the home or office, but the entire scene will tend to display strong and obvious signs of a constant decision-making process that was carried out by the perpetrator throughout the commission of the crime. With the Organized perpetrators, there is seldom if ever a point during the commission of their crimes when they are so out of control that they lose themselves in the moment and do stupid and self-incriminating things. Once such a perpetrator is captured, experience also shows that they will usually live an otherwise "normal" and acceptable life. They hold workable positions within their level of society. They will have a peer group. The general structure of their lives, in addition to the crime scenes they leave behind, can be said to be organized. The fact that they are less likely to have a criminal record than a Disorganized perpetrator results from their ability to sustain relationships and to put down roots in their community.

But a close look at the human relationships of even the most self-disciplined Organized killer will reveal them as uniformly superficial. Since an individual does not fundamentally change from one situation to the next, even if one's social behavior skillfully adapts to what is expected, the Organized killers maintain only superficial relationships in life because they do not have the time, energy, or motivation to invest much of themselves into anyone else. The obligations of honest and open relationships are too complex for this kind of person to handle. The risks of sustained contact and actual intimacy guarantee that sooner or later, something would give it all away and reveal untellable secrets.

They are able to maintain the visage of sanity for the world, so long as nobody looks too closely. This chameleon effect is how they hide in plain sight.

We read about them while knowing that the same dark energy that drives such people to their nightmarish deeds also exists in many other areas of life. Those other areas will, from time to time, present themselves to each of us.

For those bound by conscience, it is not deviance itself that has the power to titillate and thrill; instead, the compelling aspect of crime is that underneath the things we find undoable runs an unending series of glimpses into ourselves. The salient detail of difference being that, unlike the serial killer, we may think destructive thoughts, but we do not act them out. Provoked, we may feel rage, but the physical attack mode is not activated. We are restrained by religious faith, or by spiritual morality, by the desire for an ethical life. We hurt over the knowledge of the pain we might inflict, especially upon the innocent, and so we withdraw from thoughts that never become plans, from plans that never become action. Our own private journey to the brink of our breaking points is set in relief for us by witnessing the extremes of humanity, whether they are deduced from a crime scene by a trained profiler or manifested in the pages of crime fiction.

Isn't there praise deserved by all who expend the energy to push the depths of their own levels of human insight? Surely we have a solid majority for the idea that it's better to have more wisdom going around than otherwise. This remains true whether insight is employed via a recognized profiling technique, or simply through an evolving personal life—one that is composed of an ever-deeper understanding of cause and within ourselves.

So where does that leave you and me: we, who dare to love reading crime fiction in a world of interactive video games?

For one thing, it leaves us with the assurance that we cannot help but sharpen up our personal profiling skills in addition to pleasantly passing time. The nature of a story can combine with the author's manner of portrayal to take us on a tour through the mysteries of human nature, deeper than we ever get to go in everyday life. We know that a book has been a satisfying read when the insights employed in the story stick with us after we finish it. We enjoy a double payoff. First there is the initial pleasure of sitting with the book for the first time and following the story, becoming engrossed by the characters. Then there is the lingering pleasure of spontaneously recalling moments from the book later, when we are somehow reminded of them in daily life. Our own way of perceiving the world around us will be altered by the insights instilled in the unfolding of a good story. Our understanding of others is broadened, stretched by the characterizations that we follow throughout the book. Most of all, our understanding of ourselves is nudged open another notch or two, every time we recognize within ourselves that point in a character's actions where we would *never* go along—or, just as instructively, where we would . . . With luck, we walk away feeling a bit smarter about the world and ourselves.

Readers of crime fiction love more than the twists and turns of a good mystery; they love to pit their individual sense of right and wrong against the driving ethics at work in the story. These readers employ the basic elements of the profiler's skills while they match their own predictions against the plotline. Whether they are right or wrong in the outcome, the rewards to be had for sharpening up one's personal profiling skills are there for any of us. Every time we finish a book with a net gain in our understanding of human nature, we bring another contribution to society in that our decisions are then filtered through those same profiling skills that we have so recently sharpened. Everybody gains from that, except perhaps for the victimizer types, which means that it all works out fine.

All of this leaves us with one question begging to be asked, and that question is not why we love a good mystery; rather it is why anyone who doesn't, doesn't. Don't they realize that every work of crime fiction that furthers our understanding of others and of ourselves adds to our individual power to move well through this world, through this life?

Maybe some people simply find that accumulating insight into human nature is even more painful than to just hang back and continue to endure those million tiny slaps to the head.

Now there's a mystery for you.

SELECTED REFERENCES

Douglas, John and Mark Olshaker (1999). *The Anatomy of Motive*. New York: Scribner.

Egger, Steven A. (1998). *The Killers Among Us: Examination of Serial Murder and Its Investigation*. New Jersey: Prentice Hall.

Harrison, Shirley (1993). *The Diary of Jack the Ripper: The Chilling Confessions of James Maybrick*. London: Smith Gryphon.

Holmes, Ronald M., and Stephen T. Holmes (1996). *Profiling Violent Crimes* (2nd edition). Thousand Oaks: Sage Publications.

Stout, Martha, PhD (2005). *The Sociopath Next Door*. New York: Broadway Books.

Turvey, Brent E. (1997). *CP101: An Introduction to Criminal Profiling*. Course notes. Available from: www.corpus-delicti.com. (Material cited here was found at: www.crimelibrary.com/criminal_mind/profiling/profiling2/7.html.)

ANTHONY FLACCO is a 1990 graduate of the American Film Institute, where he won their Paramount Studios Award for Writing. Immediately upon leaving the A.F.I., he was hired as a feature screenwriter by the Walt Disney Studios. He later published his first of several books, *A Checklist for Murder* (Dell Books), in 1995. He has since done other books, including the internationally acclaimed *Tiny Dancer,* as well as true-crime documentary screenplays. This is his first published novel.